BOY SOLDIER

www.**boy-soldier**.co.uk

Adult titles by Andy McNab

CRISIS FOUR
DARK WINTER
DEEP BLACK
FIREWALL
LAST LIGHT
LIBERATION DAY
REMOTE CONTROL

ANDY McNAB

and ROBERT RIGBY

BOY SOLDIER

DOUBLEDAY

London • New York • Toronto • Sydney • Auckland

BOY SOLDIER
A DOUBLEDAY BOOK 0 385 60914 0

Published in Great Britain by Doubleday,
an imprint of Random House Children's Books

This edition published 2005

1 3 5 7 9 10 8 6 4 2

Copyright © Andy McNab and Robert Rigby, 2005

The right of Andy McNab and Robert Rigby to be identified as the
authors of this work has been asserted in accordance with the Copyright,
Designs and Patents Act 1988.

Papers used by Random House Children's Books are natural,
recyclable products made from wood grown in sustainable forests.
The manufacturing processes conform to the environmental
regulations of the country of origin.

Typeset in Palatino by Palimpsest Book Production Limited,
Polmont, Stirlingshire

RANDOM HOUSE CHILDREN'S BOOKS
61–63 Uxbridge Road, London W5 5SA
A division of The Random House Group Ltd

RANDOM HOUSE AUSTRALIA (PTY) LTD
20 Alfred Street, Milsons Point, Sydney,
New South Wales 2061, Australia

RANDOM HOUSE NEW ZEALAND LTD
18 Poland Road, Glenfield, Auckland 10, New Zealand

RANDOM HOUSE (PTY) LTD
Endulini, 5A Jubilee Road, Parktown 2193, South Africa

THE RANDOM HOUSE GROUP Limited Reg. No. 954009
www.**kids**at**randomhouse**.co.uk

A CIP catalogue record for this book is available from the British Library.

Printed and bound in Great Britain by
Clays Ltd, St Ives plc

GLOSSARY

Alabama lie detector	*Baton used by some US police forces*
Bomb burst	*Split up*
Contact	*In a fire fight with the enemy*
CTR	*Close target recce*
Cuds	*Countryside*
Dead ground	*Ground that cannot be seen*
DMP	*Drug manufacturing plant*
ERV	*Emergency rendezvous*
FARC	*Colombian drug traffickers*
FOB	*Forward operating base*
IBs	*The elite of the Secret Intelligence Service*
LUP	*Lay-up point*
Mag	*A weapons magazine that holds the rounds*
Maggot	*Sleeping bag*
Make ready a weapon	*To put a round in the chamber, ready to be fired*
MoD	*Ministry of Defence*
MOE	*Method of entry*
NVGs	*Night viewing goggles*
OP	*Observation post*
Pinged	*When someone is first seen*
Recce	*Reconnaissance*
The Regiment	*What SAS soldiers call the SAS*
RIB	*Rigid inflatable boat*
Rounds	*Bullets*

RV	*Rendezvous (meeting place)*
SOP	*Standard operating procedure*
On stag	*On guard*
Stand to	*Get ready to be attacked*
UGS	*Underground sensor*
VDM	*Visual distinguishing mark*

SURVEILLANCE TALK

Complete	*Inside any location – a car, building, etc.*
Foxtrot	*Walking*
Held	*Stopped but intending to move on – i.e. at traffic lights*
Mobile	*Driving*
Net	*The radio frequency the team talk on*
Roger	*OK or understood*
Stand by! Stand by!	*Informs the team something is happening*
Static	*Stopped*
The trigger	*Informs the team that the target is on the move*

HACKING TALK

Exploits	*Hackers' targets*
Root access	*When the hacker has control of the system under attack*
Script kiddie	*Novice hacker*
Script	*A program written by a hacker*
Spoofing	*Hiding a computer's IP address*

PROLOGUE

1997, Colombia

Fergus had chosen the base camp carefully. He was always careful. Being careful had kept him alive during his twelve years in the Regiment and now that he was operating alone nothing was going to change.

The jungle floor was wet and muddy and covered with decaying leaf litter. Strong shafts of sunlight, as tight and bright as spotlights, speared through the tree canopy high above, illuminating the almost airless clearing.

The morning rains had stopped thirty minutes earlier but water constantly dripped from the canopy, and every small insect that flew or crawled seemed determined to take a bite out of Fergus. It was hot and sticky and uncomfortable, but then comfort never had been the top priority in his line of work. Staying alive had.

On SAS operations Fergus had learned the hard way about the seven Ps – Prior Planning and

Preparation Prevents Piss Poor Performance – so before setting up the base camp he'd made certain that two escape routes were available in the event of a surprise attack.

Carefully disguised rat runs had been cut into the undergrowth on either side of the camp. One led deeper into the jungle; the second went towards the river, where the four inflatable Zodiacs were hidden and camouflaged, just a metre or two from the water's edge. Their fuel bladders were still connected to the engines, their bows faced the water. They were ready to be launched within seconds.

Fergus stood facing the young guerrillas. They didn't look happy.

'Again,' said Fergus, in Castilian Spanish, keeping it as simple as he could. 'We do it again. Do like I do.'

One of the Colombians sighed and muttered to his friends. Fergus didn't understand what was said – the words came too quickly – but he knew exactly what was meant. They were bored; they didn't want to spend time stripping down and cleaning their AK-47 assault rifles. They wanted to use them.

Fergus held his AK in his right hand and the curved, thirty-round magazine in the left. He checked the top of the mag to make sure the shiny brass rounds were seated correctly before placing it in the assault rifle's mag housing and listening for the reassuring click as it locked into position. Then he gave the mag a quick shake to make sure it was fully home.

'Now you,' he said to the sweat-drenched guerrillas. 'Just do what I did.'

Fergus could load, unload and strip down a weapon with his eyes closed – he had done, thousands of times – but now he kept his eyes on the twelve young men as they copied his actions. Young men? They were kids, most of them not yet twenty and the youngest maybe seventeen.

Most were dressed in ripped jeans and old Brazil or Man U football shirts. Some had thin, wispy beards. It was as though they were trying to prove they really were man enough, mean enough and brave enough to be FARC guerrillas. The younger boys were smooth-faced; they probably hadn't even started to shave.

Their faces were sullen and sulky. They hadn't left their poverty-stricken villages to clean rifles. They wanted to make their fortunes. They wanted action.

They were about to get it.

The attack came suddenly, without warning and at the worst possible moment. The government troops must have been watching, waiting for the perfect time to strike.

Fergus heard the helicopter gunships first. The deep, throaty growl of the engines, immediately followed by the ominous chop of the rotor blades. The tree canopy swayed and shifted and rainwater came cascading down.

'Shit,' murmured Fergus, as he looked up and saw the first helicopter overhead. 'Stand to! Stand to!'

The guerrillas ignored the command. Most of them simply panicked and started to run towards the boats, unaware that a gunner was already lining them up through the sights of the heavy machine gun mounted in the doorway of the gunship.

Fergus grasped the pieces of his own rifle and dived to the ground. 'No!' he shouted, rolling away through the mud. 'Not the boats! Stay away from the boats! Stay low, stay low!'

But it was already too late. Bullets thudded into the wet earth as the young Colombians hurtled towards the river, their weapons forgotten and abandoned. The youngest boy, Nino, stood rigid, petrified like a rabbit in car headlights, his eyes wide with fear.

The camp was surrounded: ground troops were approaching from all sides and shouted orders were drowned out by the sound of automatic gunfire. The attack had been expertly planned, and Fergus felt a moment of professional admiration as he mechanically loaded his AK.

He grabbed the terrified boy and dragged him towards the forest escape route. Before they had moved more than a few paces Fergus heard a stifled cry, felt Nino jerk away and turned to see him falling into the leaf litter. Blood oozed from his head.

Fergus was hit before he could return fire. The bullet smashed into his thigh and sent him spinning away, face down in the mud. Searing pain burned through his body. He lifted his head and saw blood-red bone protruding from the gaping wound in his leg.

The thudding sound of heavy machine-gun fire drifted back from the river. Fergus knew that the guerrillas who had made it to the boats would have

4

been picked off by the helicopter gunships and that, by now, their bodies would be floating downstream.

And then it was all over. The firing stopped as quickly as it had begun. Fergus tried to crawl towards the undergrowth as he heard more shouted commands and then men running towards him. He was grabbed by the shoulders and turned over. Four Colombian soldiers stared down at him, their camouflaged faces glistening with sweat as they jabbed their rifle barrels into his face and excitedly shouted to their commander. 'Gringo! Gringo!'

Two of the troopers moved aside and an officer wearing the uniform of the Anti-Narcotics Police stepped through. He smiled at Fergus, reached into the breast pocket of his camouflaged combat jacket and took out a photograph. He looked at the photograph and laughed, then beckoned to a paramedic before viciously kicking Fergus in his wounded leg.

The agonized scream echoed away into the jungle.

1

2005, Army RCB Centre, Wiltshire, England

Danny was running. His pace was as steady and constant as his breathing; he moved with a natural rhythm. This was what he'd been waiting for – at last he was really showing what he could do.

Sometimes when Danny ran, when he was training, he would wear a Walkman and sing to himself under his breath, fitting the tempo of the song to his strides. It helped maintain the pace and stopped him from getting bored on a long run. But not today. Today he was focused. He wanted to win, even though they'd been told it wasn't a race. But Danny still wanted to win. He always did.

He was way ahead of the others as he approached the stream. The muddy stretch of water was too wide to clear without the aid of the strong rope dangling invitingly from the thick branch of a tree. Danny's eyes narrowed as he neared the edge and without breaking his stride he leaped into the air, grabbed the rope with both hands and swung effortlessly across to the other side.

The watching NCO smiled his approval and checked the list of names on his clipboard. 'Good effort, Mr Watts, keep it going,' he boomed as Danny ran on towards the high wall.

Danny grinned. *Mister* Watts. Him? He couldn't remember anyone calling him Mister Watts before. A few other things maybe, but never Mister. But it was all so different here.

When they'd assembled on Day One, nervous and self-conscious, a sergeant had told them they would all be referred to as Mister. 'That's because officers are gentlemen,' he said. 'And that includes potential officers like yourselves.'

Danny wasn't bothered what they called him – General Watts, for all he cared – just as long as he got one of the Regular Commissions Board bursaries at the end of the three-day selection course. He had to get a bursary; it was the only way he could possibly afford to take up a university place and then go on to Sandhurst Military Academy.

And the weeks of preparation were paying off. Danny had sailed through the medical and fitness tests, handed in a decent current affairs essay, and if the rest of his written work wasn't exactly *University Challenge* standard, he was pretty sure he'd done well enough. In the briefings and interviews he had been confident but not cocky. He'd even laughed at the officers' bad jokes.

He knew they were being assessed at every moment, and that included their relaxation time. So when a few of the others got stuck into pints of bitter in the mess,

Danny stuck to Diet Coke. It was no big sacrifice – he couldn't stand the taste of beer anyway.

One 'real ale man' ended up making a total prat of himself, downing four pints in less than an hour. It was three and a half pints too many: he threw up on the floor before being dragged off to bed. The duty officer wasn't impressed and neither was the steward who had to mop up the vomit.

Four Pints, as the others named him, woke up the next morning to a king-sized bollocking that did nothing to make his hangover feel better.

But it was a useful reminder to Danny to get everything right. This was his one chance, he had to take it, and with the assault course run being the final event it was all working out perfectly.

He clambered over the two-metre-high wall and sprinted the final hundred metres to the finish line, where a waiting sergeant clicked a stopwatch and made a note of his time. 'Very good, Mr Watts, very good indeed. Says on your application that you've run for your county.'

'Middle distance and cross country.'

'And is that something you'd wish to continue in the army?'

Danny paused before answering, reminding himself to say the right thing. 'As long as it didn't get in the way of my other duties.'

The sergeant laughed. 'I shouldn't worry about that, Mr Watts, the army always wants to sponsor top quality athletes. Look at Kelly Holmes – she did ten years in the army and look at her now: double Olympic gold medallist. Take my advice, you stay in training.'

'I will, sir. Thanks.'

'Sir? I'm no Sir. I work for a living.' The NCO pointed at the three small green stripes sewn onto his combat jacket. 'It's Sergeant. Now get yourself off to the showers while I wait for the also rans.'

As Danny jogged away towards the changing rooms he could see the next few years panning out exactly the way he'd planned. University, then Sandhurst and then a commission as an officer in the infantry. And on top of that, they might even pay him to run. It couldn't get any better.

The selection course ended with an after-lunch debriefing from the colonel in charge. He was a red-faced, cheerful old boy who told them exactly what they expected to hear: they'd all done very well and it had been one of the best RCBs he could remember.

'Bet he says that every time,' whispered someone sitting behind Danny.

The stifled laughter died away as the colonel reminded them that with only a certain number of bursaries available, some of them were going to be disappointed.

Thirty minutes later they were in the reception area waiting for the coach that would take them to the train station. They were a mixed bunch: a few, like Danny, comprehensive kids, but the majority public school, Officer Training Corps and Army Cadet Corps.

Some were from old military families. Four Pints had boasted he could trace his family all the way back to Wellington and the Battle of Waterloo. That was just before he was sick.

As far as Danny was concerned Waterloo was the place where he changed trains on his way back to Camberwell. Military history could wait until Sandhurst. Firm footsteps sounded from along the corridor and the sergeant from the assault course approached. 'Mr Watts?'

'Sergeant?'

'Good lad, got it right that time. With me, please, Colonel's office. Leave your bag there.'

The sergeant turned away and retraced his steps down the corridor and Danny felt the eyes of the other candidates on him.

'Looks like you're in,' said Four Pints, with a wink. 'Must have been your run that did it.'

Danny hurried after the sergeant, his thoughts racing. Was that it? Was he in? The colonel had said letters to the successful candidates would go out the following day.

They reached the colonel's office at the end of the corridor and an abrupt, 'Come,' was called in response to the sergeant's firm knock. He opened the door, nodded for Danny to go through and then pulled the door shut. His combat boots echoed away down the corridor.

The man seated on the far side of the dark wooden desk was not the colonel. He was blond-haired, mid forties, and in his slick, dark blue suit and custard-yellow and red striped tie, looked every inch a top civil servant. Danny recognized the tie – he'd once been on a school trip to a Test Match at Lord's and had seen dozens of them worn by the MCC members in the pavilion.

A half-full cup of coffee stood on the desk. The man was studying a buff-coloured army RCB file with

10

Danny's photograph stapled to the front of the cover. He spoke without looking up. 'Sit.'

Danny obediently sat in the chair on the near side of the desk but felt his face flush. He wanted to say, 'Look, mate, I'm not a dog, and what happened to *Mister* Watts?' But he didn't.

A clock on the wall ticked loudly. Danny realized he was counting the passing seconds until, at last, the man looked up. 'The Regular Commissions Board will be turning down your application for a bursary, Watts.'

The words stunned Danny like a surge of electricity. 'But . . . but why? I did well on everything. I passed the medical, my written tests were good. Good enough.'

The man shrugged. 'Hardly Einstein.'

'And I won the assault course race.'

'Yes, you can run, Watts, you can certainly run. And while your predicted A-level grades are adequate for a place at one of the modern so-called universities, we all know that education standards are slipping. But the army is looking for better than average, Watts. We want the cream.'

He seemed to be enjoying it, taunting Danny, deliberately winding him up. 'On the other hand, if you made your own way through university and, by some miracle, exceeded expectations, you could apply for a commission. But . . .'

The thin smile was more like a sneer, and the way he left the 'but' dangling in mid air made it perfectly clear to Danny that he had virtually no hope of ever becoming an army officer.

'I don't have family to pay for university.'

11

Another thin smile. 'I am aware of that.'

Danny was fighting to hold back his anger. 'You knew my predicted grades. What's the point of getting me down here and putting me through all this if it's just to turn me down?'

'We believe in equal opportunities for all.'

Danny snapped. He stood up and banged a fist on the desktop. 'That's bollocks.' The man raised an eyebrow but said nothing and Danny had no alternative but to bluster on. 'It's because I'm not from the right background. I don't speak with a posh accent like you and I didn't go to the right school. I thought all that family crap was a thing of the past in the army.'

The reply was totally calm and measured. 'The working-class chip on the shoulder doesn't help either, Watts.' He let the application form drop onto the desk and raised his voice slightly. 'Now sit down.'

Danny sank back onto the chair, and the thought that perhaps all this was deliberate flashed through his mind. Another test. Of his ability to withstand pressure and provocation. If it was, he'd failed it. Big time.

'You need to learn to control your temper, Watts. And contrary to what you believe, family connections still play a very important part in the army. Your own, for example.'

'Mine?' Danny looked as bewildered as he felt. 'I don't know what you're talking about.'

This time there was no smile. The man got up from his chair, walked round to Danny, and sat back against the desk. 'When did you last see your grandfather?'

'My—'

'Fergus Watts?'

'I . . . I've never seen him. Ever.'

'Are you certain about that?' The laid-back, laconic style had gone; Danny's interrogator was now firing in questions like rounds from an AK-47. 'Has he tried to make contact?'

'Not with me, no. And what's he got to do with this?'

'Not with you? What do you mean by that?' He leaned closer. 'Answer me, Watts.'

Danny could smell the coffee on the man's breath. His own mouth went dry. It wasn't meant to be like this. 'Someone contacted social services and asked about me, when I was sixteen. I don't know who it was. If it was my granddad he never got in touch.'

The man stared into Danny's eyes. His look was almost hypnotic, probing. Finally he seemed satisfied. He moved away and went back to his chair. 'Fergus Watts betrayed his country and his regiment. You knew he was SAS?'

Danny shook his head. 'I knew he was in the army, that's all.'

'There are certain matters we need to clear up with your grandfather, and if you could help us in any way . . .' He picked up the application form again. 'Well . . . there will be other RCBs.'

2

The black-and-white photograph was yellowed and faded. Three young men in army uniforms, their arms around each other's shoulders. They were smiling, happy. Young comrades.

The photograph was the only link Danny had ever had to his grandfather. He looked at it again and then tore it down the centre and threw the two halves towards the already full wastepaper basket on the far side of the room. They missed and landed on the carpet.

Elena was standing in the doorway of Danny's bedroom. 'You might regret that.'

Danny sat on his bed, his face dark and sullen. 'Why? The only thing he's ever done for me is stop me getting into the army.'

'Don't sulk, Danny, it doesn't suit you.'

'Tough.' The journey back from Wiltshire hadn't improved his temper. He was seething, as well as

14

sulking. 'The guy kept asking questions. Did I know where my granddad was? Was I certain he'd never been here?'

Elena glanced at the two halves of the torn photograph lying on the carpet. She could still make out the smiling faces. 'But what do they want him for? After all this time?'

'He wouldn't tell me. Just said they needed to talk to him.'

'Well, don't *you* want to know?'

'I don't want to know anything about him. I hate his guts.'

The sound of voices drifted up from the floor below and Elena shifted uneasily in the doorway. 'I'd better go down. Dave the Rave's gonna go ballistic if he catches me up here.'

Danny got up from the bed. 'I might as well look in the evening paper, see if there are any jobs going for army rejects. Part time at Tesco won't do any more, will it?'

'But what about your A levels?'

'What's the point now?' said Danny, brushing past and going towards the staircase at the end of the landing. Elena grabbed the two halves of the photograph from the floor, slipped them into the back pocket of her jeans and followed him.

They lived at Foxcroft, a privately run hostel for teenagers in Camberwell, south-east London. Danny had been there for five years. It was home, or the closest anywhere had been to home for as long as he could remember.

His parents had both been killed in a car crash when he was six. Danny was in the car too, but he had no memory of the crash. Not even in his dreams. With no relatives around to look after him, he'd become a 'kid in care', a social services statistic. He'd been farmed out to four sets of foster parents over the years, but none had worked out.

It wasn't that Danny was a troublemaker. He was independent, he liked his own space, and fitting into other people's idea of family life wasn't for him. He'd lost his own family and he didn't want to be part of someone else's. So when he got the chance of a place at Foxcroft he'd jumped at it. It suited him.

Elena had been there for eighteen months, moving in soon after her mum died. There was no one else for her either; her dad had gone back to Nigeria years before, telling Elena and her mum he was going to make his fortune. He'd always been full of big ideas. Big ideas, but no result.

Danny and Elena had hit it off straight away; they just clicked, even though Elena was a year younger. And at first Danny thought they might be more than mates but Elena soon put him right on that score. 'I want a friend, Danny,' she told him when he made a clumsy attempt at kissing her. 'I'm not interested in going out with anyone. Not yet, anyway.'

So Danny settled for friendship, even though he still really fancied Elena. And sometimes he thought she fancied him too. But maybe that was just what he wanted to think.

Elena was confident, clever and sharp. No one

intimidated her, and she knew how to handle people. And that included Danny, who was looking guilty as she joined him at the top of the stairs.

'I didn't even ask about your GCSE results.'

'You're right, you didn't.'

'Look, I'm sorry. So tell me then.'

Elena smiled. 'You want me to be modest or just go for it?'

Danny laughed. Elena always did have a way of making him laugh. 'When were you ever modest?'

'In that case, I did brilliant. Six A stars and four As brilliant. Boff or what? Now, let's go down.'

Elena was a genius, her school's star pupil, but definitely no boff. She didn't spend hours and hours with her face buried in textbooks or bore you with endless streams of useless information. But she didn't mind letting her friends know how brilliant she was. In the nicest possible way, of course.

Foxcroft was an old building. Victorian, with three main floors and an attic where the below stairs maids would once have had their poky little bedrooms. At some time between the First and Second World Wars it had been the home of a government minister.

You wouldn't have thought so now. It was faded. Sad. The paintwork was flaking, the boiler down in the cellar wheezed and spluttered like an old man after a lifetime of too many untipped fags, the sash windows jammed in their runners, and when the wind blew the whole place seemed to groan and shiver. But there was something about Foxcroft that almost everyone who lived there liked. It was reassuring. Something to do with old glory that refused to lie down and die.

Danny and Elena made their way down the stairs to the first floor. The staircase was broad and grand, with a dark oak banister and a threadbare carpet that might once have been red. Boys' bedrooms were on the second floor, girls' were on the first. Telly room and living rooms were on the ground floor.

Dave the Rave appeared on the first-floor landing just as Danny and Elena arrived. There was no chance of slipping quietly by. Dave was a huge bloke. He'd been a rugby player with Saracens in his younger days and might have made it into the England team had it not been for a back injury.

But he was all right; you knew where you stood with Dave the Rave, and right now they knew they were in trouble. Dave was scowling. 'Elena, you know you're not meant to be on the boys' landing.'

'Sorry, Dave, I was giving Danny the good news about my GCSEs.'

'You can do that downstairs. You two are supposed to set an example here.'

Danny and Elena didn't usually step out of line at Foxcroft. They respected Dave Brooker and his wife Jane. They were fair, they didn't try to be like parents, or teachers, or even mates. They were just Dave and Jane: they owned the place and they made the rules.

Dave's brilliant blue eyes softened – he never stayed angry for long. And he was almost as delighted at Elena's exam success as she was. 'I think she's the first genius we've ever had at Foxcroft,' he said to Danny, who didn't reply.

'Look, Danny,' said Dave gently, 'I'm really sorry about the army. I know how much it meant to you.'

Danny shrugged as though it didn't matter. 'I'm fine, Dave. I'll find something else.'

'Yes, but . . .'

It was as far as he got. Danny had already started down the lower staircase. Elena looked at Dave, raised her eyebrows and hurried after Danny.

On the ground floor the theme tune from *EastEnders* was pumping out from the television room so they went into the room reserved for peace and quiet. Television, Game Boys and even mobile phones were banned. As usual, it was empty.

Elena threw herself onto the huge old sofa that stretched along one wall. 'You really giving up your A levels?'

Danny sat in one of the armchairs. It didn't match the sofa – none of the furniture in the room matched. 'I don't have a choice. I can't afford university and I can't stay here. I'll have to get a job and somewhere to live.'

'But Dave would let you stay.'

'He can't. I'm seventeen, over age for this place if I give up school.'

He got up from the chair and moved over to the tall sash window that looked directly out onto the street. One of the panes had a crack in one corner; it had been there ever since Danny moved in. He traced a finger over the crack and gazed out through the window. 'He's out there somewhere, Elena, and he's got no idea what he's done to me.'

The evening sun dipped behind the houses on the opposite side of the road and the room was instantly filled with shadows. Danny turned back to face Elena. 'I'm gonna find him.'

Elena had been picking at a loose thread on one arm of the sofa. She stopped and stared at Danny. 'Your granddad? But you said—'

'I know what I said, but you're right, I *do* want to know about him. I'm gonna find him and make him see how he's ruined my life.'

'Yeah, like how, Danny?'

Danny thought for a moment and then shrugged. 'You're the genius. You tell me.'

3

It was a good spot for a roadside burger bar. A busy spur from the main London-to-Southend arterial road, it was used by huge numbers of vans and lorries streaming in and out of the light industrial and residential sprawl of south-east Essex.

White-van and lorry drivers were Frankie's main customers. He got the occasional suited company rep pulling in for a secret egg and bacon sandwich with tomato ketchup. 'My wife wouldn't be very pleased if she saw me eating this,' they'd say with a guilty smile. 'She likes me to have muesli. Bloody rabbit food. Hope you can keep a secret.'

Frankie kept many secrets.

The lay-by was potholed but wide and deep, with plenty of parking space for the biggest trucks. The landscape was flat and treeless, so drivers could spot the pull-in café, with its Union Jack flying above, from at least half a mile away in both directions.

Business was good, and for regulars in a rush there was a mobile phone number painted on the side of the van. They could call in advance with their order and their ETA and then collect their takeaway and be back on the road in a matter of minutes.

But most customers liked to stop for a leisurely cuppa and a chat with Frankie. Two regulars, Reg and Terry, painters working on a factory unit in Benfleet, had arrived for their usual full breakfast baps and strong teas. Bacon, sausages and burgers were already sizzling on the hotplate.

Reg dropped his third spoonful of sugar into the steaming mug of tea. 'I dunno how you do this all day, Frankie,' he said, stirring the brown, milky tea vigorously without spilling a drop. 'Don't you ever get bored? You know, stuck all day in a six-by-four tin can with nothing to do but watch the cars go by?'

Frankie cracked an egg onto the hotplate. 'I have plenty to do,' he said, reaching for another egg. 'This stuff doesn't cook itself. And I read the papers and listen to the radio. You get to learn a lot doing a job like this.'

Terry slurped tea from his mug. 'Yeah, fair enough, but – and don't get me wrong 'cos I love your cooking – but the smell of fried food all day would drive me round the bend. It clings to you, don't it?'

Frankie cracked the second egg onto the hotplate. 'You mean like the way the smell of paint clings to you?'

Reg laughed, and pulled a copy of the *Sun* from a deep pocket in his overalls. 'He's got a point there, Terry, a very good point. He stinks of fry-ups, we stink of top coat.'

He turned to page three and studied the photograph for a few moments. 'No, I could handle the smell, no problem. What would get me would be being stuck in this little van for hour after hour. Be like being in a prison cell.'

The eggs were almost cooked and Frankie turned away to spread butter on the baps. This, a prison cell? They had no idea. A prison cell was a dark, windowless concrete cube, three paces long by five wide and crammed with twelve other prisoners. The burger bar was heaven compared to all that. You could open the door and step outside. You could look out and see the road and the grass verge and the houses in the distance. You could listen to the radio. And you could talk to people.

Frankie had acquired his new identity three years earlier, soon after he'd finally made it back to England. It had taken a long time to get back, a full nine months after he'd led the breakout from the Colombian prison.

First he had to cross the two hundred and fifty miles of jungle to the Colombian border with Panama. It took three months and he used all his skills to evade capture, living off what he could trap or pick.

In Panama he stowed away on a Japanese cargo ship as it went through the canal towards the Atlantic Ocean. He hid amongst three thousand new cars, ate only food waiting to be thrown overboard and jumped ship when the vessel docked in Turkey six weeks later. Then he hitchhiked or hid in trucks until he reached France. He finally entered England along with seven illegal immigrants hiding under the cross-Channel train.

Essex seemed as good a place as any to settle. It was teeming with people too busy with their own lives to worry about one more ordinary, anonymous-looking bloke with a limp.

He did odd jobs to begin with, casual work for cash, no questions asked. He kept every penny he earned, but when he did start to spend, he spent wisely. A new National Insurance number bought in a pub cost him just fifty quid. That was when he became Frank Wilson. Changing his name and living as another person was something he was used to from his years on covert operations in the Regiment. The rule was: always have a first name starting with the same letter as your real name. It helped you remember.

Frankie always dealt in cash; there was no bank account or credit cards to help trace him. He'd started in a bedsit, but since buying the second-hand burger bar his finances had quickly improved. Now he rented an old cottage, pretty dilapidated but very private. And that was all he wanted. Privacy. To be left alone.

Frankie placed the two full breakfast baps on the counter. 'There we are, gentlemen. Help yourself to sauce. And enjoy.'

4

The website straplines spewed out the story in graphic and horrifying detail:

> **SAS HERO TURNS TRAITOR** . . . *Fergus Watts,*
> *the former SAS hero . . .*
> **WHAT MAKES A HERO TURN TRAITOR?** . . .
> *Highly decorated SAS man, Fergus Watts . . .*

And it got even worse:

> **BRITS WHO BETRAYED THEIR COUNTRY** . . .
> *Philby, Blunt, . . . Watts . . .*

There were more. Many more.

Danny and Elena were online in the quiet room, using Elena's precious laptop. 'If what your granddad did is so terrible, we're bound to find something about it on the Internet,' she'd said to Danny. She simply typed 'Fergus Watts SAS' into Google and the details began to emerge.

They scrolled through the websites and got most of the information through old newspaper stories going back eight years. And they didn't make good reading, even though the Fergus Watts story started so well.

He'd been an excellent soldier and was eventually 'badged' into the SAS. He did tours of Northern Ireland at the height of the conflict, and in the first Gulf War was decorated for his work behind enemy lines. He rose to the rank of Warrant Officer and could have got out at the age of forty, but the Regiment was his life and he chose to stay on.

As they delved deeper into the life and history of Fergus Watts, Danny kept reminding himself that this shadowy figure was not just some anonymous stranger, but his own father's father. They were flesh and blood. Family.

Every new fact was a revelation. Fergus Watts's special skill was explosives. He had a natural flair for languages, particularly Spanish. It was like putting together a jigsaw puzzle without the box cover to guide the way.

The SAS man's skills led him to Colombia and the war against the FARC drugs barons. His ongoing mission had been to lead patrols deep into the rainforest, to seek and destroy drug manufacturing plants. Danny tried to imagine the jungle, the heat, the heroic battles.

But then hero turned villain. Fergus Watts vanished

and soon after it was discovered he'd gone over to FARC, purely for the money.

'It's true,' said Danny as they scrolled on to another page. 'It's exactly like the guy at my RCB said, he betrayed the Regiment and his country.'

A long in-depth article from a correspondent in Colombia said that the manufacture and export of cocaine to the USA and Europe was a multi-billion-dollar business, and that in selling his skills and taking the FARC 'blood money', Watts shared the responsibility for the deaths of thousands of young drug users.

'He's no better than a murderer,' said Danny angrily. 'A mass murderer.'

The newspaper stories revealed that the traitor had eventually been captured after a gun battle between his small band of FARC guerrillas and Colombian soldiers. Watts had taken a bullet in the thigh during the fighting and was later tried and thrown into a Colombian prison to rot.

After the trial and jail sentence, the name Fergus Watts disappeared from the newspapers for over four years, but then there was a dramatic return to the headlines:

SAS TRAITOR MASTERMINDS MASS PRISON BREAKOUT

Since the breakout Watts had never been seen, or heard of, again.

'He's here,' said Danny. 'He's in England.'

'You can't know that,' said Elena. 'He might still be in Colombia – he might even be dead.'

'Yeah? So who was it made the enquiry about me? It had to be him, there's no one else, and I'm gonna find him. I'll phone the SAS to start with and see what they can tell me.'

'Danny, it's a secret regiment. What you gonna do, ring one-one-eight and ask to be put through?'

Danny was in no mood to be corrected. 'Yeah, all right,' he snapped, 'it was a stupid idea. So what *do* I do?'

Normally, Elena would have snapped back, but she knew Danny was devastated by what he'd learned about his grandfather. 'Try some other army numbers – they must be listed in the phone book. And maybe you should make the calls in the garden. We don't want anyone else knowing about this. I'll see if I can find anything online. But if we *do* find him, what then? Really?'

'I'll turn him in,' said Danny, picking up the phone directory. 'I want him to suffer the way he's made other people suffer.'

The garden at Foxcroft was like the quiet room, hardly ever used. There was nothing wrong with it; it was beautiful, if you liked flowers and plants that trailed in and out of trellises fixed to the high brick wall completely enclosing the garden. But as most of the residents of Foxcroft couldn't tell a rose from a stick of rhubarb, they generally stayed away.

And that suited Jane Brooker, who tended the garden almost as lovingly as she looked after the kids in her care. The garden was Jane's escape from the stresses and strains of life at Foxcroft. She needed it.

It was almost like being in the countryside. Only the constant thunder of traffic snaking its way to and from the centre of the city and the jagged broken glass cemented into the coping on top of the crumbling brick wall gave away the fact that the garden was in a busy and sometimes dangerous district.

Dave the Rave often joked that the broken glass was there to keep the Foxcroft kids in rather than keep unwanted visitors out. But it wasn't like that. Foxcroft had been burgled many times – not that there was much worth stealing.

The garden was deserted when Danny arrived with his mobile and the phone directory. He sat on a wooden bench and started to look up numbers. He tried the local recruitment office, the Army Pensions Office and even the National Army Museum. No joy.

While Danny was on the phone, Elena went back to the online search engine. She punched in 'SAS' and was rewarded with a list of sites ranging from Scandinavian Airlines to Surfers Against Sewage.

'Idiot,' said Elena to herself. 'Use your brain, Elena, be specific.' She typed in 'Special Air Services Regiment'. There were pages and pages dedicated to the Regiment. Most were tribute sites run by wannabe warriors or SAS anoraks.

But Elena worked quickly online, swiftly deciding which sites could be discounted and which needed checking out. Eventually she logged onto the SAS Association, an organization for ex-members of the Regiment.

'Nice one,' she said, making a note of the contact phone number. She shut down the computer and hurried out to the garden.

Danny got through to the SAS Association and after a few brief words was put on hold. He paced impatiently up and down a small patch of grass between two flowerbeds and glanced over at Elena. She had taken his place on the garden bench and was staring at an unopened blue airmail letter she held in both hands. The envelope was addressed to her and bore an unusual stamp.

'Aren't you gonna open that?'

Before Elena could answer, the phone line crackled and a woman's voice came on: 'You did say *S*. Watts, caller?'

Danny sighed. 'No, *F*. F for Fergus.'

'And you say he left the Regiment about ten years ago?'

'Something like that. I think he'd be about fifty-two or -three now.'

'Just one moment, caller, I'll check again. You do realize that if he is listed I can't give you an address or number?'

'He's my granddad. I just want to know if he's still alive.'

The woman sounded sympathetic. 'Oh, dear, that's a shame. Putting you on hold, then.'

She was back in less than a minute. 'We do have a Watts, but he's much more recent. Wrong generation completely. They don't all join the association when they leave, you know. Some just seem to . . . disappear.'

'Oh great,' said Danny. 'Now what do I do?'

It was a question that he didn't expect to have answered, but the woman obviously wanted to help. 'Did you say you were calling from London?'

'Yeah, and I'm running out of credit on my mobile.'

'Well, you could try the Victory Club. A lot of the old and bold go there. Someone might remember him.'

It wasn't much, but it was a lead. 'Thanks, thanks a lot,' said Danny. 'Bye.' He went over to the bench and sat next to Elena. The envelope was still unopened. 'From your dad?'

Elena didn't sound happy. 'Who else do I know in Nigeria?'

'Don't you want to know what it says?'

'I already know. He's realized the money my mum saved is there for me now, and he wants it. Money's the only thing he's ever been interested in.'

Since turning sixteen, Elena had been allowed to use the money her mum had left her. So far, she had delved into the savings only once, to buy her laptop plus the hardware needed to turn the Foxcroft broadband connection into a hot zone. It meant she could use her machine wire-free anywhere in the building.

Elena already had her future mapped out. After university she planned to become a computer scientist, so her state-of-the-art laptop was no toy, it was an investment.

Danny reached over and checked out the stamp on the letter. 'Read it. Maybe you're wrong, and at least you've got someone who wants to be in contact.'

31

Elena hesitated. She'd been disappointed by her father so many times before. The single birthday card she'd received over the past eight years was tucked away at the back of a desk drawer in her room, along with the one letter he'd written to her mum asking for money. He'd even got Elena's age wrong on the card. But now this. She handed the envelope to Danny. 'You read it.'

'Me?'

'I've been doing things for you for hours, it's your turn to do something for me. If he mentions the money once, just once, I want you to tell me. Then I can tear it up and throw it away.'

Danny slipped a thumb under one corner of the envelope and sliced it open. It wasn't a long letter – two pages of cheap, lined paper torn from a notebook – but Danny carefully read every scruffily written word, aware all the time that Elena was deliberately looking in the other direction. When he finished reading, Danny refolded the two sheets of paper and handed them back. 'You don't have to tear it up.'

Elena said nothing but she was pleased. And relieved. She unfolded the pages and began to read.

5

About a mile upstream from the Houses of Parliament, on the south side of the river Thames close to Vauxhall Bridge, stands a strangely shaped building known as Vauxhall Cross.

It looks like a beige and black pyramid with its top cut off. There are staged levels with large towers on either side and a terrace bar overlooking the Thames. With a few flashing neon lights added it could easily be mistaken for a casino.

But Vauxhall Cross is no casino. It is the headquarters of the Secret Intelligence Service, or MI6. Those on the inside rarely, if ever, use the term MI6. As far as they are concerned they work for 'The Firm'. They are responsible for overseas intelligence gathering and for covert operations. They 'maintain the UK's influence overseas'. They keep the 'Great' in Great Britain.

George Fincham arrived early, as he did most mornings. Dressed, as always, in a smart suit, crisp white shirt and favourite MCC tie, he swiped his identity card through the electronic reader and eased open the single metal door. He carried no briefcase or papers. Staff at Vauxhall Cross do not take their work home with them, not even high-ranking IBs like George Fincham.

He walked down to reception, where the first visitor of the day was waiting to be collected after being issued with a badge that read: ESCORTED EVERYWHERE. Fincham simply nodded a good morning to the two female receptionists seated behind blastproof glass and walked on to the lifts.

His office was high up and at the rear of the building, with a river view up to Big Ben and the Houses of Parliament. Fincham reached his floor and stepped out of the lift. The long corridor kept its usual secretive silence. The only sounds were the faint hum of the air conditioning and the hardly audible electronic buzz of the fluorescent lighting.

In one of the small staff kitchens, two other early arrivals, their IDs slung on chains around their necks, stood making coffee. They spoke in soft voices. That wasn't unusual: everyone at Vauxhall Cross spoke softly when away from the privacy of their office.

Fincham arrived at his own office, unlocked the heavy wooden door and went inside. He felt at home in here. The room was functional and impersonal. There were no paintings on the walls, just plasma TVs mounted on a wall bracket in one corner. One screen constantly scrolled through Ceefax world news headlines; the other was tuned to BBC News 24, with the sound muted but with subtitles at the bottom of the screen.

The desk stood close to the picture window, which stretched the entire width of the office. Fincham went over to the window and opened the venetian blinds and the morning sunlight immediately warmed the room. There was little traffic on the Thames; not even the tourist pleasure boats had started their daily journeys up and down the couple of miles of brown, murky river water.

A sharp double knock at the door interrupted Fincham's thoughts as he stared out towards Parliament. He answered in his usual way: 'Come.'

Marcie Deveraux looked immaculate. She always did. Her black trouser suit was definitely not off the peg and was way out of the price range of most female IBs. Fortunately for Deveraux, her expensive tastes didn't depend on the salary she received from the British government. Her family was of West Indian origin and her ancestors had made their fortune way back, by cooperating with the French when they arrived to colonize their island.

With her high-cheekboned exotic looks, closely cropped jet-black hair and slim figure, Marcie Deveraux looked like a supermodel. She could have been. She had it all. Style. Class. Va va voom.

But Marcie Deveraux had always had different ambitions. Her first in Social and Political Sciences at Cambridge had led to her being recruited by the Firm, and she had quickly been identified for accelerated promotion. And she knew that within ten years, with luck and the right breaks, she could make it to 'C', the name given to the head of the Intelligence Service.

But for now she was number two in Fincham's section, which was responsible for the Firm's internal security. That included making sure that no one in the service was selling secrets to the enemy, while at the same time keeping the government from knowing too much about the Firm's activities. It was policy to keep politicians at arm's length. Whenever possible.

'Good morning, sir.'

Fincham turned away from the window, gestured to Deveraux to sit down and settled himself into the high-backed executive chair on his side of the desk.

'What do you have for me, Marcie?'

'It looks as though your plan is beginning to pay dividends, sir.'

She slid a single sheet of paper across the desktop towards Fincham. Danny's army RCB file was also on the desk. His photograph had been removed from the cover.

Fincham picked up the paper and speed-read the small type as Deveraux continued, 'He's already been a very busy boy. Four contacts reported, even the Army Pensions Office. Shows great initiative.'

'And we're watching him?'

'Oh, yes, sir, we're watching him. Closely.'

Fincham allowed himself a half smile. 'Good. Very good.'

6

A fine summer drizzle was falling. Danny zipped up his leather jacket and turned up the collar. He pulled the Foxcroft front door shut and walked towards the bus stop.

'Stand by. Stand by. That's a possible Bravo One foxtrot. He's gone left.'

The dark blue VW Golf was parked about sixty metres further down the street. It was two up, a man and a woman, both sitting back in their seats. They didn't look at each other. They hardly moved; just glanced down at the copy of Danny's RCB photograph resting on the driver's lap.

A single squeeze of the radio pressel on the gearstick activated the concealed microphone in the surveillance car.

'That's a definite Bravo One, brown leather on blue jeans, still foxtrot on the left, approaching the first junction left.'

The team was four-strong. They used first names

only – that way there was no confusion when talking on their radio net. Mick sat in the driver's seat of the Golf, Fran was next to him. They were responsible for initiating the surveillance when the target moved. They were the trigger.

Further back down the main road, Jimmy, dressed in black leathers and clutching a helmet, was perched on the saddle of a black TDM motorbike. Parked nearby in a side street was Brian, at the wheel of a silver Nissan. Both listened to the second-by-second information coming into their radio earpieces. At any moment it could be their turn to take over the follow.

'Bravo One at the junction, still straight.'

Fran got out of the Golf, checked that her jacket hadn't ridden up and exposed her pistol and the two spare thirteen-round magazines attached to her jeans belt, and walked in the same direction as Danny. Mick went on the net.

'That's Fran foxtrot. Mick still has Bravo One.'

Fran was fifty metres behind Danny as she hit the pressel sewn into the shoulder strap of her handbag to activate her personal covert radio. The mic sewn into the bag easily picked up her softly spoken words.

'Fran has Bravo One, halfway to the next junction left. He's not aware.'

Mick could see that, should Danny turn round and look back up the road, *he* was directly in his line of sight. It was time to shift. He started up the Golf, drove off and took the first turning right.

Danny reached the bus stop. Fran hit her pressel again.

'Stop. Stop. Stop. Bravo One static at the bus stop on the left.'

Fran kept walking, making sure she didn't catch Danny's eye. There was nothing unusual about the way she moved or looked. Everything was natural. Normal. Ordinary. The whole team were experts at being ordinary. It was all part of the training. Avoid causing suspicion. Make sure there's a reason for every action. Be third party aware.

On this job, 'third party' meant anyone but Danny. The last thing the team wanted was some do-gooder spotting that he was being watched or followed and then phoning the police. That would compromise the whole operation.

Fran still had her finger on the radio pressel as she neared the bus stop.

'I see bus number thirty-six, I've got to keep foxtrot, I'm gonna lose him.'

The team had to keep the target in sight at all times. Brian, in the Nissan, and Jimmy on the TDM were both about to move when Mick came onto the net.

'Mick's going for the trigger.'

Mick had taken the first right and two quick left turns. He was driving back towards the main street looking for a parking space with a sight line to the bus stop. He had to find a space quickly; Fran was too near to Danny to continue. She turned left at the side road close to the bus stop, spotted a shop and headed towards it.

'Fran no longer has Bravo One.'

Mick pulled on the handbrake and switched off the Golf's engine.

'Mick has the trigger, Mick has the trigger.'

He'd made it.

'Bravo One still static at the bus stop. Reading bus times . . . now checking his watch. That's hands in pockets, he looks unaware.'

While Mick had been racing to get into position, Brian had gone online with his Nokia and had found the information the team needed.

'The thirty-six goes from Camberwell to Victoria, Marble Arch, Paddington and ending at Queen's Park. That's along—'

Mick cut in on the net.

'Stand by! Stand by! That's a thirty-six towards Bravo One. He's getting money ready. Last three on the plate romeo bravo alpha and the back of it has a dark green Nikon advert. Here we go.'

The bus pulled into the kerbside. The air pumps hissed and the doors opened.

'That's Bravo One cash in hand. Stepping on the bus, now unsighted in the bus. Wait . . . wait . . . that's doors closed and indicators on. Stand by. Stand by . . . that's the bus mobile.'

Jimmy, the TDM rider, cut in on the radio net by pressing a button that was part of the motorbike's light selection console.

'Jimmy has the bus, mobile towards the first set of lights.'

Jimmy had taken control of the surveillance. Brian, in the silver Nissan, was also on the move as Mick drove off to collect Fran. The operation was going smoothly: the target was correctly triggered away.

The bus was crowded but Danny managed to find a seat downstairs. He glanced around at the other passengers. Most were gazing zombie-like at the television monitor at the front as it relentlessly repeated adverts for W H Smith and Woolworths.

But Danny had other things on his mind. He reached into an inside pocket of his jacket and pulled out the old photograph of his grandfather with his two army friends. Elena had carefully joined the two halves together with clear sellotape so that the tear was barely visible.

Danny looked at the bright-eyed young man smiling back at him and saw for the first time that it was almost like staring into a mirror. Fergus would have been in his early twenties when the photograph was taken, not many years older than Danny was now.

They were so alike in looks, if nothing else. Fergus was a little taller than average, just like Danny. He looked strong, but wiry rather than muscular, just like Danny. His face was lean, his smile was wide and his eyes were clear and piercing, just like Danny's.

As Danny studied the black-and-white image, he wondered again what had turned the smiling, cheerful-looking young squaddie into the cynical veteran his grandfather had become. But he knew the answer. Money. Nothing more and nothing less. It made him burn with rage. He turned the photograph over. Scribbled in faded ink was: *Watts 8654 – 2/6 to pay.* He knew that 2/6 was how old money was written but had no idea what the other numbers meant.

The bus came to a sudden halt as, up ahead, a delivery van double-parked outside a parade of shops.

'That's the bus held in traffic. Jimmy still has. Can't see Bravo One.'

Jimmy idled the TDM's powerful 850cc engine. He didn't like being in situations like this: motorbike riders don't usually hang around in traffic jams.

Fran was at the kerbside as the Golf drew up. There was no hurry as she got into the car, she did nothing to arouse the interest of any inquisitive passer-by. But the moment they were on the move she went onto the radio net.

'That's Fran complete.'

Jimmy answered.

'Roger that. Jimmy still has bus, slow moving towards the lights. Can anyone at the next bus stop?'

The silver Nissan was just three vehicles behind the TDM.

'Brian can.'

'Roger that, Brian. Lights to red, we are going to be held.'

Mick was steering the Golf through quieter backstreets, following Fran's directions as she checked the route of the 36 bus in one of their map books.

'This is Mick. We'll jump ahead on the bus route.'

The traffic lights changed and the bus pulled slowly away.

'Stand by, stand by. Lights to green. Can you now, Brian?'

'Brian can.'

Jimmy opened the bike's throttle and squeezed the bike through a gap between the lumbering double-decker and a van travelling in the other direction. On the lower deck, Danny heard the throaty growl of the TDM and glanced through the window as the bike roared by. He was into bikes in a big way and had promised himself one as soon as he joined the army. He shook his head; that was another plan his granddad had cocked up.

'Brian has the bus. That's indicators on.'

The bus came to a standstill and Brian pulled in behind a line of parked cars.

'Stop, stop, stop. Brian has the trigger. Doors open, people getting off. Wait . . .'

The rest of the team listened to hear if Danny was about to go foxtrot again.

'That's doors closed, no sign of Bravo One. Indicators on, that's the bus mobile.'

The bizarre game of vehicular leapfrog continued through the streets of south-east London and on towards the heart of the capital. As the bus neared Marble Arch, Danny got up from his seat and moved towards the doors.

The TDM passed the bus for the final time. Mick and Fran in the Golf had the trigger at the next bus stop.

'Stand by, stand by. That's Bravo One at the doors. He's at the doors ready to go foxtrot. Indicators on, bus slowing . . . Stop, stop, stop at Marble Arch. Fran's going foxtrot.'

Before Danny was even off the bus, Fran was on the pavement ready to take over the follow.

'Fran has Bravo One foxtrot on the Edgware Road, on the left towards the first junction left. He's checking a street map.'

Fran was briefly on her own while the others tried to shortcut their way towards Danny. It was a critical phase, but the pavement was busy with pedestrians, meaning Fran could continue for some time without fear of alerting any third party. Then she hit a problem.

'That's Bravo One approaching first junction left. That's Bravo One gone left. Temporarily unsighted.'

Fran quickened her pace, hurrying but not running: it was crucial to stay third party aware. But there was no need for her to worry. Just before she turned the corner, Jimmy came on the net.

'Jimmy has Bravo One. Foxtrot on Seymour Street. He's slowing – looks like he's searching for an address. Wait . . . wait . . .'

Fran turned into Seymour Street and saw the TDM parked towards the end. There was no sign of Jimmy, but Danny was standing outside a building with a glass canopy over the entrance doors.

'Wait . . . wait . . . Bravo One going into building now. Now unsighted.'

Fran cut in on the net.

'I'll do a walk past. Wait out.'

She walked slowly down the street, not stopping as she reached the building, just glancing up at the words written along the side of the canopy. They read: THE VICTORY CLUB.

1

The interior of the Victory Club took Danny by surprise. From the outside it looked old and established like most of the other buildings in the street, but once through the automatic double doors he saw that it was all black wood, steel and mirrors. Some trendy designer had been hard at work giving the place a makeover.

To the left was an open door leading into a canteen-style dining room, where a few old boys were having lunch. They didn't look much like old soldiers to Danny, but then he had no idea what old soldiers were meant to look like.

Straight ahead was a mirrored reception desk. But between Danny and the desk stood a massive security guy in a black suit. He was checking the names of three other smartly dressed men against a list he held.

Glancing down at his jeans and leather jacket,

Danny wondered if maybe he should have worn a tie. It was too late to worry, and anyway, there was a much bigger problem – his name wasn't on that list. He thought quickly. 'Use your initiative,' that's what they'd told him at the army officers' selection board. He glanced around the entrance hall and spotted an information board detailing the events in the various conference rooms. At the top it read: TRAFALGAR ROOM. ARMY RESETTLEMENT SEMINAR.

As the three visitors were given the OK to go into the club, Danny strode confidently after them. He didn't even look at the security guard and for a couple of seconds it seemed as though he'd got away with it.

Then a surprisingly high-pitched voice said, 'Excuse me, can I help you?'

'I'm here to see my dad,' answered Danny as he turned back, smiling innocently. 'He's on the army resettlement course. Said he'd meet me in the bar at lunch time.'

'And your name is . . . ?'

Danny hadn't thought that far, but there was another room mentioned on the information board. It would have to do. 'Carisbrook. Danny Carisbrook.'

The security guard studied his list. 'No Carisbrook on here. I'm sorry, your dad hasn't signed you in.'

Danny silently told himself what a dickhead he'd been. He shouldn't have made up a name; he could have just said he was looking for his missing grandfather.

But his luck was in. The security guard looked up from his list and winked. 'Tell you what, you go through to the bar and when your dad arrives get him to come and sign you in. You see, the thing is, being a military club we have to be very aware of security.'

'Yeah, I can see that,' answered Danny, trying not to laugh and moving quickly off towards the bar. 'I'll get my dad to come out.'

The bar room was smart. Gleaming. And virtually deserted, almost as though the club members didn't want to use it for fear of spoiling the newness of the furniture and fittings. The carpet even smelled new.

Behind the bar itself, an operation was being carried out with military precision. The barman was polishing glasses, patiently putting a shine on each one and then adding it to a row on the bartop. They made a perfect line, like they were on parade, a credit to the proud barman, who sighed loudly and deliberately as Danny approached. The boy was interrupting important work. 'Can't serve you.'

'Eh?'

'Not unless you're accompanied by a member.'

'But I don't want a drink,' said Danny.

Another glass was added to the row and its position was adjusted slightly. 'That's what we do here. Serve drinks. Wines, beers, spirits, even soft drinks. That's why I'm here.' He picked up another glass.

Danny sighed. 'I'm looking for someone, trying to find him.'

'Member, is he?'

'I don't think so. But he might have been.'

The barman reluctantly stopped polishing and put down the glass, realizing that Danny wasn't going to go away until his questions were answered. 'Name?'

'Watts. Fergus Watts.'

The stare was hard and suspicious. 'And you are?'

'I'm his grandson, Danny. And I need to find him, it's really urgent.'

The hard features softened. 'I'm Harry,' said the barman with a nod and a smile. His face became a mask of concentration as he scrolled through his mental filing cabinet of familiar and half-forgotten names. 'Fergus Watts . . . Fergus Watts.' Eventually he shook his head. 'Doesn't mean anything to me, and I know them all here.'

Danny reached into the inside pocket of his leather jacket, took out the photograph and handed it over. 'My granddad's the one in the middle. It's an old photo but he can't have changed that much.'

Harry studied the faded photograph and then turned it over and saw the writing on the back. He laughed. 'Two and six. Half a crown, we called it. Those were the days.'

'But those other numbers,' said Danny quickly, not wanting to be drawn into a long conversation about the good old days, 'the ones after his name – what do they mean?'

'Probably his last four,' answered Harry with a shrug.

'Last four? Last four what?'

Harry smiled indulgently. 'Everyone gets an eight-digit number in the army. There might have been a few Wattses in his unit so they just wrote the last four with the name. Last four avoids confusion, specially in the Welsh regiments with all those Joneses and Davises. No one ever forgets their number.'

He beckoned Danny a little closer and continued, 'Between you and me, I use my last four on my cash card. It's easy to get confused at my age so—'

'But do you know him?' interrupted Danny. Getting a simple answer to a simple question wasn't proving an easy task.

Harry looked at the photo again. 'I'm sorry, son, I don't. And I can tell you for a fact that he's never been in here because I go back longer than anyone. They reckon I'm part of the furniture, and I'm talking about the old furniture, not this new fancy stuff.'

It had all been a complete waste of time and the only lead had led absolutely nowhere. Danny took back the photograph and started to put it into his pocket.

Harry picked up his tea cloth. 'You need to have a word with Big Kev.'

'Who?'

'The tallest bloke in the photo, the one on the right. He's a lot younger there but I'd know Big Kev anywhere.'

Danny stared at the photograph again. He'd never taken the slightest interest in the two young men standing on either side of his grandfather. Not until now.

'That's Kev Newman,' said Harry, picking up a glass and beginning his polishing again. 'He'll be in tomorrow. There's a funeral for an ex-Regiment man and the wake's here afterwards. And Big Kev never misses a piss-up.'

8

Most days, business was over at Frankie's burger bar by mid afternoon. The white vans were heading back to their depots and the last of the reps had called in for a mug of tea and a chat. Turning off the hot water, cleaning the griddles, washing up and locking up didn't take very long.

Frankie could drive home in less than twenty minutes. But Frankie never went straight home. His anti-surveillance drill meant a long and complicated journey.

He unlocked the driver's door of his dark blue Fiesta, took a last look in both directions, climbed into the car and started the engine. The car was old and boring but in good nick, and that was just how Frankie wanted it. He never took unnecessary risks or drew attention to himself. Being stopped by the police for a routine check was taking an unnecessary risk, so the tyres on the Fiesta were legal, the lights worked, the tax disc was on display and the MOT was up to date.

On the drive towards Rochford, Frankie stuck to the speed limits, regularly checking his mirrors and taking a mental note of the make and colour of the vehicles following. Three miles from the town he pulled into a lay-by and pretended to look for something in the foot well. With no junctions for a quick turn-off, the following vehicles were committed to passing. Frankie clocked them all as they went by.

Back on the road he drove twice around the roundabout just outside the town, looking at the road signs as if he were confused. The roundabout was an obvious changeover place for a surveillance team, the ideal spot for one vehicle to peel off so that another could take over the follow. The double turn around the roundabout gave Frankie another chance to check on following vehicles.

He drove into a new residential area of flats and houses behind the town centre. The network of quiet streets gave him a wide choice of overnight parking places. He chose a different one every evening. He parked up, got out of the car and walked quickly across the road and through an alleyway towards the shops.

Frankie knew the surveillance game only too well. The most difficult time for a team is going foxtrot, so the quicker he got out of sight the harder it was to get the trigger on him. He moved as swiftly as he could but remained third party aware, never looking back to see what was happening behind.

Hiding his limp completely was impossible, and the

faster he walked the more apparent it became. He'd been stuck with it ever since the bodged operation in Colombia. It was with him for life and a real bonus for any watching surveillance team. A VDM that helped pick out Frankie in a crowd.

He went into a shop and bought an evening newspaper. Standing in the queue to pay, he glanced out through the windows, looking for even the smallest sign that he was being followed. Signs like someone hovering for a moment too long by the doorway or apparently talking to themselves when walking by – a basic error. Surveillance operators are trained in not moving their lips when talking on the radio net.

Frankie saw nothing suspicious, but that didn't necessarily mean he wasn't being followed. It could mean that the team was good.

He left the shop and crossed the small town square. He went through another alleyway into a small car park, pulling from his jacket a green nylon waterproof and a rolled-up flat cap. His ancient, three-gear bicycle was locked to a railing. He quickly unlocked the bike, put on the waterproof and flat cap and cycled away.

It was a long ride home, but Frankie was used to it.

The bustling modern commuter towns of east Essex gradually give way to a flat, marshy landscape, where ancient villages like Canewdon, Paglesham and Creeksea could still almost be a million miles from the twenty-first century.

The cottage was in remote farmland, off a quiet B-road and down a long muddy track. Around it were small patches of woodland and further out were the marshes and then the river Crouch.

Frankie reached the track and stopped to check that no vehicles had made any ground sign in the mud. It was clean of tyre marks.

He walked down the track, pushing the bike by the saddle. Halfway down and off to one side stood an old, disused chicken coop. Underneath it, attached to a wire, was a mini Maglite torch. The front glass had been covered with tape so that when the torch was on it showed just a pinprick of light. Frankie checked under the coop. There was no beam of light, which meant that the motion detectors in and around the house had not been tripped during the day. If they had, Frankie would simply have turned round and never come back. The only rule was survival.

Walking towards the cottage, he made sure he tripped the four further concealed detectors. Their wiring was dug into the mud and their monitors were hidden in the branches of stunted and wind-blown trees lining the track. They were at shoulder height – that way they couldn't be tripped by a fox or a dog.

The detectors were connected to normal domestic security lights placed along the track and around the house. Normal, but specially customized by Frankie. They were covered with layers of infra-red filter paper, meaning that if they were activated there would be no flood of white light. Instead, IR security cameras hidden beneath the lights would relay pictures back to the small bank of TV monitors inside the house.

The house was like a fortress. Fortress Frankie.

Everything used in its defence had been bought at either the local B&Q store or an electrical repairs shop and then been adapted by Frankie for his special requirements. He had security down to a fine art.

He reached the cottage. All seemed in order: the garden gate was still closed. He ran one hand down to a point just below the latch and felt the tip of the match head he had wedged there while closing the gate that morning. No one had opened the gate. No one had reason to: Frankie never got any mail.

He took the bike inside, locked the front door, and went into every room, checking that nothing had been disturbed.

Most of the rooms had bare, original floorboards or old carpet, but in the kitchen Frankie had fitted a cheap vinyl covering in an imitation marble tile pattern. In front of the sink unit a thick rug was super-glued to the vinyl. Frankie grabbed one edge of the rug with both hands and pulled, lifting the rug, the covering and the hidden trapdoor beneath.

The rotting wooden steps disappeared into darkness. A torch lay on the first step. Frankie switched it on and descended into the cellar. It was damp and musty, and because of the closeness to the river, a few millimetres of water covered the floor even in the summer months. But apart from the isolated location of the cottage, the cellar had been its major attraction.

Against one wall was a stack of wooden boxes. Frankie moved them to one side and shone a torch into a small hole halfway up the wall. The piercing beam picked out the coffin-sized cave a metre and a half into the tunnel. In it was a bin liner full of clothes, tinned food and most of Frankie's savings. Beyond the cave, the narrow tunnel stretched away into darkness for nearly twenty metres. At the far end, a camou-flaged escape hatch went up to ground level in the tree line to the right of the cottage. If ever the house came under attack Frankie's best chance of survival would be concealment. The cave was one of his hides; there were two more out in the woodlands.

He went back up to the ground floor and looked at the TV monitors to make sure the detectors had tripped on the way in. The reassuring green glow of the muddy track from the IR cameras told him all was well.

That was it. Drill over. Frankie could relax, as much as he ever relaxed. He would make himself a meal and then settle down to another night in front of the telly.

9

'Your granddad was a good bloke.'

'Was?'

Kev Newman shrugged, took a long drink from his pint of bitter and sat back in his chair. It seemed to have difficulty in containing him. 'Figure of speech.'

It was easy to see why he was known as Big Kev. He was massive. He'd looked tall in the photograph but in the years since then he'd bulked up in a big way. Now muscle was gradually turning to fat, but with hands like shovels, Kev still looked like the wrong man to pick an argument with.

The Victory Club was heaving, very different from Danny's first visit. The 'old and bold', the name given to ex-SAS men, had turned out in their droves to give their mate a good send-off. Ties were loosened, jackets were draped over the backs of chairs, the beer was flowing and the room was alive with animated conversation and laughter. The funeral was over and the wake was well and truly underway.

Getting into the Victory had been easier for Danny second time around. He'd arranged for Harry the barman to sign him in under the name of Carisbrook and it had been no problem, specially as he was more suitably dressed in jacket and tie.

He spotted Kev Newman as soon as he walked in with a bunch of his mates. Big Kev wasn't easy to miss. The group got in their first round of drinks, and as they made their way towards a corner table, Kev was waylaid by another veteran. Danny waited until Kev was alone and then moved in and introduced himself.

If the big man was surprised he didn't show it. He looked at Danny and nodded, as if seeing the similarities between grandson and grandfather. Then he shook hands, almost crushing Danny's fingers in his giant fist, and invited him to join the group at the table. When they pulled up their chairs Kev simply said to the others, 'This is Danny.' Nothing more.

Since then they'd been talking quietly, sitting slightly apart from the rest. But the conversation wasn't getting very far. Danny leaned in closer to Big Kev. 'Do you know where my granddad is?'

The answer came immediately. 'Haven't a clue.'

'But you were his friend.'

'Best mates. That photo you've got was taken before we even made it into the Regiment. We went all the way together, joined up at the same time and then—'

Whatever Kev was about to say went unspoken as

he stood up, almost spilling his beer in the process. As Danny looked on, bewildered, the other veterans stood up too. Then he saw why.

'No need to stand, chaps. Not any more.'

Kev was almost standing to attention. 'Old habits, sir.'

'Sir' was tall, grey-haired and distinguished-looking, and he had such a presence that, without knowing why, Danny found himself standing as well.

'Just wanted to let you chaps know that my wife and I are leaving now – long drive back.'

'Good of you both to come, sir,' said Kev.

'Not at all, least we could do.' He noticed Danny. 'Hello, who's this? A new recruit?'

'Friend of a friend, sir,' answered Kev before Danny could speak.

Sir smiled at Danny. 'Don't let this lot of reprobates lead you astray. Goodbye to you all then.'

The veterans chorused their 'Bye, sir's and retook their seats.

Big Kev finished his pint and Danny took a swig of his Coke. 'Who was that?'

'Old CO. Colonel. A good bloke.'

Danny couldn't stop himself from replying, 'Like my granddad?'

Kev didn't answer. He was a man of few words, and most of those he seemed to want to keep to himself. But everyone else had plenty to say. The room was getting noisier by the minute; the old and bold were enjoying sharing stories and memories of their glory days.

Danny almost had to shout. 'I know what he did. In Colombia.'

'Do you?' said Kev, so softly that Danny struggled to hear. 'Well, maybe you do and maybe you don't.'

Kev was giving nothing away and Danny's temper was building. 'Look, I've got to find him.'

One of the men on the far side of the table heard Danny. 'Find who? Who's he on about, Kev?'

The noise in the bar was so loud now that Danny did have to shout. 'My granddad.'

An outburst of raucous laughter from the group at the next table gave the veteran no chance of hearing. He shouted back, 'Who?'

What happened next was one of those freak moments: it probably wouldn't have happened again if it had been rehearsed a hundred times. But just as Danny cupped his hands to his mouth and shouted there was a total drop in the level of chatter and laughter.

The two words boomed out: 'Fergus Watts!'

A great swathe of the room went completely silent and all eyes turned towards Danny. He turned to Kev. 'What? What did I do?'

The answer was softly spoken. 'Not a very popular name in the Regiment these days, son.'

Gradually the conversation and laughter resumed but two tables away one man kept his eyes firmly fixed on Danny. 'Fergus Watts,' he whispered. 'Now there's a name I haven't heard in a long time.'

Maybe it was the intensity of his stare that made Danny turn and look, maybe it was just chance. Whatever the reason, their eyes met. The staring man gave Danny an exaggerated smile, raised his glass and silently mouthed, 'Cheers.'

It was unsettling, spooky, and Danny looked away as Big Kev stood up and called over to one of his friends, 'I need a gypsy's. Get a round in, will you, Tone, and one for the lad?' He glanced at Danny. 'Unless it's time for you to go?'

Danny wasn't going to be pushed out. 'I'm not in any rush.'

Kev shrugged and moved off and Tone collected the glasses and headed for the bar.

Danny sat back in his chair and gazed around at the old and bold. They were a tough-looking bunch, but in some ways they were as different as they were similar.

He had half expected them all to be like Kev Newman: big, brawny, muscular; but physically they came in a variety of shapes and sizes. They had one thing in common though, they all looked hard. More than that, they looked *hardened*, as though what they had seen and done had given them a different attitude to life from ordinary people.

Danny couldn't figure out what it was that made them want to join the SAS. The regular army was different; he still desperately wanted that for himself. The army meant a career, a lifestyle, worldwide travel. There was the possibility of danger, but not on an almost daily basis, and maybe never at the same level as in the SAS.

But the SAS was like saying, 'Put me in danger. I want to risk my life every time I go on an operation. I want to go into the most dangerous places and face up to guerrillas and terrorists and whatever they can throw at me.'

As the noise got louder and the booze flowed faster,

Danny decided that maybe there wasn't any special quality that marked out an SAS man, just a special kind of madness.

His eyes rested on the door leading out to the lobby. Danny stared. Through the glass section at the top of the door he could see Big Kev. He hadn't gone to the toilets at all. He was talking on a mobile.

That was when Danny realized. Big Kev *did* know where his granddad was. And the phone call he was making – it was to Fergus Watts. Danny knew that for sure, but even as he thought of running out to the lobby to confront Kev, the big man came pushing his way through towards the table.

He slipped his mobile phone into a pocket of his jacket, which was hanging over the back of his chair, and glanced towards the crowded bar. 'What's wrong with that Tone? He hasn't even ordered the drinks yet.'

Tone was standing near to the bar, empty glasses in hands, talking to two other veterans.

'If you want something doing, do it yourself,' growled Big Kev and stomped off towards the bar.

It took no more than three seconds. A glance around to check that no one was watching and Kev's mobile was out of the jacket pocket and in Danny's hands. He didn't hang around but slid the mobile into one of his own pockets and headed off towards the toilets. He had to find the last number called on the mobile.

The toilets were empty but Danny went into a cubicle and locked the door. Finding the last number dialled was simple, even though Kev's mobile was ancient, a total brick.

But Danny had no way of keeping or storing the number. His own mobile had run out of credit and he hadn't bothered bringing it. He didn't even have a pen on him. 'Think, Danny,' he whispered. 'Think.'

At the bar, Big Kev had taken over the drinks order and was being served. The last pint was pulled and placed on a tray full of glasses. It was an expensive round and Kev handed over two twenty-pound notes. He had a lot on his mind and was deep in thought as he pocketed the change and picked up the tray.

As Danny emerged from the toilets he saw Kev turn from the bar and start to make his way back to the table. Danny had to get there first; he had to get the mobile back into Kev's jacket.

Kev was closer to the table but he also had a tray full of easily spilled drinks to manoeuvre. He reached his friend Tone, who was still with the two veterans.

'Please stop and talk to them,' whispered Danny, looking at Kev and trying to appear as normal as possible. He couldn't rush – someone would want to know why.

But Kev didn't stop, he obviously needed his pint. He moved steadily towards the table: he was going to get there first. Then he heard the shout: 'Kev? Kev?'

Kev turned back as Harry the barman approached. 'You gave me two twenties, didn't you?'

The big man nodded. 'Yeah.'

'Sorry, mate, I gave you change for thirty. We're so busy behind there I don't know my arse from my elbow.'

Kev grinned. 'Leave it on the tray, Harry.'

By the time Kev placed the tray on the table, the mobile was back in his jacket pocket and Danny was sitting in his chair trying to look a lot more relaxed than he felt. 'Think I will make a move after all.'

'What about your drink? Took me long enough to get it.'

'No, I'd better get off.' He stood up and was more prepared for the crushing effect of Kev's handshake this time, but he still winced as the big man gripped his hand.

'I'm sorry about your granddad, Danny. If you want my opinion the best thing you can do is forget all about him.'

Danny nodded. 'Yeah, maybe you're right. Thanks anyway.'

On the way out Danny stopped at the bar and borrowed a pencil from Harry. He went back to the toilets and into the cubicle he'd used before. The telephone number was still there, scrawled in soap on the cubicle wall. Danny copied the number onto a scrap of paper and wiped the wall clean.

He was feeling pleased with himself as he left the bar and headed for the lobby. He'd done it: he had the number and got one over on Big Kev. He'd got away with it. Then he felt the tap on his shoulder. 'Hang on.'

Big Kev wasn't so easily fooled after all. Danny had been rumbled. Slowly, he turned round. But it wasn't Big Kev; it was the staring man, smiling that same exaggerated smile. 'Name's Eddie Moyes. I thought we might have a little chat.'

10

Danny made his phone call to Elena from a public phone box. The conversation was brief, and fifteen minutes later he was in an Internet café. He bought himself a Coke and chose a computer with a view out onto the street. When he went online and logged on to MSN, Elena was waiting for him. She regularly changed her screen name and since her GCSE results had started calling herself 'A star'. Modest as always. Danny stuck to Danny.

```
A star says: (4:34:09 pm)
so wots all the mystery. yor call spooked me
Danny says: (4:34:18 pm)
think im being followed
A star says: (4:34:26 pm)
o yeah right
Danny says: (4:34:47 pm)
im serious. a motorbike, u know i always
```

spot bikes. Saw it twice yesday & more
today. same bike same rider
A star says: (4:35:01 pm)
y should any1 want 2 follow u
Danny says: (4:35:13 pm)
dunno . . . really freakin me tho

Danny glanced out through the window. He was
sure he'd seen the black TDM at least three times that
day, the last time soon after he left the Victory Club.

A star says: (4:35:28 pm)
danny calm down yr making me nervos. tell
me what happened @ club
Danny says: (4:35:43 pm)
saw big kev. got a mobile number, sure its
my gdads
A star says: (4:35:51 pm)
wot big kev gave u the number
Danny says: (4:36:06 pm)
not exactly. kev called him, i got number
from his mob
A star says: (4:36:15 pm)
r u gonna call
Danny says: (4:36:27 pm)
dunno. not sure wot 2 do
A star says: (4:36:40 pm)
don't call. might scare hm off. give me
number
Danny says: (4:36:48 pm)
y

```
A star says: (4:37:13 pm)
mayb i can trace where kev made call 2, I
mean the location, where yor gdad woz wen
he took call
Danny says: (4:37:24 pm)
like how
A star says: (4:37:36 pm)
police do it. if plod can A star can. gimme
number
```

Danny fished out the scrap of paper and sent the mobile number over to Elena.

```
A star says: (4:37:56 pm)
wot u do while i go 4 this
Danny says: (4:38:28 pm)
this bloke at club, said he might be able
help find fergus. names eddie moyes, said
id meet 2morrow but dunno if I trust him,
gonna check something
A star says: (4:38:43 pm)
u r getting para!!!!!!
Danny says: (4:38:54 pm)
maybe but dnt trust any1 but u
A star says: (4:39:06 pm)
w8 there & dnt panic!!!!
```

They both stayed logged on to MSN but set their status to 'away'.

Danny still felt edgy. At any moment he expected to hear the growl of the TDM as it passed the window or see a man in black bikers' leathers walk through the door. The café wasn't busy – just a youngish businessman checking or sending e-mails and a couple of Australian girls online to friends back home. Their online conversations must have been interesting: the two girls kept shrieking with laughter and then whispering to each other.

Elena was always up to speed with the latest developments in online technology. She knew all about companies providing GSM location services. It was a relatively simple operation. They just traced which mobile mast the phone was connected to, and from that could locate the phone to within a hundred metres. The police had been operating the system for years and had used the location of tracked mobiles as evidence in court cases.

Now the system was available to the public, and Elena was ready to give it a shot. There were plenty of online companies offering the service. She logged on to one and read the welcome-page boast that from now on parents could keep track of their kids and companies could always know exactly what their employees were up to.

Elena went to the main page and got the bad news: to use the system, subscribers needed not only the phone number but also the phone user's four-figure PIN number. 'Should have realized they wouldn't make it easy,' she said to herself.

She decided to take a chance. She paid her £4.99 fee online using her cash card and got four attempts at the correct PIN number.

'Maybe he's stupid,' said Elena as she tried the obvious combinations: 1234, 4321, 1111, 2222.

But Fergus Watts obviously wasn't stupid. For another £20 she could try twenty more times.

Danny was going back over the website pages about his grandfather.

Ever since Eddie Moyes had introduced himself at the Victory Club, Danny had felt sure he had heard or seen the name somewhere before. And very recently.

Moyes certainly didn't look ex-SAS. He was over-weight and well out of condition. But that didn't necessarily mean he wasn't a former soldier, and at the back of Danny's mind there was something telling him he'd seen the name in at least one of the stories about his grandfather.

And there was something else about Eddie Moyes that didn't feel right. At the Victory Club Danny had told him he was the grandson of Fergus Watts and that he was searching for his grandfather.

'Really?' Moyes answered with barely concealed excitement. 'I think I can help you. Look, why don't we get out of here and find somewhere we can speak in private? I know a nice little pub just down the road.'

Danny almost said yes, but something told him to back off. While everyone else at the Victory had recoiled in horror at the name Fergus Watts, this bloke was almost falling over himself to help. It didn't add up, specially as Danny had already convinced himself he was being followed.

He stalled Moyes by saying he had to get away but that they could meet the following morning at a café near Foxcroft. Moyes didn't press him to stay, just smiled, and agreed to everything he said. That worried Danny too.

'Maybe Elena's right,' he whispered, as he trawled through the pages. 'Maybe I am getting paranoid.'

He sat at the computer and went through page after page of newspaper stories, but the name Moyes didn't feature in any of them.

He was just about ready to give up when he came to a headline he'd read before:

SAS TRAITOR MASTERMINDS
MASS PRISON BREAKOUT

But this time it wasn't the headline that drew Danny's attention, it was the by-line underneath:

By our correspondent Eddie Moyes

Danny smiled. 'He doesn't want to help me, he wants to find Fergus for himself. Well, nice try, Eddie Moyes, but you're not getting to him through me. No way.'

A soft ping on the computer informed Danny that Elena was back on MSN.

```
A star says: (5:06:01 pm)
this could take 4ever and seriously damage
my fundz
```

69

```
Danny says:  (5:06:19 pm)
wots happening
A star says:  (5:06:29 pm)
on site bt need pin no, 4 figures. dyu no
his bthday, might b start or end of it. i
dunno, im just guessing now
```

Elena was right, it could take for ever. The chance of randomly hitting the right combination was about as likely as winning the lottery. But then Danny had an idea. He took out the old photograph and turned it over.

```
Danny says:  (5:07:12 pm)
try 8654
A star says:  (5:07:21 pm)
y
Danny says:  (5:07:29 pm)
just try
```

Elena went back to the site and punched in the four numbers. The web page changed immediately and told her that it was locating a number. In less than a minute a map came onto the screen with a circle around an area in Essex. Elena could zoom in on the map and in seconds she was writing down the details. She went back to Danny.

```
A star says:  (5:08:08 pm)
GOT IT
```

They logged off quickly. Danny wanted to get back

to Foxcroft to share the information and decide what to do next.

He was feeling better as he left the Internet café. He'd sussed out Eddie Moyes and there was no sign of the TDM. Maybe no one was following him at all. Maybe it was just his imagination. He turned to the right and walked towards the bus stop.

'Stand by, stand by. That's Bravo One foxtrot, he's gone right from Internet café. Fran's foxtrot.'

11

'I don't understand. He's in the same place as before but it's in the middle of nowhere. It's just a road. No buildings. Nothing.'

Danny and Elena had skipped breakfast and had logged on to the phone search company again. It clearly showed that Fergus – and Danny was convinced that it was Fergus – was in the same spot as on the previous day with his phone switched on. But the onscreen map showed no houses or larger factory buildings, not even a roadside filling station. Just road.

Elena was sitting at her laptop, frowning at the screen. 'Maybe he parks his car in the same place every day and waits for his calls. But why?'

The question went unanswered. Danny leaned against the door frame in the open doorway of Elena's room. They were bending the Foxcroft rules again. He wasn't supposed to be in the room. And he wasn't, not actually *in* it.

Elena turned from the computer. 'So what next?'

Danny had already made up his mind. 'I'm going there. Today. I can get a train from Liverpool Street, and then a bus, and then walk or hitch if I have to.'

'To a bit of road? It might be a total waste of time.'

'I'm going, Elena, and I'll find him.'

'I'll come with you.'

Danny shook his head. 'No way. But I do need your help.'

Elena logged off from the website, shut down her computer and they went down to the quiet room. It wasn't very quiet. Lucy, the Jamaican woman who helped Jane with the cleaning, was doing her best Kylie Minogue impression as she danced round with the hoover.

She spotted them in the doorway and broke off from singing just long enough to shout, 'Five minutes, darlings, that's all I need. Then it's all yours.'

Without waiting for an answer, Lucy went back to her version of 'Can't Get You Out of My Head'. When Lucy liked a song, she liked it, it didn't matter how old it was, and the Kylie classic was an all-time favourite. Danny and Elena didn't hang around for the chorus – it wasn't easy listening. They went out into the garden and sat side by side on a bench.

Danny had made his plans. 'You stay here, check the site again during the day and let me know if he takes any more calls.'

'But what about that reporter bloke? You're meant to be meeting him.'

Danny smiled. 'That's what he thinks. But Mr Eddie Moyes is in for a long wait.'

Mr Eddie Moyes was used to waiting. He'd spent countless hours hanging around, drinking endless cups of coffee while he waited for the little titbits of information that sometimes led to a major exclusive. They'd been a lot harder to come by in the last few years.

He'd been made redundant. Eddie Moyes, the man who'd broken more exclusives than the last three governments had broken promises. He'd been The Man. Top Dog. Numero Uno. He'd worked for all the red-tops in his time and was known as one of Fleet Street's finest.

Until the last job. All right, he'd turned forty-five. All right, he liked a drink. But that was all part of the profession, and most of his best bits of information had been skilfully extracted over a friendly pint or three. And a few beers never affected the quality of his work.

His last news editor hadn't seen it that way. He was a whiz kid, one of the new breed who'd taken the cushy university route instead of doing their time on a local rag. He didn't like Eddie from the off and quickly started sending him on stories more suited to an office junior.

They clashed more than once, and when the management announced that redundancies were needed, the whiz kid struck. Eddie had been one of the last in, so he was one of the first out. They could have made him a special case, but they didn't. His record and reputation counted for nothing.

Since then he'd scraped a living as a freelance. But now that he had the chance to get back where he belonged, he was determined to take it. Fergus Watts had cemented his reputation once before and he could do it again. He just had to find him.

Eddie arrived very early at the café down the road from Foxcroft. He got himself a black coffee, ordered a bacon sandwich and found a seat at a vacant table by the window. He could see Foxcroft from where he was sitting.

He pulled out rolled-up copies of the *Sun*, *Star* and *Mirror* from his jacket pocket and, with one eye on Foxcroft, speed-read the news pages. Eddie was feeling good. Soon they would all be begging for his services.

His bacon sandwich arrived and Eddie lifted the top slice of soggy white bread and splashed on huge dollops of thick brown sauce. He replaced the bread and hungrily bit into the greasy sandwich. It was delicious, just the way he liked it. A thin stream of brown sauce ran down onto his podgy chin.

Forty minutes and a second coffee later, Eddie was still waiting. He wasn't surprised and it didn't matter. It was just one of those setbacks all reporters have to cope with. He knew he'd been a bit too eager when he met Danny Watts the previous day and had sensed him backing off. That was no problem. He'd found out where Danny lived.

The bacon for another sandwich was already sizzling in the frying pan. Eddie kept his eyes fixed on Foxcroft. A couple of kids had left the building during the past forty minutes, neither of them Danny.

'Bacon sandwich!' called the woman behind the counter.

As Eddie stood up he saw Danny walk out of Foxcroft and turn up the street in the opposite direction.

'Make that to go, will you, love?' said Eddie, slapping a two-pound coin onto the countertop. 'Quick as you can.'

12

It was happening again. Danny was convinced he was being followed on the way to Liverpool Street Station. There was no sign of the TDM motorbike; it was more of a gut feeling. He was being watched.

On the street, on the bus, everyone seemed to be looking towards him and then turning away as he returned their stare. He got off the bus before it reached the station and walked. A man in a brown bomber jacket was following him, Danny was certain. But when he stopped and looked back, the man went into a shop.

Danny thought about running, but decided it would only draw more attention. So he walked faster, went straight past the entrance to the station and kept going. Then he doubled back on himself through side streets and entered the station through the bus pull-in entrance. He went quickly to the ticket office, got a return ticket and went to the platform where the train was waiting.

Late morning was one of the quieter times at Liverpool Street and Danny had the section of the carriage he chose to himself. Within a few minutes the train was pulling away and quickly gaining speed as it moved through east London.

The carriage was grimy and drab, with ripped seats and WEST HAM ARE CRAP – TOTTENHAM RULE gouged into the glass of one of the windows. The train didn't stop as it went through Stratford and Ilford and past the greyhound track at Romford and then out into the commuter land of Essex. First stop was Brentwood. A few people got off and even fewer got on, and Danny was relieved when no one chose the same compartment as him.

The train stopped at every station after that. Shenfield, Billericay, Wickford, and then his stop, Rayleigh. Judging from the website maps, it was the closest to where he wanted to be, but not quite close enough.

Danny jumped from the compartment and ran towards the exit as soon as the train came to a standstill. He didn't look back to see who was following but rushed past the ticket collector and out into the street. He expected to be in the town centre. He wasn't. A long, uphill climb past semi-detached houses eventually brought him to the shops and a one-way traffic system.

He went into a shop and bought a road map for the whole of the area, and a shop assistant told him he had to go back down the hill to pick up the bus he needed. On the way he called Elena.

'Did he make any calls?'

'No, none made or received. Are you all right?'

'Yeah, but I'm being followed again.'

'Have you seen someone then?'

'Well no, but . . . it's just a feeling.'

Danny could hear the irritation in Elena's voice as she answered. 'Danny, you are really winding me up, *and* making me nervous. I sit here worrying and waiting for you to call and then all you can say is you *think* you're being followed. You're not. You're imagining it. Just call when you've got something useful to tell me!'

She hung up. She'd never done that to Danny before. He didn't like it.

The bus carried Danny out of town, past a housing estate and then into a less built-up area. He got off near a large roundabout which connected with the trunk road he'd seen on the website map.

From there it was a question of walking or hitching. He decided to hitch. It was another first: hitching a lift isn't an option in south-east London.

Cars and lorries roared by; the road throbbed with traffic, and then a battered pick-up truck loaded with building material pulled in ahead of him. He ran to the truck and the passenger door creaked open on rusty hinges. The driver was leaning over, his hand still on the door, and Danny spotted the letters H A T E tattooed on the knuckles.

The driver smiled when he saw Danny's look. 'Don't worry, mate, the other one's more friendly.'

He stuck out his right fist. It read L O V E. The driver

shrugged. 'Seemed like a good idea at the time. Where you going?'

'I don't know, somewhere down this road.'

It didn't seem an adequate answer, and it wasn't. 'You taking the piss?'

'No. No, honest. I'm not sure where I'm going till I get there.'

The truck driver laughed. 'Sounds like the story of my life, mate. You'd better jump in. I'm Colin.'

They drove for nearly ten minutes while Danny gazed out at the flat, open landscape and listened to Colin's story of how his girlfriend, Cheryl, had almost dumped him when he first revealed L O V E and H A T E.

'She's got used to them now, but it was a nightmare for a while. Wouldn't even talk to me, and as for her mother—'

'Stop!' yelled Danny.

Colin stood on the clutch and brake pedals. The brakes screamed in protest and the truck skidded into the grass verge in a cloud of blue smoke. The smell of burning rubber leaked into the cab and Colin turned to Danny with his eyes blazing. 'What the hell are you playing at? You could have killed us.'

'I'm sorry, I've got to get out. That's it – that place back there.'

They'd driven past a lay-by on the opposite side of the road. At the back of the lay-by stood a roadside café with a mobile number painted on the side and a Union Jack flying above it. Parked alongside was an old blue Fiesta.

Danny opened the door and jumped out. 'I'm sorry about . . . Thanks.' He pushed the door shut and watched as Colin shoved the truck back into gear and drove away. Then he took out his phone and punched in a text to Elena:

IVE FOUND HIM.

He switched off the phone. He didn't want to be disturbed now, not even by Elena.

13

Frankie didn't make many phone calls. There was no need. He called the cash-and-carry one morning each week to place his regular order of bacon, burgers and whatever else was running low. His pay-as-you-go mobile was switched on during the day for phone-in orders but was always turned off before he left for home.

He was on the line to the cash-and-carry again, checking that the order was ready for collection, when he heard the footsteps approaching. No vehicle had pulled in and Frankie didn't get pedestrian customers. He hung up, put down the phone and let his hand rest on the Alabama lie detector he kept under the counter.

This was the moment Frankie had feared ever since arriving back in England. He hadn't expected it to happen this way, but then he'd been trained to expect the unexpected. He didn't panic. Frankie never panicked.

The footsteps got closer and louder and then

stopped completely, just out of Frankie's line of vision. He waited, his fingers tightening on the baton, and then his unexpected, unwanted visitor moved towards him again.

It was Danny – he recognized him instantly. But there was no sense of relief; it simply meant they were both in terrible danger.

Danny's moment of recognition was just as instantaneous. His grandfather looked older, but the face that stared back at him was the face he'd seen so many times over the past few days in the old photograph. And the eyes were just the same as the eyes that stared back at Danny from the mirror each morning.

'Thought I'd never find you, didn't you?' he snarled. 'Thought you could run away from me, didn't you, Fergus Watts?'

Fergus had to try to bluff it out. He smiled. 'I'm sorry, son, I think you're mistaking me for someone else. The name's Frankie, like it says on the van. Frank Wilson. Do you want a cuppa tea or something?'

But Danny was too pumped up and certain to be sidetracked. 'I don't care what you're calling yourself now, but you're Fergus Watts. My granddad. I wish you weren't, but you are.'

It was pointless trying to continue with the subterfuge. Frank Wilson the smiling, friendly roadside tea-bar owner instantly disappeared and Fergus Watts, highly trained and skilled SAS veteran, took over.

The shutter slammed down and Danny heard the click of a heavy padlock. The side door opened and

Fergus emerged carrying his jacket and a bunch of keys.

'Get in the car,' he ordered as he locked the van door and fixed another padlock.

Danny pulled his mobile phone from his jacket. 'Piss off! I'm not going anywhere with you. I'm calling the—'

He got no further. Fergus grabbed him by his jacket collar, snatched the phone away and shoved it into a pocket. As Danny struggled, Fergus dragged him to the blue Fiesta, pulled open the door and threw him inside. 'Stay there!' he yelled and slammed the door.

'Stand by, stand by. Jimmy has Bravo One and a definite Fergus towards the car. That's a positive ID on Fergus. He's limping. Jimmy still has the trigger and can give direction at the main. Wait . . . wait, that's both complete in the car . . . engine on. That's the car mobile towards the main . . .'

The Fiesta roared away, spewing up gravel and dust as it raced from the lay-by.

'That's blue Fiesta gone left on the main . . . repeat, left on the main . . .'

Another voice burst into Jimmy's earpiece.

'Mick has the Fiesta . . . mobile on the main.'

The team had been all over Danny from the moment he left Foxcroft that morning. It had been difficult once he'd taken the train at Liverpool Street. Fran had followed Danny onto the train, taking a different carriage. She checked at each station to see if Danny had got off and constantly relayed details to the others.

The two cars and a motorbike had undertaken a high-speed chase from station to station through the streets of east London and Essex as the train ploughed through the suburbs and into the countryside.

The TDM was no longer part of the operation. Jimmy had realized the machine had become too hot for the follow. He crawled out from under the tangle of bush and scrubby grass fifty metres down the road from the lay-by and ran towards his new vehicle, a Ford Focus.

He'd been following Danny when he was in the pick-up truck and had watched it swerve off the road. He pulled the Focus onto the grass verge round the next bend and then tracked back on foot, finding what little cover he could.

Now, as he ran, he ripped off the Gore-Tex jacket he wore to protect his clothes. He ran hard: the rest of the team needed him back on the follow as soon as possible. Mick was still driving the dark blue Golf, with fresh number plates. He'd picked up Fran at Rayleigh Station, and Brian was now on a motorbike, a Suzuki Ninja. But the third vehicle was vital if Fergus was heading for one of the nearby towns.

Jimmy smiled as he ran back to the Focus. He'd done good work, thinking quickly and reporting everything that happened in the lay-by to the rest of the team. And George Fincham and Marcie Deveraux would have been alerted by now and would be on their way.

Sweat ran down the side of Jimmy's face as he reached the car. He gulped in air as he lifted the tailgate and listened to Fran on the net.

'Stop. Stop. Stop. That's the Fiesta static in a lay-by. He's aware, he's checking vehicles passing him.'

Jimmy threw the Gore-Tex jacket on top of two bags that sat in the boot. One contained Gore-Tex trousers, wellington boots, extra warm clothes and enough canned food and water for two days. If a follow turned into a surveillance on an isolated building there had to be a trigger on that building 24/7; there was never time to go away and fetch kit.

The other bag held an MP5 automatic machine gun, loaded thirty-round magazines, body armour, night viewing goggles and a trauma pack. The team had to be ready to deal with any situation, including wound-ings. Plastic litre bottles of plasma were part of the pack: if a team member was shot the others knew how to plug the holes and replace the lost blood.

Jimmy slammed down the boot, jumped into the Focus and pulled off the verge and onto the road. He squeezed the radio pressel on the gearstick.

'That's Jimmy mobile and with you in five.'

14

It wasn't working out quite the way Eddie Moyes had planned.

The first part had been easy. Jumping into a cab and telling the driver to 'Follow that bus' felt good, like old times.

Even when the cab driver moaned at him about getting bacon fat on his upholstery, Eddie just mouthed a quick, 'Sorry,' and kept his eyes glued on the bus Danny had taken from close to Foxcroft.

But Eddie had no idea it would be such a long journey, right into the heart of the city. When he saw Danny get off the bus, he quickly drew some crumpled notes from his pocket and thrust them at the cab driver. Parting with that much cash was painful, but it would be worth it.

Trailing Danny on foot was more difficult, specially when he seemed to sense he was being followed and increased his pace. Eddie struggled to keep up and lost

Danny completely as he passed Liverpool Street Station. But a few minutes later, as he hung around outside McDonald's, he saw Danny enter the station by the side entrance.

Eddie didn't bother with a ticket, he just followed Danny to the platform for the Southend train and got on, one carriage back. All went well until Rayleigh, where Danny leaped from the train and sprinted through the barrier. But when Eddie tried to follow he was stopped by a ticket inspector. By the time he'd paid his fare and been warned that 'attempting to avoid payment was a serious offence', Danny was gone.

The out-of-condition reporter puffed his way uphill to the town centre, realizing he'd blown it. He asked around in a few shops but no one admitted to seeing a boy fitting Danny's description. So Eddie went to a cashpoint, withdrew enough money to see him through the day, and then did what he always did when a story hit a brick wall: he went for a pint and a pie. Hunting an exclusive always made him hungry.

A couple of hours later he was back near the station. He found himself a patch of grass in the shade of some straggly bushes by the car park, unfolded a copy of *The Times* he'd bought in the town and sat down to do the crossword, and to wait. Danny had to come back at some time, and if Eddie missed him, he'd go back to Foxcroft first thing in the morning, ready to start again.

He was puzzling over seven down when an old blue Fiesta pulled into the car park. He took no notice at first but when the driver got out and looked around, he seemed vaguely familiar. Then the passenger door opened and Danny emerged. Eddie smiled, looked up to the heavens and mouthed a silent 'Thank you.'

He watched as Fergus locked the car, took Danny by the arm and pulled him to the bus lay-by in front of the station where two buses were waiting. They got on the first and a couple of minutes later it pulled away. Eddie was already at the taxi rank, and for the second time that day he told a cab driver to 'Follow that bus'.

Fergus was heading back to the cottage. In the short term, at least. He could pick up cash and emergency supplies and decide on what to do next. He had to figure that Danny had been followed, but there was no point in grilling him about it, he just wouldn't know.

'Listen to me, boy,' Fergus had said as he drove. 'There are people looking for me, and thanks to you, they're probably very close. If they find me I'm dead, and so are you!'

'Me?' said Danny in amazement. 'It's *you* they want. As soon as you stop this car I'm going to the police—'

'The police can't help you now! No one can, no one but me. So just shut the fuck up and do what I say!'

Danny did shut up, stunned into silence.

Fergus concentrated on trying to see if they were being followed. There were no give-away signs but that meant nothing. He knew they couldn't go all the way back by car: it would give any following surveillance team too much time to lock onto them. He drove to Rayleigh – there were buses that went close enough to the cottage.

They took seats near the back of the bus. Fergus pushed Danny into the window seat so that he couldn't try to make a quick exit. But Danny wasn't planning on trying to get away. Not any more. He was scared.

Fergus spoke quietly. 'How did you find me?'

Danny didn't answer.

'I need to know, boy,' hissed Fergus. 'Don't mess me about.'

'Your phone,' said Danny at last. 'I got the number from Kev Newman's mobile and traced where you were on the Internet.'

'But how?'

'A phone location company.'

'But . . . but you'd need my PIN number for that.'

'It's your army number, last four.'

'How did you . . . ?' Fergus shook his head. 'Kev warned me that you were a persistent little shite.'

The bus was deep in the countryside when Fergus leaned across the aisle and pushed the stop button. 'This is us.'

They got off and hid in the tree line that followed the road. Soon after, two cars went by, one of them a mini cab. Fergus watched them disappear into the distance. The smell of the nearby salt marshes hung in the air and the only sounds came from the cawing of huge black crows as they wheeled their way across the early evening sky.

Danny's anger was growing again. 'Are we just gonna stand here?'

'Shut it,' answered Fergus as he started to walk quickly along the road. Danny noticed his grandfather's limp for the first time and realized it must be the result of the gun battle in Colombia. It made him even angrier.

They reached a long, muddy track leading off the road. Just visible down at the end of the track was a cottage, and when Fergus headed towards it, Danny had little alternative but to follow. He watched, bemused, as Fergus looked under the old chicken coop and confirmed for himself that the mini Maglite wasn't on. He moved on and Danny trailed behind, not spotting any of the cameras, lights or motion detectors.

At the gate Fergus checked that the matchstick was still in place. It was. He opened the front door, pulled Danny inside and closed the door. The sitting-room door was half open, exactly as it was meant to be. Danny could see through to the small bank of TV monitors showing the muddy track. He turned to his grandfather. 'What is all this?'

Fergus didn't reply but grabbed Danny by the collar of his jacket, dragged him into the kitchen and pushed him against the wall. 'Stand there and don't move. Don't even think about moving.'

He stomped away and went upstairs. Danny heard his footsteps moving from room to room. A couple of minutes later he came thundering down the stairs and back into the kitchen, not even looking at Danny as he lifted the rug and revealed the opening to the cellar. He picked up the torch on the top step. 'Stay there,' he growled, disappearing into the gloom.

Danny leaned against the kitchen wall and looked at the back door, thinking about making a run for it.

Then the bleepers began to sound, loud and shrill and piercing.

Fergus came hurtling up from the cellar and rushed to the monitors. Two cars were coming down the track at high speed. Mud flew from their wheels and the beams of their headlights seemed to bounce off the trees. The front vehicle was a Ford Focus. Fergus cursed, turned back to Danny and pushed him towards the open trapdoor. 'Get down there, quick!'

Danny stumbled down the stairs into the cellar and stood in semi-darkness and a pool of water as Fergus pulled shut the trapdoor, turned on the torch and went straight to the boxes against the wall. He yanked them aside and shone the torch into the tunnel. 'In there, boy, get in!'

It was no time to argue. Danny scrambled into the hole and Fergus followed, pulling the boxes back against the wall and switching off the torch to save the batteries. They were plunged into total darkness and Fergus pushed Danny further into the cold, wet, muddy tunnel. 'Get going, boy, hurry up!'

Eddie Moyes was feeling pleased, tired and hungry as he leaned against the chicken coop and stared up towards the cottage. The first hint of night was beginning to slither over the landscape. That suited Eddie: it would make his approach easier. He took a Snickers bar he'd kept in reserve from his pocket and decided to enjoy it before continuing on up the track. Before the chocolate bar had even reached his mouth, Eddie heard the cars screaming up the road and saw the first one turn towards him. The Snickers bar dropped into the mud as Eddie ducked down behind the chicken coop.

Brian and Jimmy were in the Focus, Fran and Mick barely bumper distance behind in the Golf. All four members of the team wore dark blue body armour and had MP5s on slings across their chests. Jimmy also had a sawn-off, pump-action shotgun with seven solid-shot rounds in the tubular magazine below the barrel. He was the MOE man.

Both cars skidded to a halt just short of the garden fence. Jimmy was first out, even before the Focus had stopped. He jumped the fence and ran to the front door, not looking to see what was around him, totally focused on the door. He looked for the hinge side, knowing he had to get it right first time. The slightest delay would give anyone inside priceless escape time.

He heard Brian behind him as he jammed the muzzle of the shotgun into the frame a third of the way down the door where the top hinge should be. He pulled the trigger. The shotgun roared and jolted back and splinters of wood sprayed over Jimmy and Brian. Jimmy was already on his knees reloading as Brian waited, his eyes and MP5 trained up at the first-floor windows.

Mick and Fran came running up as Jimmy jammed the shotgun muzzle into the lower hinge area of the frame, a third of the way up from the bottom. The second shot seemed even louder, and showers of jagged splinters flew into the air. Jimmy dropped the shotgun and moved away as Mick charged the door. It fell away easily and Mick tumbled into the hallway with it.

Fran was directly behind. With her weapon up in the aim, she jumped over Mick and moved into the hallway. She stayed right, clearing the door area, so the others could make their entry. Jimmy and Brian went by, into the kitchen. Their job was to clear the ground floor while Fran and Mick took the upstairs.

Fran kept low, safety catch off and finger on the trigger, looking for any sign of movement from the top of the stairs. She took the stairs two at a time, weapon now up high and pointing at the landing. Mick was close behind.

They could hear the other two as they checked each ground-floor room. 'Clear!'

Fran reached the landing and stayed there, covering the two doors in front of her. Mick went past, reached the first door and pushed it open so that Fran could move into the room. 'Clear!'

They reversed roles for the second room. Mick had the door covered as Fran went by, grabbed the handle and pushed open the door. Mick could see inside immediately.

Weapon up, both eyes wide, chest heaving for oxygen, safety catch off and finger on the trigger, he pushed his way into the bathroom. 'Clear! Top floor clear!'

An answering shout came from below: 'Ground floor clear!'

Eddie wasn't a brave man, but he was a reporter through and through. His nose for news meant he had to get closer to find out exactly what was going on inside the cottage.

It was getting darker. Eddie scrambled over the rough ground, lost his footing and slid into a muddy ditch before he was halfway to the cottage. He was wet through and covered in mud but it didn't matter. This was the story he'd been waiting and praying for. He couldn't wait to offer the exclusive to one of the nationals. He couldn't wait to see the faces of the so-called journalists who'd rejected him, especially that jumped-up little apology for a news editor.

He moved closer and sheltered in a hedgerow fifteen metres from the cottage. As he considered his next move he saw the headlights of a third vehicle approaching along the track. Sweaty and muddy, Eddie ducked down low to await the new arrivals.

The car was drawing to a standstill as Fran led the team from the house to their vehicles. They went to their ready bags and took out NVGs in preparation for a long night in the cuds searching for their targets.

A man and a woman got out of the car. Both were smartly dressed – Eddie could see that these were no knuckle-draggers like the other four. The governors had arrived.

Marcie Deveraux walked towards the house, shouting out to the team, 'Stop! You won't find him, he's gone. There'll be an escape route from the house some-where. Find it.' She turned back to Fincham. 'Should we go back and get a trigger on the car, sir?'

Fincham stared out across the fields. Trees and bushes were merging into the darkness as the night swiftly closed around them. 'The car's history, he won't go anywhere near it now.'

Twenty metres away, the camouflaged manhole cover was raised just a few centimetres above ground level, but Fergus heard the voice and saw George Fincham clearly in the light that spilled from the cottage windows.

Danny sat a couple of metres back along the tunnel. He was trembling, with fear and from the cold. The black, wet mud on all sides closed in on him; the air was stale and rank. He could hardly breathe. The sounds of the shotgun had terrified him. The yells and crashes from inside the cottage had terrified him. But most of all, Fergus terrified him.

Fergus raised the manhole cover a little more as he watched Deveraux and then Fincham follow the team back into the house. He turned to Danny. 'They get one sight of us now and we're dead. We've got to get away from here before they find the tunnel. Understand?'

Danny nodded and Fergus slowly moved the manhole cover to one side and climbed out, taking with him the black bin liner containing his escape and evasion kit. Then he reached back into the tunnel and hauled Danny out of the damp, black hole.

The sound of voices wafted over from the cottage and Fincham appeared in the front doorway. Fergus pushed Danny down into the mud, fell down by his side and hissed into his ear, 'Stay down.'

They could both see Fincham, framed in the doorway, as he peered into the gloom. He stood still, looking in every direction. He seemed to look straight at them for heart-pounding seconds. But then he turned away and went back into the cottage.

'Move, now,' breathed Fergus, pulling Danny to his feet.

'I've seen that man before,' whispered Danny as they dodged into the tree cover.

'Just shut up and move,' answered Fergus.

It was also exit time for Eddie Moyes. He knew that the assault team, whoever they were, had missed the chance to capture Fergus and that from now on they would be cleaning up and searching for clues. Eddie had the beginnings of a major exclusive and it was time to go. And quickly. He made his way towards the road, keeping low, being as cautious as possible. But not cautious enough.

Fran was at an upstairs window, checking out the surrounding area with her NVGs. She shouted, 'We've got a runner!'

Fincham, followed by Marcie Deveraux, came bounding up the stairs. He grabbed the goggles from Fran. 'Is it the boy or Watts?' He didn't wait for an answer but pulled the NVGs to his eyes.

Through the green haze he saw Eddie Moyes

stumbling about in the mud. 'It's neither. Too fat to be the boy, and no limp.' He held out the goggles for Fran to take.

'Do we kill him, sir?'

It would a simple operation. The body would be taken back to London and frozen so that it could be cut up more easily. That way there was less mess for the team to clean up. The remains would probably then be distributed around London hospitals, to be burned with other body parts that are routinely incinerated. No one would ever know what had happened to Eddie Moyes. He would become a statistic, another name on police missing persons lists.

Fincham nodded and Fran started to leave, but Deveraux gestured for her to wait and spoke to Fincham. 'Sir, perhaps it would be better if we let the runner go.'

Fincham turned from the window. 'Why?'

'We don't know who he is. Get the team to follow him and there's a chance he'll lead us to Watts. It would be a waste to kill him now, don't you think?'

Fincham considered for a moment and then nodded again.

15

It was first light. Danny sprawled, exhausted, just off the road by a clump of bushes, but his grandfather was still standing. Watching. Listening.

Through the long hours of darkness Danny had discovered the difference between walking quickly and a forced march. Fergus was fit and strong and, despite his limp, his pace was relentless.

They cleared the immediate area of the cottage and then travelled in what seemed to Danny to be a straight line across fields and open countryside. They made a brief stop while Fergus delved into his black bin liner and took out a brand-new, compactly folded day sack, still in its packaging. Most of the contents of the bin liner were transferred to the day sack. Smaller items and cash went into pockets.

Then they moved on, and just when Danny was beginning to think they were out of danger, Fergus told him they were doubling back – 'looping the track', he called it. That way, he said, they would know, and possibly even see, if they were being trailed.

There was no sign of followers and eventually Fergus was satisfied that they could head in the direction he wanted to take. Not that Danny knew what direction that was. He had no idea. Fergus walked in silence, and on the few occasions Danny tried to speak he was abruptly told to shut up and save his energy. After a while he realized it was wise advice.

They didn't stop again until first light broke the skyline.

Fergus took the day sack from his shoulders and looked over at Danny, who was lying back in the rough grass, eyes closed. 'No time for sleep, I want you awake.'

'I'm not sleeping, I'm resting my eyes,' answered Danny, eyes still closed.

Fergus allowed himself the slightest of smiles. He sat down next to Danny on the grass and then delved into the day sack and pulled out a couple of small tins. Baked beans with mini sausages. He took the ring-pulls off both tins and placed one tin on Danny's stomach. 'Breakfast. Get it down your neck.'

Danny opened his eyes. 'I don't do breakfast.'

'You do now. Need to keep your strength up.'

Danny sat up, clasped the tin in one hand and looked at the beans and sausages. 'But they're cold.'

'That's right, they're cold. And I'm not a boy scout so I won't be building a fire to heat them up. And before you ask, no, I haven't got plates or cutlery or a bottle of Daddies sauce. So just eat.'

'But I don't like—'

'Eat!'

They sat in semi-darkness and ate. Slowly. It wasn't a pretty sight. But as Danny devoured the sausages and beans he realized he was ravenously hungry.

And while he ate, he looked at his grandfather. Studied him for the first time. There hadn't been a chance before. He looked just like any other bloke. Middle-aged, ordinary, past his prime. His face was lined, and his short, cropped hair was mostly grey. The sort of man you'd expect to see taking his grandchildren for a walk in the park. Or talking to his mates about retirement and the football results.

But Danny knew his grandfather was no ordinary bloke. He'd done terrible things. Almost unimaginable things. He'd killed people on battlefields and in back streets. Shot them. Fought with them. Life-and-death stuff, hand to hand, face to face. He'd seen for himself the results of his awesome combat skills. The gaping wounds, the ripped flesh. He'd watched men die, seen their blood, smelled it, tasted it.

Danny had had a few fights in his time – most had been of the playground variety. A lot of posturing, barging, shoving, threats. But once there had been a real fight. A kid called Peter Slater had goaded him into it for weeks. In the end he couldn't back down. It was set up for after school, behind the gym. Slater boasted all day about what he was going to do to Danny. Everyone in the school was talking about it, everyone wanted to be there.

There must have been a couple of hundred watching when the time came, as many girls as boys. They gathered, shouting and cheering, in a huge circle, with Danny and his mates on one side and Slater and his on the other.

When it began, they both prowled around the circle, feinting, advancing, throwing a few punches that mainly missed or brushed against raised arms or fists. The crowd bayed for more action. The blows got harder and found their target more often as the fighters started to tire.

Slater did the first serious damage, thumping Danny in the guts, forcing out every bit of his breath. Danny staggered back, gasping, and a shout went up: 'Finish him! Finish him! Finish him!'

Slater grinned as he moved in for the kill. Maybe he was over-confident: his guard was down and he walked straight into the hopeful punch that Danny threw. Pain jarred up through Danny's arm into his shoulder as his fist smashed into Slater's nose. It crumpled and squashed like a rotten tomato, exploding in a fountain of blood. Slater went down, blood everywhere – on his face, on his clothes, staining his white school shirt. And all over Danny's throbbing hand.

A girl screamed and turned away and then the whole crowd went silent, staring at Slater, pale-faced and spark out on the ground with blood pumping from his busted nose.

This was real fighting. It was bloody. It was horrible. And it was there, in their faces. Not on a cinema screen or a video game.

Slater came round quickly enough. All he said to Danny afterwards was, 'Respect.' Pretty soon he was boasting about his permanently damaged and crooked nose. It was like a battle honour, a medal.

But Danny knew that his one experience of real violence was another world, another planet, another universe to the things his grandfather had seen and done.

Fergus seemed to sense that Danny was staring at him. He looked up. 'What?'

Danny shook his head and went back to finishing the beans while Fergus delved into his day sack again and took out two small bottles of water.

'There's a bus stop a couple of hundred metres down the road from here,' he said, giving Danny one of the bottles. 'First bus is in an hour. We'll be on it.'

'To where?'

'Southend. Plenty of people there to get lost in.'

'I've had enough of this, I'm going home.'

Fergus laughed. 'You don't get it, do you, boy—?'

'Stop calling me *boy*!' yelled Danny. 'Just 'cos you're a killer it doesn't mean you're a man. I'm more of a man than you are. I haven't worked for drug dealers and made a fortune out of people's misery.'

When Fergus replied his voice was almost a whisper. 'I see you've been doing your research . . . Danny. You know, I was younger than you are when I joined up. Sixteen. They called us boy soldiers in those days.'

'I don't give a shit what they called you then,' snarled Danny, 'just what they call you now. A coward and a traitor. You're family, the only family I've got, and I'm ashamed of it.'

Fergus took a swig from the bottle of water. 'Maybe

you are, but if you want the truth I'll tell you. And if you want to survive, you've got a lot to learn. And quickly.'

'I know the truth, I've read it all. And there's nothing you can teach me, nothing worth knowing.'

Fergus's mind went back eight years, to the hot, humid Colombian jungle and the group of surly, ill-tempered boys standing in line, none of them wanting to learn a thing from him. And then he saw the youngest boy lying dead on the jungle floor, with a bullet through his brain. He wouldn't let that happen to Danny, no matter what his grandson thought of him.

'Just listen to me. You can have your say when I've finished.'

'I don't wanna hear—'

'Shut it!'

The way Fergus glared at Danny gave him no option but to do as he was ordered.

'I was SAS, I'd been in Colombia for two years. We were chasing FARC, the Revolutionary Armed Forces of Colombia. They're drug traffickers; they control all the cocaine coming out of their country.'

'I know all that,' snapped Danny. 'I've read all about you. Everything.'

Fergus ignored him. 'We were trying to destroy their manufacturing plants but getting nowhere fast. That's when I was recruited by the Firm.'

'The what?'

'The Firm, the Secret Intelligence Service, MI6. Different names, same set-up. When I went over to FARC, I was actually working for our side, for the Firm.'

'You were a traitor, it said so in the papers,' said Danny. 'Everyone knows it, even your old mates.'

'Forget what it said in the papers, I was—'

The sound of an approaching vehicle stopped Fergus mid sentence. He grabbed the day sack in one hand and Danny with the other and they ducked down low behind the bushes. A few seconds later a milk van went by, bottles shaking and rattling and radio blaring.

Fergus continued the moment the van turned the corner. 'I was what's called a K, a "deniable operator". That meant—'

'You're just trying to confuse me,' said Danny angrily. 'Baffling me with words, and excuses.'

Fergus moved like lightning, grabbing Danny's jacket in both hands and yanking him forward so that their faces were just inches apart. 'This is not bullshit! I told you you'd get the truth and you are!'

He pushed Danny away and took a long drink of water. 'Deniable operator means what it says. It's dirty work, stuff that can't be officially sanctioned by our government. So if your cover is blown, you're on your own. It's the risk you take. My job was to gain the rebels' confidence, locate the DMPs and get out. I was almost there, nearly ready to come out. And I'd discovered something else, something even more important.'

Fergus paused as he drank some more of the water. He glanced at Danny, who was staring back with a look of scorn and disbelief. 'So what was it? What was so important?'

'The FARC leaders were being fed information about anti-drug operations against them by the Firm's desk officer back at the British Embassy in Bogotá. He must have been copping a small fortune, and that was why the rebels had always been one step ahead of us. What I didn't know was that by the time I was ready to move, the desk officer had found out I'd been sent in as a K.'

Fergus finished the last few drops of water and wiped the back of his hand across his mouth. 'He lets his friends at FARC know and suddenly I'm sent on this training mission with a bunch of kids. FARC don't give a toss about losing a few raw recruits so they tip off the anti-narcotics police, exact location, everything. We didn't stand a chance.'

'Why should they do that?' said Danny. 'If FARC found out about you from this desk officer, why didn't they just kill you?'

'Because it all worked out perfectly for them. What better way is there to protect a traitor than by exposing a traitor? I was the fall guy, and best of all, I was a deniable operator. No one was gonna come to my rescue. That's the truth, Danny, believe it or not. It's up to you.'

Danny got up and walked to the roadside, turning the story over in his mind. He wanted to believe it. He wanted to believe every word. He wanted to believe that his grandfather was a hero and think of him with pride instead of shame. Slowly, he turned back and stared at Fergus. 'You're a liar. *You* were the traitor. You were then and you are now. And you'll never make me believe anything else.'

16

George Fincham stood in his office, cradling a delicate, bone-china cup in both hands and staring out through the window, upriver towards Parliament.

He never tired of this view, his personal picture of the home of government, the seat of all power. Power which he had long ago pledged to protect and maintain. Fincham had worked tirelessly and ruthlessly for many years to achieve his own position of power and influence.

As head of the security section, he was an important figure within the Firm. And if he hadn't risen quite as high in the set-up as he believed he deserved, there was still time. As long as there weren't too many repeats of last night's botched operation to be rid of Fergus Watts.

Watts was an irritation, like a fly buzzing around Fincham's head. But soon the fly would be swatted. Squashed. Killed. The cover story would be that he died trying to avoid capture. No fuss. Cleanly and efficiently over, just as Fincham liked it. He prided himself on the efficiency of his section.

He could depend on the loyalty of all his operators, particularly the four assigned to the Watts operation. They had been with him for a long time and he had selected them personally for this job. They knew his methods and never questioned them, and they took pride in the reputation of the section.

And then there was Marcie Deveraux, the latest recruit to the section, but already invaluable. Fincham could depend on Marcie too. She was like him. Ambitious. Ruthless. And she knew that he was her route to the top.

Fincham finished his coffee, turned away from the window and sat at his desk. He was an intensely private man who never revealed even the smallest detail of his personal life within the Firm. Only his few close acquaintances – Fincham had acquaintances rather than friends – knew that he was a collector of things of rare and exotic beauty. His bachelor flat contained his small but stunning collection of Pre-Raphaelite paintings as well as many exquisitely bound, first edition antiquarian books. They were rarely seen by anyone but their owner.

There was a knock at the door. 'Come.'

For someone who had worked throughout the night, Marcie Deveraux looked incredible. Fresh and totally unruffled. She took the seat on the opposite side of the desk. 'We have the identity of the runner, sir.'

'Tell me.'

'Eddie Moyes. Freelance reporter, bit of a has-been. Hangs around the Victory Club quite a lot looking for SAS stories, which probably explains how he latched onto young Danny. We've pulled old stories he did about Fergus Watts off the Internet.'

Fincham nodded. 'And?'

'The team followed him to a pub. He stayed there for a while and then got a taxi back to civilization. Then a train home. He's there now – sleeping, I would imagine.'

Fincham looked at the plasma TV churning through its Ceefax list of news headlines. 'I do not want anything appearing in the press, Marcie.'

Deveraux shook her head. 'I don't think it will, sir. He's only got half a story, and being a freelance he's got to make the most of his information. Once he files his first report he'll have the whole of Fleet Street chasing this.'

'So what do you suggest?'

'Surveillance, sir. His phones, his PC. And a CTR on his flat. I went there at four this morning and carried out a locks recce. Let's find out what he knows and use it to our advantage.'

Fincham stood, went to the coffee machine that sat on a small side table and poured more coffee into a fresh cup. 'Excellent, Marcie. Moyes will never get to file this story.' He glanced over at her. 'Coffee?'

17

The bus journey passed in silence, both Fergus and Danny deep in their own thoughts.

But when they arrived in Southend, Fergus surprised Danny by leading him straight to another bus. 'Too many CCTVs here,' he said as they took their seats at the back, out of earshot of the few other passengers on board. 'We'll pick up a train somewhere quieter.'

'You do what you want,' said Danny as the bus drew away. 'The only train I'm getting is the one back to London.'

Fergus spoke quietly. 'You still don't get it, do you, Danny? You can't go anywhere without me any more. You know the truth, even if you don't believe it yet. And if he catches you now, he'll kill you.'

'Who? Who will?'

'George Fincham, the man you said you'd seen before.'

'But . . . but how do you know him?'

'Because George Fincham was the desk officer in Bogotá. George Fincham was the traitor, *he* was the one giving the information to FARC. You think he'll let either of us live, when we know that?'

Danny looked stunned. 'You are unbelievable. You've been sitting there inventing all this stuff because I don't believe a word you say. The guy was at my army RCB: he was the one who told me about you.'

'Yeah, and I bet he was the one who gave you the idea of finding me. They've been tailing you – how else did they turn up at the cottage?'

The bus lurched to one side as the driver swerved to avoid a cyclist. 'Bloody bikes,' yelled the driver. 'Ought to be banned from the road.' There were a few murmurs of agreement from the front of the bus.

'I met Fincham too,' said Fergus quietly. 'At an embassy do, long before I was recruited as a K. I thought he was a clever, cunning bastard then. And he was; clever enough to find out that I had been recruited, even though it was meant to be classified. Face it, Danny, he set you up, and you fell for it.'

'Even if he did set me up, that doesn't mean he was the traitor,' said Danny. 'Why should I believe you?'

'Because it's the truth.'

Danny sneered. 'You wouldn't know the truth if it came up and punched you in the mouth.' But he was no longer quite as certain as he sounded. George Fincham – if that really was his name – *had* planted the idea of finding Fergus; Danny *had* sensed he was being followed; and the cottage *had* been raided.

Fergus knew there was more than just the question

of truth or lies standing between the two of them. There was also their history, or their lack of a history. They had to talk it through. 'Look, I understand the way you feel about me, Danny. I was a total disaster as a dad, and I've been no better as a granddad.'

'I stopped worrying about that a long time ago.'

'You really expect me to believe that?'

'Yeah,' answered Danny angrily, 'like you expect me to believe everything *you* say!' He looked away. 'Why? Why did you leave my dad?'

Fergus took a deep breath. He was a loner, a man who'd spent a lifetime keeping his feelings and emotions in check. A man who'd avoided justifying many of his actions even to himself, let alone to the grandson he'd only just met. 'I was eighteen when I got married. Your dad was on the way, so we had to – that's what happened in those days. But I was too young, just a kid. I wanted to be off soldiering with my mates. So I left. I'm not proud of it, but that's what I did. After I left, it was the odd visit, and later on the occasional letter.'

Danny stared out through the window as the bus ploughed through the suburbs of Southend and his grandfather continued with his halting, hesitant confession. 'I got this letter from your dad, first one for a long time. I was in Malaysia, up in the north. He told me that he was getting married and that your grandmother had died of cancer. I was . . . I was sorry about it, of course I was, but . . . it was like another life. There didn't seem any point in coming back for the wedding.'

'But he was your son.'

'Yeah, and he must have hated me.'

Danny turned back from the window and glared at his grandfather. 'Don't expect me to feel sorry for you! You always had a choice in all this; I never did.' He fumbled in his jacket pocket for the old photograph he'd been carrying around for days and handed it to Fergus. 'And he didn't hate you. He always kept that.'

Fergus was still looking at the photograph when he spoke again. 'I didn't even know he had it. I was in Colombia when I got news of the car crash. The funeral had already happened. It was too late to say I wish it could have been different.'

They were silent for a few moments as Fergus stared at the old photograph. He turned it over and saw the numbers written there. 'My last four.' He looked at Danny. 'That's how you knew.'

Danny said nothing as Fergus handed back the photograph.

They got off the bus at a place called Westcliff. To Danny it seemed just an extension of Southend. A bit quieter, more old fashioned. There were a lot of old people out for their early morning stroll along what was exotically named the Boulevard. Most seemed to be wandering aimlessly, stopping every now and then to gaze into the same shop windows they'd probably gazed into a thousand times before.

It was the perfect place to do a runner. Fergus couldn't have stopped Danny, not with his limp and not without stirring one of Westcliff's finest into calling the police.

But Danny didn't run. 'Can I have my mobile?' he asked as they walked slowly away from the bus stop.

'You know you can't,' answered Fergus without looking at him.

'Don't worry,' said Danny. 'I'm not planning on calling Fincham. I have to let Elena know what's happening.'

Fergus stopped walking. 'Who the hell is Elena?'

'She's my friend, at Foxcroft. She helped me find you.'

'Oh, terrific. And who else knows about this?'

'No one. Just Elena. And I trust Elena a lot more than I trust you.'

Fergus reached into a pocket and took out the phone. 'Is this pay as you go?'

'Course it is, I can't afford a contract phone. I'm an orphan, remember?'

'Don't make any calls, just check your messages,' said Fergus, handing Danny the phone. 'If *you* can find a way of locating phones, I'm sure Fincham can. But we'll be well away from here long before it's any good to him.'

Danny switched on the mobile. He had five new voicemails and three texts. 'They'll all be from Elena.'

'Just check the texts, the voicemails will take too long.'

Danny checked the first text and Fergus read it with him:

Wher r u & y dont u ans fone. Its v l8.
Im worried

'Stupid bloody language,' said Fergus as he worked out what the message meant.

The second text read:

> Danny!!! Wots going on?? DTR asking questions.
> Please call!!!

'What's DTR mean?' asked Fergus.

'It stands for Dave the Rave, the bloke who runs Foxcroft. He's all right.'

The final text had been sent at nine o'clock that morning.

> Something bad must hve hapened 2 u. If i dnt
> hear in nxt hour im telling dave wots bin going
> on. I must so please please call.

Fergus looked at his watch. It was nine forty-two. 'She sounds a bit flaky.'

'Flaky?' said Danny angrily. 'Elena's not flaky, she's worried about me. A lot more worried than you've ever been.'

'Yeah, all right, enough,' snapped Fergus. 'You've done the hurt grandson bit and I've got the message. But what I am worried about now is keeping us both alive.'

'Us? You keep saying *us*. Nothing's gonna happen to me. I'm out of this. You do what you like, I'm going back to London.'

'I can't let you do that.'

Danny laughed. 'How you gonna stop me? Tie me up? Shoot me? Fill me with cocaine?'

Their raised voices were beginning to attract the attention of Westcliff's strolling pensioners and Fergus decided to take a different line. 'All right. Maybe I'm wrong. Maybe once Fincham knows you're back home and I'm nowhere around he'll question you and then leave you alone.'

'He will. And . . . and I won't tell him anything. I'm not saying I believe what you've told me, but . . .'

Fergus nodded. He had absolutely no intention of letting Danny walk into danger. For the moment, he was buying time. 'Tell you what, I'll come with you. Just to see you safely back.'

'There's no need.'

'Probably not, but let me anyway. Then I'll get out of your life. Send your friend one text. Tell her not to worry and that you'll be back in about three hours. And tell her—'

'Yeah, I know,' interrupted Danny. 'Tell her not to make any more calls or send texts to this phone.' He switched on the phone and punched in his text, knowing that Elena would be furious at getting such a brief message.

When Danny had finished, Fergus took the phone and removed the simcard. 'I'll get you another one later. But now I'm going to buy you some new clothes.'

'What?'

'You want to look your best when you get back, don't you?

They obviously had very different ideas on what constituted 'looking your best'.

On the main shopping drag Fergus found a charity shop, and after checking there was no CCTV installed, led Danny inside. He went straight to the racks of clothes.

'See anything you fancy?'

'I'm not wearing these rejects.'

Fergus grabbed an anorak from the clothes rail and thrust it into Danny's hands. 'Do this for me, Danny. I don't want you picked up outside Foxcroft. You were followed all day yesterday, so they know what you were wearing. So choose some gear and let's get out of here.'

Five minutes later they left the shop with a carrier bag full of clothes. 'We can change on the train,' said Fergus, who was already wearing a newly purchased flat cap.

'You look a right dickhead in that,' said Danny as they walked down to the small station.

'Maybe,' answered Fergus. 'But that's the idea. Mr Average, the bloke no one ever gives a second glance.'

Danny went onto the platform and waited while Fergus got tickets from the machine outside. He insisted they stay third party aware so they began the forty-five-minute journey into Fenchurch Street Station in separate carriages. The early morning commuter scramble was over and when Fergus thought it was safe, he moved into Danny's carriage.

Danny had put on his newly acquired bomber jacket and baseball cap. And he'd been thinking. 'I'm still not saying I believe you, but . . . if you were set up, why haven't you tried to clear your name?'

'Like I told you, "deniable operator" means just that:

you get caught and you're on your own. Once I was captured, the story of me being a traitor was perfect for the Firm. But when I escaped I became a potential embarrassment, to the Firm and the government, and they don't like loose ends. But it's worked out perfectly for Fincham; he'll have full backing to get rid of me and he'll be covering his own arse at the same time.'

'But isn't there anyone else who knew you were a K. Anyone outside the Firm?'

Fergus shrugged. 'My old CO, Colonel Meacher – he had to sanction the move and—'

'I met him,' said Danny quickly. 'At the Victory Club. We could find him and he could clear you.'

'He hasn't up until now.'

'But he's out of the army now. If we went to him and told—'

'Look, Danny,' said Fergus, 'I appreciate what you're saying, but I'm not up to it any more. I'm fifty-three, I can't walk properly and I came back to England to keep my head down and stay out of trouble.'

'Yeah, well, you've lost that option now,' answered Danny angrily. 'And what's wrong with you? I read the stories. You were a hero in Ireland, and in the Gulf. You got medals. Now you reckon you're not up to it. Don't you want to live?'

Fergus smiled. 'Yeah, I want to live. And I thought you didn't believe me . . .'

The train was starting to slow as it began the approach into Fenchurch Street and Danny glanced out at the grimy city buildings. He spoke quietly. 'I don't. And maybe you're not up to it, but I am.'

18

Mick and Fran had drawn the short straw. They were on surveillance outside Foxcroft but as far as they could see there was no way Danny would return. Fergus Watts was far too experienced to allow that.

But they had to be there, just in case. Resources were stretched. Jimmy and Brian were with Marcie Deveraux, preparing for the CTR on Eddie Moyes's flat. George Fincham had chosen not to bring in extra manpower on this job. And if the governor had his reasons for keeping this one to his chosen few, that was fine by them. It was a compliment.

The lack of sufficient manpower on the surveillance meant they were using technology to plug the gaps. Earlier, Mick had parked a white Transit van on the corner of a side road close to Foxcroft.

The back of the van faced the building, and in one of the rear doors were several tiny holes, so small they were invisible to the naked eye. Fibre optic cables ran from the holes into a sophisticated camera system with face-recognition software, rigged inside the battered van. The ends of the fibre optics were trained towards Foxcroft, and Danny's image had been loaded into the system.

A single click of recognition would be enough to alert Mick and Fran, who were in the blue Golf, cruising the area. Staying close, but not too close to alert any inquisitive third party. But if Danny was pinged inside, or coming out of Foxcroft, they could be there in seconds.

Fergus tried everything he could to persuade Danny not to go back to Foxcroft. He asked, argued, bullied and almost begged, but by the time they were half a mile from the building he knew it was pointless.

Danny was adamant. He had to go back. He had to explain the situation to Elena. He had to straighten things out with Dave the Rave.

And he had a plan. He would tell Dave he was going to stay with a mate while they looked for jobs. It made sense, he said, as he had to leave Foxcroft soon anyway.

And with Dave squared it meant they could go off and track down Colonel Meacher.

It all sounded so easy. To Danny. Daylight, and the thought of clearing his grandfather's name, had driven away the horrors of his experience in the escape tunnel.

Fergus would have agreed to anything at that stage. All he wanted to do was get Danny in and out of Foxcroft and away. He had always had contingency plans for his cover being blown, but his grandson had never figured in his thinking. Until now.

And as for Danny's own plan? It was crazy. It was stupid. But maybe. Just maybe . . .

They were in a street that ran parallel to the rear of the building, less than five hundred metres away from Foxcroft. Fergus had let Danny make a quick call to Elena from a public call box. By now she should be waiting by the back garden gate, ready to unlock it.

'Be as natural as you can but keep that cap pulled down over your eyes,' said Fergus. 'And when you're inside stay away from the windows. You got that?'

'You've told me three times.'

'Have you got it?'

'Yes!'

'And you leave by the back gate too. I'll be around, never far away and we meet here again in forty-five minutes.'

Danny nodded.

'We need to fix the ERV.'

'The what?'

'The emergency rendezvous, in case either of us runs into a problem. Somewhere public we can both find easily and not too far away.'

Danny shrugged. 'Burger King at London Bridge Station?'

'Fine. Let's move and I'll tell you what to do if you need to use the ERV.'

A few minutes later Danny knocked once on the wooden gate at the back of Foxcroft. Two heavy bolts slid back and the gate creaked open.

As soon as Elena saw Danny she laughed. 'What *are* you wearing?'

Danny didn't have time to discuss his second-hand bomber jacket and faded baseball cap. He pushed past his friend, shut the gate and slid back the bolts. 'Never mind that now, just listen to me before I go to see to Dave. My granddad was set up, he wasn't a traitor.'

The flat cap Fergus wore was pulled low; beneath the cap his keen eyes were scanning the surroundings, taking in parked and moving vehicles and pedestrians. He had moved to the front of the building and was about fifty metres away.

A teenager wearing a Walkman passed by. Fergus heard the distorted thump of a bass drum and the tinny rattle of the snare. Three giggling girls, arm in arm, approached from the opposite direction, and one of them made some sort of comment as they passed Walkman Boy. He either ignored it or didn't hear, but it made the girls' day as they burst out laughing.

On the opposite pavement two young mums were deep in conversation as they struggled along with pushchairs weighed down with their offspring and fully loaded supermarket carrier bags.

It all looked perfectly normal. Everyday. But Fergus was looking beyond the everyday, searching for the slightest sign that Fincham's team had surveillance on Foxcroft. While Danny was inside the building and in potential danger, Fergus had to be the eyes and ears out on the street.

He checked the parked vehicles, looking to see if any were occupied or had steamed-up windows. That might only mean that a thoughtless dog owner had left little Rover without enough air, but it could also mean a tired operator on surveillance had got careless. But there was no sign of anything unusual.

Further down the street, parked on the corner of a side road, Fergus noticed a white Transit van. Blacked-out rear windows would be an obvious sign of danger, but the rear doors were windowless. The vehicle still had to be checked out. He would do a walk-by and try to see inside through the windscreen.

First, though, he wanted to look at the buildings and windows on either side of the road. Eyes trained on Foxcroft might not only be human eyes.

Danny was getting a bollocking. And when Dave the Rave gave a bollocking, all the unfortunate person on the receiving end could do was sit back and take it. Dave was barely pausing for breath as words like *irresponsible, immature, inconsiderate, thoughtless* and *selfish* were strung together in a stream of wounding sentences.

They were in the small first-floor office at the front of the house. The door was closed because what Dave had to say was for Danny's ears only.

Danny explained that he'd met an old mate and had gone back to his place. They'd been so engrossed in catching up and making plans, he'd completely forgotten to phone to say he was staying the night.

Dave swallowed the story and was all in favour of Danny going off to search for a job. But he still wanted to have his say. 'While you live under this roof, you let us know what's going on. You don't stay out all night without even a phone call. Jane and me have got better things to do than worry about selfish, inconsiderate, brainless idiots who only think of themselves.'

Brainless. That was a new one.

'I really am sorry, Dave. I know I should have called – I will in future.'

'Future? You're lucky to have a future after what you got up to last night!'

Danny shuddered as he thought back to the previous night. Dave had no idea how close to the truth he was. But fortunately for Danny, the volcanic eruption of fury was beginning to subside, just as it always did.

'Danny, you are certain about giving up your A levels?'

'I've got a week or so to decide,' said Danny with a shrug. 'It can't hurt to see what jobs are around.'

'We'll miss you if you go.'

'And I'll miss this place, and you and Jane. You've done a lot for me.'

Dave was getting embarrassed. Bollockings he could handle, but compliments and gratitude were another matter. 'Go on, get out. We'll keep your room for a couple more weeks.'

Danny stood up to leave, forgetting his grandfather's order to stay away from the windows. He looked outside, trying to see if Fergus was nearby. It was a big mistake.

The fibre optics picked up the movement and in less than a second the camera system inside the Transit van clicked and immediately sent a signal of recognition to the blue Golf. Fran and Mick exchanged a look. 'Bingo,' snarled Mick. He dropped a gear and accelerated towards Foxcroft.

Fergus saw Danny move away from the window just before he spotted a blue Golf speeding down the road. It was caked in mud and Fergus instantly realized it was one of the cars that had been at the cottage. The vehicle was two up and he saw the woman in the passenger seat glance at Foxcroft. He knew they'd pinged Danny.

He moved quickly towards the house, no longer bothering about trying to hide his limp. He had to get Danny out, and fast. But then he saw the Golf turn left where the Transit was parked and come to a halt further down the road. The tailgate sprang open. It could only mean one thing. Fergus changed direction: he had to stop the operators from removing what was in the back of the car. There was no time to think, he just had to *do*.

The two operators' faces were set as they went to the back of the Golf and leaned in to grab their ready bags. The prearranged plan was simple: they would carry the bags containing their MP5s into Foxcroft and kill Danny. And Fergus, if he was there. And they had no reason to believe he wasn't there; he wouldn't have abandoned Danny. A 'drugs deal gone wrong' cover story was ready and waiting for the tabloids. It wouldn't be the first time Fran and Mick had been part of an operation such as this in broad daylight.

But they had given Fergus a chance. There was no way he could fight it out with them on the street. But in the next few seconds, while they were bent over with their heads and backs inside the car, he had one opportunity to use his own personal SAS mode – Speed, Aggression and Surprise.

His injured leg was almost giving way as he lurched towards the rear of the Golf. A couple more seconds and the two operators would have been clear, but as they grasped their bags, Fergus took his full weight on his good leg and leaped into the air. His arms and body arched over the tailgate and brought it crashing down.

There were yells of pain and shock. Mick dropped the car keys on the ground and Fran screamed in agony as her shoulders and neck took much of the force. Fergus felt his leg buckle as he landed. But he made himself to stay upright, lifted off the tailgate and slammed it down again and again on his two victims.

The muffled screams coming from the vehicle were a mixture of agony and anger. Shouting furiously, Mick tried to reach back to the pistol he had on his jeans belt. But Fergus saw the movement and, grasping the tailgate for support, kicked him between the legs with his right foot. There was an anguished yell and Mick temporarily forgot all about the pistol.

Fergus slammed the tailgate down once more, picked up the car keys and staggered round to sit in the driver's seat. He heard Mick and Fran moan as he slid the key into the ignition. The engine revved and Fergus shoved the car into reverse. It jerked backwards and Fergus stood on the brakes. The tailgate flew open and Mick and Fran were thrown out onto the road.

The Golf's gearbox crunched in protest as Fergus

struggled to locate first gear. Fran had blood running down her face but managed to get to her knees and go for the pistol in her belt holster as the car sped away. It was too late to fire. Fran cursed and glanced at Mick. He was still curled up on the road, groaning, as blood poured from his mouth and started to form a small puddle on the tarmac.

Fergus steered the car with his left hand and felt under the seat with his right. Nothing there. He tried the door compartment. Still nothing. He reached under the dashboard and found what he was searching for – the car pistol. It was in a holster glued to the underside of the dash.

He swerved right at the first junction, knowing he had to dump the car soon. There would be a tracking device fitted and at least one of the operators he'd left in the road would be on their personal radio by now, calling the drama in.

But they wouldn't go into Foxcroft now, even if they were able to. Their mission had been compromised. Big time.

Fergus took the next left, found a parking space, got out of the car, locked it and walked casually away. He felt calmer, and safer, especially now he had a Sig 9mm semi-automatic pistol tucked into his jeans. There was only one thirteen-round magazine. Better than nothing. A little insurance.

At the next junction was a bus stop. One of the new bendy buses was approaching. Fergus got on, going nowhere in particular. He would take a ride before heading to the ERV.

19

London Bridge Station was getting busier by the minute. Thousand upon thousand of homeward-bound commuters bustled and pushed their way in and glanced up at the departures board to see if the train they were hoping to catch was still on the platform.

The lucky ones went sprinting onwards in the faint hope of getting a seat rather than having to stand as usual. Others gave a sigh or a shrug of resignation and settled for finding a little comfort in a drink or a burger and some fries.

The crowded station made perfect cover. Fergus stood by the ticket machines, watching. He was over an hour later than the agreed rendezvous time.

He'd ordered Danny to wait by Burger King but to move on after thirty minutes. After that, he was to walk past every half hour for the next three hours until he saw Fergus. He was simply to make eye contact and keep walking. Fergus would catch up.

Fergus saw Danny just as the station announcer seemed to take particular delight in the news that another departure was delayed due to a signalling failure. When Danny spotted his grandfather there was a flicker of recognition and for a moment it looked as though he was going to change direction and walk straight towards him. Then he remembered his instructions. He's learning, thought Fergus. There was a lot to learn.

They were well outside the station when Fergus caught up. Most people were walking in the opposite direction so it was a few minutes more before they were actually side by side. Danny didn't look at Fergus when he spoke. 'I thought you'd be at the back of Foxcroft. Was there a problem?'

Fergus smiled to himself before answering, happy to let Danny remain ignorant of the events near Foxcroft. 'No. No problem at all. I just fancied a ride on one of those bendy buses.'

Danny had to stop himself from staring at his grandfather. 'Yeah?' He shrugged. 'Dave was cool about me being away, so it all went pretty easily, didn't it?'

'Piece of cake.'

'Where we going now, then?'

'We need to buy a few things,' answered Fergus softly. 'Then we find a desirable residence for the night to hide up in. And then we'll talk about this Colonel Meacher plan of yours.'

Danny grinned. 'Oh, that's sorted, Elena's finding him for us.'

'What!' Fergus moved swiftly, grabbing Danny by

the arm and bundling him into a shop doorway. 'What the hell have you done now?'

Danny shook himself free. 'If we have to hide like you keep saying, we need someone to find out things and get us what we need.'

Fergus looked around, anxious not to draw the attention of any passer-by. 'It's bad enough having you with me; now you're dragging someone else into it. If you want to survive, just do what I tell you, and that's all.'

'You weren't there, so I made a decision,' snapped Danny. 'And I'm not dragging her into it, she wants to help.'

'What have you told her?'

'That we have to find Colonel Meacher. She'll search on the Internet and then be online between eight and nine in the morning to report back. Seemed a good idea to me.'

Fergus pushed Danny away from the doorway and they started to walk again. 'You've got to learn to obey orders. Operational security. The less anyone knows, the safer it is for us. That's the way we operate, so get it into your head.' He reached into a pocket, took out a sheet of paper and handed it to Danny.

'What's this?'

'A shopping list. Maybe you can get that right. Just get what it says on the list.'

Danny departed towards a Spar shop with the list and two ten-pound notes, while Fergus went off to a camping and ski shop that stayed open late and made most of its money from frustrated commuters dreaming of distant holidays.

In the Spar, Danny kept the baseball cap pulled low, aware of the CCTV and the eyes of the two men behind the counter. It was a weird shopping list. The ring-pull cans of food and bottled water made sense, but cling film and baby wipes? But Danny obeyed orders and bought everything on the list. And nothing more.

When they met up again Fergus headed away from the station, following the line of the railway tracks that snake out of the terminus. The tracks were thirty metres above, perched on top of grime-covered, brick elevations, with massive arches supporting the whole structure.

Over the years front and back walls had been added to the arches, creating instant business premises. Close to the station they were trendy wine bars and shops, but soon Fergus and Danny had left the lights, the noise and the crowds behind them.

'Start counting your paces from here.'

'What?'

'Just count.'

Rain began to fall as they started to walk along a narrow, dark road with potholes and years of grease. There were still converted arches to their right; high above, the trains rumbled away towards commuter land.

Trucks lined the dingy road. They had moved quickly into a different world, where cash-only businesses operated and no one ever noticed what was happening around them. There were garage workshops, car radio installers and locked-up arches without any identifying signs. It was dark and damp and threatening.

'Where are we going?' Danny's voice was unnaturally loud as it bounced back off the towering brickwork.

'You'll see when I find it,' replied Fergus quietly.

They continued down the narrow street until they reached an open archway full of wooden pallets. On the wall a hand-painted sign said the owners would pay good money for more of the same.

'Stop counting and remember the number.'

'But what's it for?'

Fergus didn't even glance at him. He pulled Danny behind a rubbish skip full of flattened cardboard boxes and then looked carefully at the archway and up and down the road. He leaned closer to Danny and whispered, 'I'm going in there. If you hear any shouting, or if I don't come out in fifteen minutes, go back to the ERV and do the same drill until we meet up.'

Without waiting for a reply, he put down the sleeping bags and the other kit bought from the camping shop, walked over to the arch and disappeared into the darkness.

The minutes dragged by as Danny waited. He heard the rumble of trains and the occasional blast of a car horn from distant streets, but he kept his eyes fixed on the archway as raindrops dripped steadily from the peak of his baseball cap.

After ten long minutes that felt more like an hour, Fergus emerged from the dark archway. He walked quickly to Danny and picked up his bags. 'Come on.'

They went into the archway. Inside there was a strong stench of wood and grease from the pallets. It was completely dark and reminded Danny of the nightmare experience of being in the tunnel back at the cottage. 'I can't see,' he whispered.

Fergus put a hand on his shoulder. 'Stand still – we'll wait for our night vision to come.'

After a few minutes Danny could make out the shapes of the pallets, the brick walls – even his grandfather's face. He nodded and Fergus began to climb up the pallets; Danny clambered after him.

They reached the top of a high stack with a gap of only two metres between them and the top of the arch. Fergus moved about, checking out his lines of sight and his potential escape route. When he was satisfied they were safe, he sat down next to Danny. 'We're staying here tonight, this is our LUP.'

'Our what? Don't you ever speak normal English?'

'I am – *my* English, and you'd better start learning it. All you need to know now is that if we really are going to find Meacher, we have to live like this. And there are SOPs you've got to learn and stick to. Like tonight, one of us has to be awake at all times. On stag.'

He saw Danny's confused look. 'On guard. And if we get bumped we leave everything and get out the back way. I'll show you.'

Danny didn't bother asking what 'bumped' meant: he had a pretty good idea. They crawled to the rear of the stack where, many years earlier, a back wall had been added to the archway. There was a hole in the

133

brickwork where at one time there had been a window. 'Stick your head out and look to the right,' said Fergus.

A rusty old ladder was set into the brickwork. It went up to the railway track as well as down to the ground.

'We go down that and bomb burst, you right, me left. Then we RV at Burger King.'

They went back to the front of the pallets so that they could see out to the front of the archway. 'LUP means lay-up point,' said Fergus. 'Always check out the area of a possible LUP first. There could have been a couple of homeless guys in here wanting to get out of the cold and wet.' He nodded towards their entrance point. 'Make sure that from the LUP you can see if anyone is approaching so that you can escape. To do that, you need an escape route, like the one I just showed you.'

There was a lot to take in, but Fergus was far from finished with Danny's lesson in SAS fieldcraft skills. 'Everything you take into the LUP goes out with you. You leave absolutely nothing to show you were there.'

He delved into a heavy-duty carrier bag from the camping shop and handed Danny a brand-new Leatherman knife. 'I never gave you anything before and you ought to have one of these. Look after it. There's an old saying, "You're only as sharp as your knife." It's true.'

'Thanks,' said Danny. He was examining the knife when Fergus threw over a small day sack, followed by a sleeping bag and an empty water bladder. 'Get comfortable, we'll eat soon.'

Danny unravelled the sleeping bag and then held up the water bladder. 'What's this for?'

'Think about it. You'll probably need it before you turn in for the night.'

As Fergus unfolded his own sleeping bag, his grandson worked out the precise purpose of the bladder. And as he did so, he was struck by another thought. 'But what if . . . what if . . . ?'

Fergus grinned. 'You got the baby wipes and the cling film, didn't you?'

'I got everything on the list.'

'Good. So, like I said, we leave absolutely nothing to show we've been here.' He glanced towards the carrier bags Danny had carried up to their hideaway. 'Shall we eat?'

Danny had suddenly lost his appetite.

But they did eat. As the trains rumbled by overhead, they consumed the contents of the ring-pull cans, followed by chocolate bars. When they finished, Fergus packed the empty cans, wrappings and bottles into a carrier bag as the rain bounced off the tarmac outside. Danny watched as his grandfather checked and then double checked that not a scrap of evidence of their makeshift meal had been left behind.

'I just realized something,' said Danny. 'I don't know what to call you.'

Fergus shrugged. 'It's a bit late for Granddad, and it's not a good idea anyway. Neither is Fergus. Don't call me anything if you can avoid it, but if you have to, stick to Frankie. And I'll call you . . . Derek.'

'Derek!' said Danny, horrified. 'No way, I'm not being called Derek.'

'You pick something then, beginning with a D. It's easier to remember it that way.'

Danny thought for a few moments. 'Dean. I don't mind Dean.'

'Fair enough, Dean it is.'

'And there's something else,' said Danny.

A train passed overhead, the first for several minutes – the rush hour was long over. Fergus looked out to the front of the archway to check that it was clear before settling down on his sleeping bag. 'Go on, then, ask.'

'If we have to use the ERV again and you're not there, I have to walk by every half hour for three hours, right?'

'That's right.'

'So what if you don't turn up after three hours? What does that mean? And what do I do?'

Fergus nodded. 'It would most probably mean Fincham and his team have got me. If it happens, you don't go to the police, they'd only hand you over to Fincham. You go to the press, one of the tabloids, the *Sun* or the *Mirror*. And you tell them everything I've told you and everything that's happened. It'll cause such a stink that Fincham won't dare come after you. Now get some sleep. I'll take first stag.'

20

Marcie Deveraux parked the battered old Mazda in a line of cars that looked in even worse condition. She switched off the windscreen wipers and looked across the road towards the drab, rundown housing estate. It made a depressing view, but Marcie Deveraux wasn't concerned with that. There was a job to be done and she was dressed and kitted out to do it.

Her designer clothes had been replaced with trainers, jeans and black cotton jacket – cotton rather than nylon because nylon meant noise. Her hair was unusually ruffled, almost scruffy, and fell over her ears. But there was a reason for that too. There were earpieces in both her ears and the tousled hairstyle hid them perfectly. One was connected to the personal radio that kept her in contact with her team. The other was blue tooth and was connected to a mobile she wore on a cord around her neck. That was for Fincham. He wanted to know everything Deveraux was about to learn, as she learned it.

The rain beat down on the windscreen as she checked that the Nike bag on the passenger seat was zipped up. Then she made sure the cord attaching the Maglite torch to her jacket was firmly fixed. She had to be certain that nothing would be left behind when the job was complete. The Maglite lens was covered with black duck tape, with a hole cut in it. She wouldn't need much light, and the more light the bigger the chance of compromise.

Deveraux had to be sterile of any ID, so she checked her pockets were empty. She already knew they were, she'd been through them before leaving her flat, but as always, she double-checked.

A couple out walking a dripping dog went by, heads bent low. They didn't look into the car – they were much too anxious to get home and out of the rain. Deveraux watched them hurry away into the dark night as she pulled on a pair of clear plastic surgical gloves. She was ready.

The message she was waiting for came a few minutes later.

'Brian has Moyes now complete the Victory Club. Marcie acknowledge.'

With Mick getting treatment for broken front teeth and Fran nursing a busted nose, the surveillance team was down to two tonight. It was lucky for them that Eddie Moyes had travelled to the Victory Club by car. Deveraux pressed the small button that led from a wire under her watchstrap into her hand.

'Roger that. Marcie's foxtrot.'

She grabbed her bag, got out of the car and locked

up before crossing the road towards the housing estate and Eddie Moyes's flat. Jimmy and Brian had followed him to the Victory Club; they had the trigger and would warn Deveraux when he left. There was plenty of time for her to get in and out of the flat for the CTR.

It wasn't much to look at from the outside. In his glory days Moyes had been the proud owner of a loft apartment in Docklands. Now he could just afford the rent on a housing association flat in east London.

Deveraux climbed the stairs, passing a teenager sitting in the rubbish-filled stairwell, his face pushed into a crisp packet. The bag moved in and out as he breathed and the strong smell of glue drifted upwards.

Moyes lived on the first floor. Rain had dampened the front half of the exterior balcony so Deveraux walked close to the doors as she headed for number 34. She didn't want to leave any wet marks inside the flat. The windows of the flats she passed had metal grilles covering them; some even had them in front of the doors.

Deveraux had learned which two locks were on the front door of number 34 during her four a.m. recce. There was a standard Yale, the normal pin tumbler type. That would take seconds to defeat. The second one would take longer and needed to be tackled first. It was the four-lever type, the sort that had to be turned into the locked or unlocked position. Deveraux had used her mini Maglite during the recce to peer into the lock and decide which master keys to bring. She unzipped the bag and brought out three lever-lock keys on a ring.

As she reached the blue front door, Brian came back in her earpiece.

'That's Moyes no change. Still complete the Victory Club. His vehicle still static.'

Entry to the flat had to be quick. Deveraux slid in the first key. It didn't work. She quickly tried the second and the key turned and unlocked the four-lever. The keyring went back into the bag and Deveraux pulled out a Yale gun. It looked a bit like a chunky pistol with two thin-bladed picks instead of a barrel. She pushed the picks into the top lock and began to squeeze the trigger repeatedly. The picks rattled about and on the fourth squeeze the lock turned and Deveraux pushed open the door.

She slipped noiselessly into the dark hallway, gently closed the door and the Yale clicked back in position.

Five miles away at the Victory Club Eddie Moyes was watching Harry the barman go through his glass-polishing routine. The glasses were lined up, as usual, on the bartop.

Eddie nodded his approval. 'You're very proficient, Harry. Precise.'

Harry adjusted the position of one of the glasses slightly. 'If a job's worth doing, that's what I always say. We learned to do things right in the army.'

'I can see that.' Eddie finished his drink and stood his glass at one end of Harry's line-up. Harry swiftly moved it away.

'I'll have the other half in there, Harry,' said Eddie before the barman had the chance to consign the glass to the washing-up tray. Eddie didn't like drinking halves, but he'd lost his driving licence once before and had no intention of letting it happen again. So when he was driving, his limit was two halves.

'Never eaten out of a mess tin or been on the wrong end of a rifle, have you, Eddie?' Harry asked the question as he pulled the second half, knowing perfectly well that Eddie had never served in the army or any other of the armed forces.

Eddie smiled at the hint of disdain in the barman's voice. He lifted his glass, gave the beer an admiring look and downed almost half of it in one go. 'Sadly not, Harry. But you know how much I admire the army. And our boys and girls who serve in it.'

'I know you've made a living out of writing stories about them. Some of them more true than others.'

Eddie was anxious to move the conversation on to safer ground. He glanced around the bar: there were only two other customers, sitting together at a table in one corner. 'Quiet in here tonight.'

The barman shrugged and Eddie took another mouthful of beer. But he wasn't there purely to enjoy the beer. For much of the day he'd been checking through his cuttings and notebooks, reminding himself of the details of the original Watts stories.

A name had leaped out at him, someone he'd spoken to briefly by telephone then, the obvious person to comment on the SAS man's treachery. That person was Colonel Richard Meacher, Watts's commanding officer. And Eddie reckoned he was worth talking to again.

Back in '97, after Watts had been captured in

Colombia, Meacher had stuck to the official line, trotting out all the expected clichés: Watts had betrayed his country and his Regiment; he was the rotten apple in the barrel; the Regiment would go on producing brave men prepared to lay down their lives in the defence of their country. All standard stuff, carefully phrased to reassure the great British public.

But at that time Meacher had been the Regiment's CO. Now it was different. He was retired and might be prepared to say a lot more once Eddie told him that Watts was back in Britain and on the run.

'So,' said Eddie as nonchalantly as he could, 'you were telling me about Colonel Meacher.'

Harry continued polishing. 'Was I?'

'Come on, Harry, you and me are old mates. I need to contact him.'

Harry put the glass he was polishing down on the bartop. 'I wouldn't exactly call us mates, Eddie. And I'll tell you exactly what I'd tell anyone else. He's a member here. That's all.'

Eddie finished his drink and placed his empty glass on the bar. 'I'll bid you goodnight then, Harry. Always a pleasure to chat with you.'

Harry picked up the empty glass and turned away to put it in the washing-up machine. Eddie looked at the perfectly lined-up row of glasses. Then he smiled and pushed two of the glasses a few centimetres out of line before walking out.

Marcie Deveraux stood perfectly still in the hallway of Eddie Moyes's flat. Tuning in. Allowing her eyes to become accustomed to the darkness. Next door a television blared out. A woman shouted to her kids. 'Turn that bloody thing down!'

Deveraux smelled the microwaved remains of a Chinese meal. The odour of sweaty socks was even stronger.

Noiselessly she put down the unzipped bag, took out two plastic foot covers and slid them over her trainers. Next she drew a police-issue telescopic steel baton from the holster on her belt with one hand and removed her earpieces with the other. She needed to hear even the slightest movement because before the CTR could be carried out the flat had to be 'cleared'.

Moyes lived alone. She had checked. And there was no girlfriend. It appeared that there were no friends at all. But anyone unfortunate enough to be inside the flat now would be dropped.

It would be made to look like a burglary gone wrong. Deveraux would take something on the way out and make a run for it. The car would be abandoned and the pre-planned escape route would be utilized. Every contingency had been considered and covered.

Deveraux moved. She was good. Textbook good.

Short, dark corridor first. Slowly. Cautiously past the kitchen to her right. Glimmer of the streetlights down below penetrating the dirty grey net curtains just enough to show the room is clear.

Living room next. Dark. Curtains drawn. The small beam of the mini Maglite illuminating the room as the gentle tapping of the rain hits the window. The Maglite picks out a PC on a tabletop, a TV and a worn-out settee. Room clear.

Single bedroom and bathroom clear. A mess, but clear.

Deveraux went back to the front door and relocked the lever lock with the master key. Then she took out two wooden doorstops and jammed them into the door frame. If Moyes were to slip away from the club unnoticed and return to the flat everything would appear normal until he tried to push open the door. Deveraux would have time to drop Moyes and maybe take his wallet before escaping.

A pair of high heels clicked along the exterior landing. A woman was on her mobile. 'But it's raining. Can't you pick me up?'

The earpieces went back into Deveraux's ears and she got on the net. She spoke softly but clearly; whispering could cause confusion and waste valuable time.

'That's Marcie secure and complete the target.'

Brian came back instantly.

'Roger that, Marcie. No change here. Moyes still complete the club and the car still static.'

Deveraux picked up her bag and, with the Maglite held between her teeth, took out a camcorder. Using its infra-red capability, she filmed her route from the door into the living room. She scanned the whole room, even the carpet, before moving over to the PC. Everything on the tabletop was filmed from different angles, every scrap of paper, the anglepoise lamp and the half-drunk mug of tea to the right of the keyboard.

She put away the camcorder and took out what

looked like a Discman. It was a Discman of sorts: a box containing a CD. But instead of earpieces it had a multi-connector that enabled it to link up with any computer. Moyes's computer had USBs. It was switched off, but the box of tricks didn't need the PC powered up to find out what was on its hard disk.

Deveraux connected it to the PC and soon heard the slight hum of the CD disc spinning. The machine would break through any firewall or password Moyes might have on his PC and download his complete hard drive onto the disc. Five small red lights would light up one by one to indicate the progress of the download.

The machine began its work and Deveraux turned her attention to the other items on the desk.

Eddie Moyes wasn't so particular about the way he searched for information. He just got what he wanted in whatever way he could and didn't worry about the consequences. Harry the barman had given away little, but it was enough. He'd confirmed that Meacher was a member of the Victory Club and that was all that Eddie needed.

He knew his way to the office – he'd been there before. It wasn't locked and Eddie slipped quietly inside. The club's officials probably kept the membership records on computer but Eddie was banking on there being hard copies as backup.

And there were. He found them in a filing cabinet, all neatly and alphabetically filed. It couldn't have been easier. Eddie thumbed through to the Ms and removed the file bearing the name *Meacher, Richard, Col.*

Eddie smiled and took out an old and highly prized notebook. *July '97 – SAS Traitor Watts* was scrawled on the front cover in Eddie's untidy handwriting. It was the notebook he'd used when covering the original Fergus Watts stories, and inside were the notes he'd made then during the brief telephone conversation with Meacher.

Eddie jotted down the address and telephone number on the back of the notebook and slipped the file back into the cabinet. He was feeling very pleased with himself. And hungry. Everything they said about Chinese meals really was true.

Deveraux was reading old newspaper articles about Fergus Watts, many of them written by Eddie Moyes. But she was learning nothing new. Once each piece of paper was read, she replaced it in exactly the same position.

The disc was still turning, soaking up every piece of information on the old PC. She opened up her mobile and dialled. Fincham answered immediately. 'What have you got?'

'Nothing useful. Just printouts of information we know he got online and old newspaper cuttings. Maybe we'll learn more from the download and—'

Brian burst in on the other earpiece.

'Stand by, stand by. That's Moyes foxtrot from the Victory.'

Deveraux had no time for Fincham now. 'He's on the move. Got to go.' As she powered down the mobile she went on the net to Brian.

'Marcie needs more time. I have only two lights.'

'Roger that. Brian foxtrot.'

Eddie's old blue and rust Sierra was parked a couple of streets away from the club. As he slowly ambled back towards it, Brian was well ahead of him. Jimmy, in his vehicle, took the trigger.

'Jimmy has Moyes. Still foxtrot towards car.'

Brian was already at the car. He took his Leatherman from a pocket, stuck it into the valve of the nearside front tyre and heard the escaping gush of air. The tyre was flat before Moyes turned the corner and Brian stood up and walked away.

In the flat, Deveraux was watching the playback of the tabletop on the camera, and checking that everything was in place. Then she filmed in front of herself as she moved back out to the corridor and into the bedroom.

Brian came onto the net.

'Brian has Moyes approaching his car. He hasn't seen the flat tyre yet.'

Deveraux filmed the bedside cabinet with the Maglite in her mouth. There was nothing of interest on top of the cabinet, just a few petrol receipts and an overdue gas bill.

She opened a cupboard and saw a stack of used reporter's notebooks. She took out the top two and read the titles scrawled on the front covers: *Nov '95 – Footballer's shame; March '99 – Used car scam.*

'That's Moyes kicking the car, he's found the flat tyre. Now opening boot. How's it going, Marcie?'

'Wait out. I'm in the bedroom.'

The flat tyre had given Marcie valuable time. She

carefully removed the notebooks, filmed the covers and replaced them in the correct order before moving on to the wardrobe to check through coat pockets.

'That's Moyes now tightening the last nut. Nearly mobile.'

Deveraux wouldn't be rushed, even though she knew she had to be quick.

'Marcie, roger that. Still in the bedroom.'

She reached the bedroom door and made a final check. The carpet was a thick shag pile and she had left a few footprints. She moved back into the room and bent down to smooth them over with a hand.

'Stand by. Stand by. Engine on, that's Moyes mobile towards the main. Marcie acknowledge.'

'Roger that. Marcie's still in the bedroom.'

'That's Moyes at the main and indicating right. I need a quick pick-up, Jimmy.'

Deveraux could hear Jimmy's vehicle engine gunning as he came on the net.

'Nearly there.'

Deveraux moved back to the living room and went to the PC as Jimmy calmly relayed what was happening on the follow. He was two vehicles behind Moyes.

'Brian's complete. Jimmy has Moyes. He's gone right at the main. Looks like he's heading home. Marcie acknowledge.'

'Marcie has three lights up.'

'Roger that, Marcie. I reckon he's got another ten minutes to home.'

Deveraux checked out the kitchen. There was nothing of any use to her and the smell drove her back to the living room.

'Marcie has four lights up.'

'Roger that. Moyes is turning into the estate now. There's blue lights ahead, outside the target block. Marcie acknowledge.'

Deveraux moved quickly back to the kitchen, which was being bathed in blue flashes from down on the street. Briefly she wondered whether someone had seen her break in and had called the police. But as she looked out of the window she spotted an ambulance. Then she saw Eddie Moyes's Sierra pull into a space just behind it.

Jimmy came back on the net.

'Stop. Stop. Stop. He's outside the target now. Door open, he's out, now locking up.'

Deveraux saw none of that. She was back at the PC.

'Marcie's got fives. I'm coming out.'

Quickly but calmly she pulled out the USB. And then, checking that everything was in her bag and the Maglite torch was still attached to her jacket, she walked to the door.

Jimmy gave her a step-by-step picture of exactly what Moyes was doing.

'That's Moyes held at stairs. A stretcher's coming out. Still static by the ambulance.'

Deveraux pulled out the doorstops and opened the lever lock.

'Stand by. Stand by. Moyes foxtrot up the stairs. Now unsighted. I'll get him on the landing. Marcie acknowledge.'

Deveraux gave the acknowledgement with two presses of the SEND button by her watchstrap. The team would get two hisses of air. It was quicker that way.

She took off the plastic covering her trainers, opened the door and stepped out onto the balcony.

As she relocked the lever lock Jimmy came back on the net.

'Stand by. Stand by.'

Deveraux knew what that meant. She moved away from the door and walked towards the staircase. It was the only way out.

Moyes appeared ahead of her at the top of the stairs. He looked down at the ambulance as it pulled away but glanced towards Deveraux as they passed. She kept her head down and made it to the stairs.

Eddie was glad to be home. He was hungry and was hoping that there was still a can of baked beans in the kitchen cupboard. He took out his keys and slipped one into the lower lock. As the key turned Eddie tried to think why the woman he'd just passed seemed familiar. But it didn't come. He opened the Yale lock and stepped into his flat.

At the bottom of the stairs Deveraux saw that Glue Boy had gone. Someone, maybe the woman who'd clicked past the flat in her high heels, had called the ambulance. Glue Boy had got lucky. This time. Deveraux reached the Mazda, got inside and started the engine.

'That's Marcie mobile. Meet you back at the office.'

21

Fergus and Danny left their archway LUP at 0745 hours. They took everything with them, even though the plan was to return later that day. They left by the escape route, climbing down the rusted metal ladder fixed to the brickwork.

Between the arches and the already busy main road was a stretch of open waste ground strewn with empty cans and takeaway food cartons. But they were hidden from inquisitive eyes by the towering advertising billboards that fronted the road.

By 0805 hours they had found an e-mail phone at London Bridge and were ready to go online to Elena. The station was heaving: the same weary-looking commuters who had pushed and battled their way out of the city the previous evening were now pushing and battling their way back in.

'Do you use your real name on that?' asked Fergus as Danny prepared to log on.

'Usually. I never know what name to expect with Elena. Depends what mood she's in.'

Fergus frowned. He hadn't told Danny, but he was prepared for this to be the first and last contact with Elena. To ignore her now would be a mistake: she might panic and start shooting her mouth off. But depending on how she responded this could well be a 'thanks but no thanks'.

'Use a different name.'

'No one can get into this, it's just me and Elena.'

'I know that, but do it anyway.'

'She'll laugh if I call myself Dean.'

'Then use your imagination, think of something else.'

Danny was still thinking as he went online, but as usual Elena was one step ahead.

```
Oakeley says:  (8:10:15 am)
have info
```

Fergus was looking over Danny's shoulder. 'Oakeley? What's that?'

Danny smiled. 'We have these houses at school – you know, meant to encourage teamwork and all that. Oakeley is Elena's house. I'll use mine.'

```
Stockwell says:  (8:11:19 am)
good. how did u find it
Oakeley says:  (8:11:49 am)
internet whos who, easy. will get other
stuff u need now, travel arrangements, etc.
how do u want it delivered
```

Fergus nodded. He was impressed. 'Good. She's thinking, not rushing in and blurting everything out.'

'I told you we could trust her.'

'Tell her I'll speak to her next.'

```
Stockwell says: (8:15:24 am)
my friend wants 2 talk now
Oakeley says: (8:15:35 am)
ok
```

Fergus replaced Danny at the keypad. He typed slowly, deliberately and precisely. To him, it was the information that mattered, not the speed or the way it was typed.

```
Stockwell says: (8:17:06 am)
Put what you have in black bin liner secured
with elastic band. Go to London Bridge
station, then to top of Magnis Street, station
end with station on your right. Start walk-
ing down street between 1755 and 1800 hrs.
That's between five to six and six pm.
```

He sent the first part of the message and then turned to Danny. 'What was the pace count last night?'

'One four seven.'

Before Fergus could start typing, Elena came back to him.

```
Oakeley says: (8:17:26 am)
i have heard of the 24 hour clock
```

153

Danny grinned but Fergus simply ignored the interruption and continued with the information.

```
Stockwell says: (8:19:11 am)
Count the paces as you walk. After 147 paces
you will see on your left a rubbish skip
filled with cardboard boxes. An archway with
wooden pallets will be on your right. Toss
the bin liner into the skip and keep walk-
ing. Don't look around or look nervous. Be
natural, you're just on your way somewhere.
Think of it as acting, but don't overact.
Got that?
Oakeley says: (8:19:24 am)
i'll try mi v best 😟
```

Fergus looked at Danny. 'What does that mean?'
Danny laughed. 'She's winding you up.'
Once again, Fergus ignored Elena's sarcasm.

```
Stockwell says: (8:20:43 am)
Keep walking to housing at the end of the
street and then make your way back home.
And make sure the bin liner is secured tightly
so no rain gets in. That's it. And thanks.
```

Fergus made Danny sign off before Elena had the chance to ask any questions. She had all the information she needed and it was time for them to move on.

'You've never thanked me for anything,' said Danny as they headed out of the station.

Fergus didn't look at his grandson. 'I'm waiting for you to get something right.'

He didn't see the V sign Danny made behind his back.

'So this Elena,' said Fergus as they walked, 'she's a real computer buff, is she?'

'Yeah,' answered Danny. 'You could say that.'

22

Eddie Moyes had ordered breakfast. The Big One. Double eggs, bacon, two sausages, beans, mushrooms, fried bread and three rounds of bread and butter. He preferred bread and butter to toast. It made mopping up the egg yolk, beans and tomato sauce that much easier.

He was working while he waited. A half-drunk mug of tea stood on a table next to the pay phone in one corner of the café. Eddie's 1997 notebook rested on the shelf beneath the phone, and he was writing as he spoke. He was using the remaining pages of the notebook he'd used on the original stories so that he could refer back quickly and easily if necessary.

Eddie Moyes was no fool, he'd been around far too long for that. He was trying to track down Fergus Watts and he knew he wasn't alone in that. The others, whoever they were – and he suspected MI5 or MI6 – might well know by now that he was also on the hunt. Nothing escaped the security services for very long.

So just in case, Eddie was being careful. This call was important: better to make it from a public box than use his home phone or mobile. And Eddie had struck lucky – not quite the result he wanted, but he was making definite progress. He was writing quickly. 'Sailing? . . . No, you wouldn't even get me on a rowing boat in the park . . . Yes, I've got that, the morning tide . . . You've been very helpful, Mrs Meacher, thank you . . . The day after tomorrow, then . . . Yes, I'll call first . . . Goodbye.'

He replaced the receiver with a satisfied smile. And then his breakfast arrived. He was chewing slowly on his favourite combination of egg yolk and sausage when the door opened and a young woman walked in. Eddie noticed the cuts and bruises on her face but paid her little more attention. It was a busy café, used by all sorts of people, and they usually had a story to tell if anyone was prepared to listen. All the tables were in use, so it was no surprise when Eddie glanced up from his plate a few minutes later and saw the young woman standing there with a mug of tea in one hand.

She smiled. 'You look as though you're enjoying that.'

Eddie swallowed the final mouthful of sausage. 'Always get a good breakfast here.'

'D'you mind if I sit down?'

'Be my guest,' said Eddie, picking up the last slice of bread and butter and commencing the mopping-up operation. It didn't take long, and the young woman was polite enough not to look until it was all over.

Eddie had enjoyed his meal. He was full – replete, as he liked to call it. He picked up his mug and drained the last of the tea. As he put it down he saw that the young woman was looking at him. He smiled. 'You not eating?'

The young woman returned the smile and gently touched her face. 'Bit difficult at the moment.'

'Oh, yeah, sorry, I, er . . . well, I couldn't help noticing the bruises. Accident, was it?'

'Mmm, I walked into a door.'

Of course you did, thought Eddie. I've heard that one a thousand times. But it was nothing to do with him. If she had an abusive boyfriend – Eddie had already clocked that there was no wedding ring – and chose to let him get away with it, that was up to her.

'Actually,' said the woman softly, 'it was my boyfriend. I dunno why I should protect him.'

Oh no, thought Eddie, a talker. Still, he was in a good mood and in no great rush. If she had something she needed to say, Eddie was prepared to sit and listen. 'You shouldn't stay with him, love. In my line of work I've seen this sort of thing happen too many times.'

'Really? What, are you a social worker or something?'

Eddie smiled. 'Hardly. I'm a reporter.'

The young woman was wide-eyed. 'Honest? Oh, that must be so exciting. D'you do murders and things?'

'Well, I don't actually *do* them,' said Eddie with a laugh. 'I report them. I report all sorts of things.'

The notebook Eddie had been using was on the tabletop and the young woman glanced towards it. 'Do you know, I wondered why you had a notebook with you.'

Eddie picked up the notebook and slipped it into his coat pocket. 'You're very observant,' he said with a smile. 'Make a good reporter yourself.'

Forty minutes later the woman was sitting in her car, dialling a number on her mobile. It rang three times.

'Yes?'

'You were right, he's got the missing notebook with him. It's got *July '97 – SAS Traitor Watts* written on the front.'

'Well done, Fran. Good work. Where is he now?'

'Back at his flat with all the dailies. Looks like he's settled in for a while.'

'And how are the bruises, and the nose?'

'Painful. I can't wait to meet up with our friend Watts again. Did Mick call in?'

'Yes. He'll join you later, once the swelling goes down a bit.'

Fran smiled. 'It's his own fault – should have kept his legs together. How about the governor? Has he got over us losing Watts for a second time?'

'He's not happy, Fran, but this should convince him that last night's CTR wasn't a complete waste of time. Wait out and I'll come back to you.'

She hung up. It was true, George Fincham wasn't happy, and wouldn't be until Fergus Watts had been eliminated.

Marcie Deveraux, on the other hand, was not un-happy with the way the operation was progressing.

23

'This girlfriend of yours—'

'She's my *friend*. Can't you just accept that?'

'All right, friend. She was the one who located my phone?'

'Yeah, and it was her idea.'

'Could she do more than that? Like . . . like listen in on calls?'

'I doubt it. Why?'

'We need information, Danny. If we can find out anything, anything at all, about what Fincham's doing, we can maybe stay one step ahead.'

They were on the way back to the LUP. It had been a long day. After the MSN conversation with Elena they couldn't return to the LUP while people were on site, so Fergus said they should split up for a while. Fincham's team were looking for the two of them. Together. Apart they were less conspicuous. He gave Danny some cash, told him to 'keep his head down and not talk to anyone', and arranged to meet later at the usual RV.

Danny followed his instructions. He wandered around, got himself a pizza at lunch time and saw a film during the afternoon.

Fergus drank a lot of coffee and later did a couple of walk-bys of the archway. There wasn't much activity. The first time he saw a man on a fork-lift shifting a few pallets from one place to another while his workmate leaned against a wall and sipped tea from a mug. The second time, just after four thirty, the two men were getting ready to leave.

There was nothing happening at any of the neighbouring arches, so by five thirty Fergus and Danny were making their way back.

'What about e-mail?' said Danny. 'What if she hacked into Fincham's?'

'Could she do it?'

Danny smiled. 'I bet she'd wouldn't mind having a go.'

Elena began counting her steps as she started to walk down Magnis Street. She was exactly on time. Under one arm she carried a black plastic rubbish sack, tightly secured with strong elastic bands.

Inside the sack was an Ordnance Survey map for the area of Norfolk where Meacher lived. His address and telephone number and even his wife's name were written carefully and clearly on a single sheet of paper. Elena had been out and bought the map earlier in the day. Train and bus timetables for the journey to and around the county had been downloaded from the Internet.

She spotted the rubbish skip and the open archway with the stacked wooden pallets long before she finished the count. But she kept counting. As she came alongside the skip she casually tossed the black bag inside and continued walking, wondering where Fergus and Danny were, and if they had seen her.

Before leaving Foxcroft, Elena had checked a London *A–Z* and worked out the quickest route back to the station. She took a left. Elena didn't scare easily, but the gloomy and dismal street made her uneasy. It was empty. Deserted. A couple of battered cardboard boxes lay in the middle of the road. A door to one building was wide open but as Elena glanced towards it she could see there was no one inside. That was the problem. There was no one around. It was like the place had been abandoned in a big hurry. Elena just wanted to get back amongst the crowds.

Then, ten metres ahead, someone stepped out of a doorway, head down. He turned towards her. Elena tensed but kept walking, ready to leg it if he made a grab at her. He came closer, walking quickly, head still down. They were less than a couple of metres apart and Elena was about to run when he finally lifted his head.

'All right?'

'Danny! You . . . you . . . dork.'

'What's wrong?'

'You had me brickin' it, that's what's wrong!'

Danny didn't see what all the fuss was about. 'Did you leave the stuff?'

'Of course – I should have kept it to hit you with.'

'Look, you might have been followed and we

couldn't take the chance of someone seeing you make the drop. And *he* said if you'd spotted me near the skip you might have panicked.'

'*He's* got a really great opinion of me.'

'You should worry, he treats me like I'm about five. We need you to do something else.'

They stood by a car with a smashed-in windscreen while Danny explained the plan of hacking into Fincham's e-mail.

'D'you think you can do it? It's bound to be a secure site – firewalls, the lot.'

'Danny, I thought you knew by now, nowhere online is secure. I'll give it a go tonight and let you know what I've found when we MSN in the morning.'

They didn't hear the footsteps approaching. They didn't see a thing. The first they knew of the attack was when Danny was roughly shoved in the back and sent sprawling into the road. Elena felt herself being grabbed around her arms and body and held tightly in a bear-like grip. All the breath was squeezed out of her; she couldn't even scream.

Danny had taken the weight of his fall on his left shoulder and it hurt like mad. He rolled over, expecting to see a couple of burly MI6 guys standing there with pistols pointing at his head. But they were kids. Three of them. Younger than him by the look of it, but mean looking all the same. And the one holding Elena was enormous.

Danny tried to get to his feet.

'Stay down!' yelled the closest of the three, kicking out at him. Danny saw it coming and tensed as a trainer thudded into his ribcage. He tried to roll with the kick, but didn't make it. The pain screamed through his body.

'Phone!' shouted the kicker. 'Give us your phone, and anything else in your pockets. Cards. Cash. Quick.'

'I haven't got a phone,' gasped Danny as two of the attackers loomed over him, poised to kick out again.

'Don't talk shit, everyone's got a phone! Give us it, quick!'

'It's true!' yelled Danny. 'Someone else beat you to it.'

The attackers were momentarily thrown. They stared at each other, highly pissed off that other muggers had got in before them. 'Cards then, and you must have cash!'

'Give it to them, Danny,' shouted Elena, struggling to free herself from the big guy's grip. She was getting nowhere. He grasped her even more tightly and shouted at Danny, 'Do as she says, dickhead. I'm getting bored with this and if I come over there I'll kick the crap out of you.'

'All right! I'll give it to you! Just don't hurt us.'

'That's better,' smiled the one who'd done the kicking. 'You know it makes sense.'

It did make sense. Everything Danny had ever heard about how to react in this sort of situation told him to do exactly as the attackers demanded.

He didn't do it. He was angry, he was hurting and he wasn't going to give in. Not without a fight. He thought about going for the Leatherman knife in his jacket but forced the idea from his mind. That was a step too far, and anyway, for all he knew his attackers might be carrying weapons of their own.

'My wallet's in my pocket,' he said, moving one hand towards his jacket. The two thugs closest backed off slightly. As they did, Danny drew back his leg and stamped as hard as he could into the kicker's leg, catching him directly below the knee.

He went down, fast, screaming, 'Wanker! Wanker!' as he hit the pavement. Danny swivelled and kicked out at his second target. His foot thudded into his victim's thigh, sending him staggering backwards. Danny leaped to his feet.

'Oh, Danny, no!' yelled Elena. 'No!' But she had to go for it too now. The big bear was holding her off the ground, but his brain obviously wasn't as fast as his hands: he couldn't decide if he should drop Elena and go for Danny. Elena made up his mind for him. She swung her right foot and brought her heel back into his shin.

He let go, squealing like a pig.

'Run, Elena!' screamed Danny. 'Run!'

She was already running. Danny was at her side and two of the attackers were after them. The third was still on the ground, holding his knee and spitting out words of fury. But he wouldn't be running for a long time.

'Stupid, stupid, stupid!' shouted Elena as they hurtled down the road and into the next on the left.

The chasers were close, but not gaining, and up ahead was the main road. And people. Hundreds of people. Exactly what Elena wanted.

They were almost there. Safe among the crowds. Pedestrians passing at the end of the street had turned to stare as the four youngsters came tearing towards them. And then, when they were just metres from the junction, a police officer stepped out from behind the building on the corner of the street.

He saw the four runners. They saw him. The muggers skidded to a halt and turned on their heels. Danny glanced at Elena, shook his head and went tearing off up the main road, away from London Bridge. Elena came to a standstill.

'What's going on?' demanded the police officer.

'They . . . they . . . they tried to mug me.'

The officer looked towards the figures disappearing in two directions and thought about giving chase. Then he reached for the radio at his collar while keeping his eyes fixed on Elena.

'Name?' he said.

Elena shrugged. 'I dunno,' she said with a grin. 'I never met any of them before.'

The officer wasn't amused. '*Your* name.'

Danny stopped running as soon as he was safely swallowed up in the crowd. He felt bad about running out on Elena, but he'd had no choice. The last thing he needed was his name and details fed into the police computer. And he knew Elena would give nothing away.

He took a long route back to the LUP, and entered the arch by the ladder at the back. Fergus was pleased about that, but less than delighted when he heard what had happened out on the street. 'Where do you keep your brains?' he snarled. 'Combat should always be your last option. You talk your way out of it, or run away, but you never go looking for a fight.'

'But I couldn't help it, and we did get away.'

'*You* got away. What about your friend? She's probably sitting in some nick now telling the nice policeman all about you!'

'She won't be, and she wouldn't.'

She wasn't. Elena was on her way back to Foxcroft. She'd given the police officer her name and address, which he confirmed while she waited, and told him a tale about the *four* boys who'd tried to mug her. She gave accurate descriptions, or as accurate as she could remember, of the real muggers, and then told him the fourth attacker 'looked a bit like that footballer, Will Rooney'.

'I think you mean *Wayne* Rooney, don't you?'

'Yeah, that's the one. He was just like him. Only shorter. And fatter. I'm not sure, really.'

The officer looked bemused by the description of the fourth mugger, but seemed satisfied that Elena was telling the truth. He warned her of the dangers of young girls going alone into dodgy areas and said they'd be in touch if they found any suspects. Then he let her go.

She walked back to London Bridge and waited fifteen minutes for a train. She wanted to get back to Foxcroft and her computer. She had no idea if she would really be able to hack into Fincham's e-mail, but she was up for the challenge.

The journey home took less than half an hour. She

opened the front door and saw Dave the Rave standing in the hallway. 'We've been waiting for you,' he said without smiling. 'There's someone here to see you.'

Elena couldn't believe it. They couldn't have found Danny, not after the description she'd given. Maybe they'd traced one of the real muggers.

'You'd better come with me to the office,' said Dave, and he turned towards the stairs.

Elena followed Dave upstairs to the office. The door was closed. Dave turned the handle and pushed it open. 'In you go.'

'Aren't you coming in with me?'

Dave shook his head. 'I'll wait out here.'

Elena stepped inside. A man dressed in a suit was standing by the window looking out to the street. Slowly he turned round. 'Hello, babe,' he said with a huge smile. 'Surprised?'

Elena could hardly believe her eyes. 'Dad!'

24

Fergus was impressed when he saw the contents of the black plastic bag. It was similar to a target pack he would have been given when he was in the Regiment. Elena had given them the exact position of the target, with maps and information on how to get there.

They'd waited until dark before fetching the sack from the skip and then Fergus decided there was no point in taking the risk of hanging around in London for another night. They had everything they needed to locate Colonel Meacher. It was time to move.

On the late train to Norwich, they took all the operational precautions that were by now beginning to become familiar to Danny. Staying third party aware, travelling in separate carriages until Fergus was confident they were not being followed.

When he eventually took the seat opposite Danny he nodded but said nothing. The train ploughed on through the night. They didn't speak, but caught snatches of conversation from other weary travellers. The final stop before Norwich was at the small town of Diss. Doors opened and slammed shut and the train moved slowly away. Danny stood up and looked around the carriage. They were alone. He slumped back down onto the seat and felt his bruised shoulder jar, painfully reminding him of his meeting with the three muggers.

'You told me I should run away from a fight,' he said, shifting in the seat to get comfortable. 'But you were SAS, you didn't run away. You . . . you killed people.'

Fergus reached into his bag, took out a couple of pre-packed sandwiches and handed one to Danny. 'The Special Forces aren't all about killing. It happens, but mostly it's about gaining information and destroying strategic targets. Most times, if you get into a contact with the enemy, it's because they're blocking your mission or your escape route and you've run out of other options.'

'A contact?' said Danny. 'You mean a fight?'

Fergus nodded.

'And what then?'

'Then you react with extreme speed and violence, so they're scared shitless. And you kill them before they kill you.'

He saw Danny's eyes widen and he smiled. 'You asked, Danny,' he said. 'And seeing me limping around now probably makes it hard to believe. But that's what I was trained to do. Listen, when I was in the Regiment, every soldier I knew would rather dig a hole and hide than get involved in a contact with the enemy. It's all about survival, staying alive – exactly what *we* have to do. Now, are you gonna eat that sandwich or are you gonna sit there gawping at me all night?'

Danny finished his sandwich just as the train arrived in Norwich. The station was quiet; the shops and bar were closed. They found a computer phone they could use to go online to Elena in the morning and then made their way out into the night.

The city lights bounced off the dark river. Hordes of young people headed noisily towards nearby club-land. Girls wobbled along in micro skirts and high heels and shouted even louder than the leering, jeering lads shouting at them.

Fergus took in the new surroundings. 'We need to find a—'

'I know,' said Danny. 'LUP.'

Behind the station was a Big W superstore. At the back was a bin area, filled with plastic wrapping and empty boxes. It would do.

They went through the security drill before settling down and Danny volunteered for first shift on stag. He was feeling anxious. Uneasy. And when it was his turn to rest he found it impossible to sleep. Eventually he did drift off, but his dreams were troubled and violent, dreams of 'contact with the enemy'.

As Danny slept, Elena worked at her computer. For hours she'd had to sit and listen while her dad amused and entertained Dave and Jane with his endless stream of jokes and stories.

Joey was exactly as she remembered him and how her mum had described. Only more so. He was handsome and funny and as charming and cunning as a campaigning politician.

He said he'd come to England on business. Elena knew what that meant: the business of getting his hands on as much of the money her mum had left her as he could.

But not immediately. He was far too clever for that. That night was just the beginning of the operation. He was smooth. As smooth as a baby's arse, thought Elena as she watched him give Dave and Jane the full treatment. Carefully flattering. Gently flirting. It was no surprise when they offered him the use of the visitor's room for a couple of nights.

His 'I couldn't possibly put you to all that trouble' was sincerely spoken because he knew full well they would insist. And they did.

'Well, if you're absolutely certain,' he said with a smile worthy of a television toothpaste advert, 'it would mean I can spend as much time as possible with my darling daughter.'

Elena wanted to throw up. She got away as soon as she could, saying she was tired. It was gone eleven when she went online. At two thirty in the morning she was still online. And getting nowhere.

Maybe what she had told Danny was true. Maybe no site was safe, but hacking into the Intelligence Service was proving harder than she'd ever imagined.

From the outset Elena knew that the Firm would never be accessed through the normal, surface Internet. She had to go to dark corners of the Deep Web to find the information she would need.

She'd been there before, not as a hacker, but to find facts, to explore, to learn. Elena still had a printed-out paragraph she'd read online a couple of years earlier:

> Searching the surface Internet is like dragging a net across the surface of the ocean: much is caught in the net but much, much more remains deep on the ocean floor. There are more than two hundred thousand Deep Web sites, and sixty of the largest ones contain more than forty times the information of the entire surface web.

The words had inspired her when she first read them and had continued to inspire her ever since. Elena had her future mapped out. After university she was going to make a name for herself as a computer scientist, but in the meantime she absorbed Internet information like a sponge sucking in water. And that included finding out how hackers operated, the language they used and the tactics they employed.

She'd visited websites like attrition.org, where hackers receive credits for their successful attacks; securityfocus.com, where details of what's happening in the hackers' dark world and how they have been stopped can be found; and even cybercrime.gov, where the American Justice Department relates its successes in prosecuting hackers.

But now she was trying it for herself. For real. It was dangerous, it was risky, it was illegal, but Danny and Fergus were existing outside the law and Elena was prepared to run any risk for them.

First she had to hide her online identity, spoof her IP address, cover her tracks. Finding and downloading a program that enabled her to mask her IP address was relatively easy, but it took time, valuable time. And this was the easy bit.

The minutes became hours as she hunted in dark corners for a script that would give her root access to the one place she wanted to go. She needed a script already written by an experienced hacker, an expert who would probably laugh at the tentative and fumbling efforts of a script kiddie like Elena.

At three forty-five she heard a noise outside her bedroom window. She looked towards the chink in the drawn curtains and saw that the sky was beginning to lighten. The noise was birdsong.

Elena was suddenly aware of how desperately tired she felt, but there was no way she was giving up. She found scripts of successful exploits and ran them, but nothing was right; she was getting no closer.

Her eyes were red and sore and her brain was telling her to stop. She made herself focus and carry on, but tiredness crawled over her, sewing seeds of doubt and disappointment.

'Why won't someone out there help me?' she whispered as she logged on to another site.

It was the last thing Elena was aware of until the alarm clock on her desk started to ring. She'd set it for seven thirty to make certain she was online for Danny. She reached for the alarm clock and fumbled for the off switch, then looked at her dark computer screen. The machine had long since logged off and gone into standby mode.

When Elena went online to Danny her latest screen name told him exactly how she was feeling:

```
Useless says: (8:07:16 am)
im sorry, I cant do it
```

Danny looked at Fergus and saw him frown. 'It was worth a try.'

Fergus nodded and Danny started to type, not bothering to change his screen name.

```
Stockwell says: (8:08:02 am)
not useless, if u cant no1 can
Useless says: (8:08:31 am)
swot I thought. big head or wot? O yeah, n
my dads here, all I need, it's a nightmare
```

'Danny, we haven't got time for this,' said Fergus. 'You'll be talking about the weather next. If she's got nothing for us, then we're off.'

'But she hasn't seen him for years.'

'Well, then let's hope their reunion goes a bit better than ours has. Now, come on!'

'Two minutes, that's all.'

Danny went back to the keypad.

```
Stockwell  says:  (8:09:05  am)
u  ok  wiv  that
Useless  says:  (8:09:18  am)
just.  look  I  wanna  try  again  l8ter.  2morrow
might  ave  something  4  you
```

'Tell her no,' said Fergus. 'We're visiting friends tomorrow and can't make contact like this. If all goes well, you'll be online the day after.'

```
Stockwell  says:  (8:09:47  am)
cant  do.  visiting  2morrow.  day  after.  got
2  go,  take  care
Useless  says:  (8:10:04  am)
u  2.  bye  then  xx
```

Danny logged off and ten minutes later they were on a local train to the seaside town of Cromer.

'Why stop here?' asked Danny as they walked from the station into crowds of late season holidaymakers. It was hot and clammy, as if a summer storm was slowly building up its forces.

'Because it's too early to get to where we're staying tonight. If we have to hang around it's better to do it in a crowd. We need a whole day for Meacher, time to recce and then make the approach. We do that tomorrow.'

At the clifftop they looked down on the beach, where brave swimmers were splashing about in the grey, choppy North Sea. They moved down to the pier. Huge posters with pictures of 'stars' Danny had never heard of promised a night of fun, glamour and excitement at the 'Seaside Special'. It must have been popular with Cromer's elderly visitors: there was a long queue at the ticket office.

Fergus found an empty wooden bench, gestured to Danny to sit next to him and then took out the map Elena had provided.

'I know this area,' he said. 'Came here when I was a kid. I think we can find somewhere close to Meacher's place for tonight. He lives further along the coast. Very remote.'

Danny stared out to sea. A huge freighter slowly moved across the horizon; closer to the shoreline white-sailed yachts ploughed through the waves.

'What's up with you?' asked his grandfather.

'I'm worried about Elena.'

Fergus refolded the map and replaced it in his day sack. 'Look, she's all right. It's only her old man who's turned up, not the police. And you'd be better off worrying about yourself.'

'You would say that. You've only *ever* thought of yourself. Never gave a toss about anyone else.'

Fergus stood up and beckoned for Danny to follow him to the very end of the pier. They leaned on the railings. 'You're right, I never did care – not enough, at least. Not until I got back to the UK this time.'

Danny turned to his grandfather. 'What, you're saying you cared about me?'

'I wanted to know you were OK. I made enquiries, found out where you lived. I saw you a couple of times, outside Foxcroft.'

'But why? What was the point if you never meant to meet me?'

Fergus shrugged. 'Getting old, maybe. Or maybe I needed to know that not everything I was part of had turned out badly. I dunno, I wanted to, isn't that enough?'

'No,' said Danny angrily, 'it's not enough. It's what you wanted, as usual. What about what I wanted? You never thought of that, did you? And what's the point of telling me now, anyway?'

'What do you mean?'

'Well, suddenly I've got this caring granddad and guess what, he might well be dead tomorrow or the day after.'

Fergus looked out at the freighter on the horizon. It seemed hardly to have moved. 'D'you fancy some fish and chips? Cromer's famous for its fish and chips.'

Danny nodded.

'Good,' said Fergus. 'And after that we need to get some more supplies and go to a garden centre.'

'A garden centre? You taking Meacher some flowers?'

Fergus smiled. 'Something like that.'

25

Elena was having the day from hell.

Joey didn't come straight out with it. He spent the first few hours 'getting to know his beautiful daughter', as he put it.

They went out for that big English breakfast he'd been looking forward to ever since he stepped off the plane from Nigeria. And then his 'get the cash' campaign began. Joey was smiling, joking, saying how wonderful it was they'd found each other again.

And at first Elena was almost taken in. She did enjoy being with her dad. They went sightseeing and he told her stories of the family she'd never met back in Africa. She was fascinated and intrigued, just as he meant her to be.

It wasn't until mid afternoon that the subject of money and her inheritance came up. He was so pleased that her dear mum had managed to leave a few pounds for her and he only wished he had money to spare too.

'It doesn't matter, Dad,' Elena replied. 'It's just great to see you after all this time.'

But Joey wasn't finished. 'But I can help, darling, and I want to – it's my duty as a father. There's an investment I have lined up that will double your money, guaranteed, maybe even treble it. Much better than leaving it in the building society with its miserable couple of per cent interest.'

Elena's heart sank. If only he hadn't said that. If only Joey really had made the long journey back to England to see her and be with her.

She listened in silence as he went on and on about the great wealth *they* would make by investing in his friend Sonny's scheme to export second-hand 'white goods' – fridges, freezers and washing machines – back to Nigeria.

'You see, darling, in Africa we repair old white goods so they can be reused. It's not like the UK, where people throw them out after a few years because they want a new style or colour. It's a winner, babe, I'm absolutely certain of it. And believe me, I wouldn't risk your inheritance if I didn't trust Sonny like a brother.'

Elena nodded and smiled and eventually agreed to go and speak with Sonny. There was no way that Joey or his friend were going to get their hands on a single penny of her savings, but at that moment she was too tired, disappointed and disillusioned to even argue.

'We'll go now then, shall we, darling?' said Joey with a huge grin. 'No time like the present.'

'Yeah, all right.' Elena just wanted the whole thing over and done with.

They set off with Joey convinced he was at last on the way to the fortune he deserved, and with Elena wishing that he would go home and never come back.

She liked Sonny exactly as much as she had expected to – not at all. He was loud and self-important and dripping with chunky gold. And he spent most of their visit telling them how lucky they were to have the opportunity of coming in on his moneymaking scheme.

They wandered around his lock-up, staring at old fridges, freezers and washing machines that looked as though they should have been carted off to the rubbish dump instead of taking up valuable cargo space on a freighter to Africa.

And as far as Sonny was concerned it wasn't just Joey and Elena who were benefiting from his benevolence. 'The people back home in Africa are fortunate I can provide this service for them. Of course I make money, I'm a businessman, but I also consider I'm doing my bit for the third-world countries.'

'Yeah, you're all heart, Sonny,' whispered Elena to herself. After nearly an hour she couldn't take any more. She tugged at Joey's sleeve and spoke quietly to him. 'Dad, I'd like to go now. Tell him we'll think about it.'

'Sure, darling,' answered Joey. 'But you sure you learned enough?'

'Yeah, more than enough.'

Sonny wasn't pleased about them leaving; he'd

obviously been expecting a quick and easy kill. 'Don't be too long making your mind up,' he called as they went. 'There are other investors looking to get in on this.'

The north Norfolk coastline stretches away from the resorts of Cromer and Sheringham in a long semicircle of flat beaches of fine sand or shingle. The wind blows in from the Russian Steppes, driving away many of the bucket-and-spade brigade.

Serious hikers stride along the shingle banks to catch a glimpse of the seals basking in the sunshine off Blakeney Point. And birdwatchers gaze out through powerful binoculars, hoping for a sighting of some rare feathered visitor to British shores.

But most visitors leave as the sunlight starts to fade. That's what Fergus was counting on. Darkness was approaching as he and Danny walked down the narrow road leading to the isolated stretch of beach he had chosen for their overnight stop. At the bottom of the road was a small deserted car park.

Danny was tired. They'd had a long walk since getting off the train at its end-of-the-line halt. 'There's nothing here,' he said irritably.

'That's the idea,' replied Fergus. 'We won't be disturbed and we're close enough to Meacher's place to get there early in the morning.'

But they weren't quite alone. As they reached the top of the sandy bank that met the beach they spotted two vehicles that had been driven through a gap in the bank onto the beach itself. One was an old Transit, its sides painted with multi-coloured flowers. The other was an even more battered-looking VW camper van, with curtained windows and a roof that opened to give standing room inside.

Near the vans, straggle-haired children played in the sand and a ponytailed guy threw bits of driftwood onto a bonfire.

'Hippies,' said Fergus. 'They won't bother us.'

Fergus led Danny further down the beach where three salt-stained, dark wooden sheds stood. 'Fishermen use these to keep their gear in. It'll do for the night.'

Danny looked at the three doors, each one protected by a heavy padlock. 'And what about the locks?'

His grandfather went to the door of the last shed. The lock was a large round combination with a black disc on the front and numbers from one to a hundred. 'Take off one of your trainers.'

Danny was learning not to question his grandfather's orders, however weird they might sound. As he slipped off one of his Nike Airs, Fergus twisted the lock to expose the shiny steel back. 'Now hit the lock with the heel of your trainer.'

Danny slapped down the trainer, hitting his grandfather's hand as much as the lock. 'Go on, keep hitting it.'

The trainer thumped down on the lock a second and then a third time, and as Danny lifted his arm for a fourth attempt, Fergus unhooked the lock and handed it to his grandson. 'The springs inside these things shake about if you hit them with something soft, like a rubber mallet. Or the soles of trainers.'

Inside, the shed was dark and gloomy. It smelled of fish and looked as though it was rarely used. There were curled lengths of rope, fishing nets, buoyancy floats and a rusting anchor on the floor. But there was plenty of room for Fergus and Danny to spread out their sleeping bags. It would be a reasonably comfortable night.

26

Eddie Moyes was enjoying himself. He'd taken a slow and leisurely drive up to north Norfolk and was comfortably settled in for the night at a pub with a reputation for good beds and great food.

He was well pleased with his accommodation. Now it was time for dinner. As he sipped his second pint of real ale, there was only one important decision to make: whether to go for the steak or the seafood platter.

The menu informed him that the seafood was locally caught and famed throughout the county. It was tempting, very tempting, but then there was nothing Eddie liked more than a thick, juicy steak, rare to medium and served with onion rings, chips and just a little salad. He didn't like too much green stuff getting in the way of his steak. Eventually he decided to ask for a smaller version of the seafood platter as a starter. Not too much smaller, of course.

During the long drive up Eddie had thought a lot

about his recent night out in the country, when Watts's cottage had been hit. He reckoned the hit team were most likely MI6: they were the ones with the ongoing interest in Fergus. But what he couldn't figure out was the total silence ever since. Why no official announcement that a dangerous fugitive was on the run? Eddie's reporter's nose smelled cover-up. And if that was true it made an even better story.

Tomorrow he would talk to Meacher, even though Mrs Meacher had given no guarantees that her husband would agree to an interview. But Eddie was confident that his skills at flattery and persuasion would win through. He reckoned that everyone liked to see their name in print, as long as they were talking about someone else.

According to Mrs Meacher, the colonel was due back on tomorrow morning's tide, but Eddie had changed his mind about telephoning before turning up at their home. That would give Meacher time to think about things and maybe refuse to talk. Eddie's new plan was to be waiting on the quayside when the colonel arrived.

The pub was pleasantly crowded and Eddie was seated on a stool at one end of the bar with his back resting against the wall. He preferred to drink at the bar until his food was ready.

A youngish man walked up to the bar with two empty glasses and ordered two halves of lager. Eddie was in the mood for conversation. 'Nice place, eh?'

The man smiled. 'Very nice. Local, are you?'

Eddie laughed. 'Me? No, I'm up from London on business for a couple of days.' He picked up the bedroom key with its large wooden fob that had been resting on the bar. 'I'm staying here, though. Lovely room they've given me. Ensuite bathroom, double bed, view over the garden, the lot.'

'Sounds tempting.' The man paid for his drinks, nodded a goodbye and went over to a table on the other side of the bar where a second man was already seated. 'Room three. It's just a two-lever key. Easy.'

Fincham's team had followed Eddie from the moment he'd left his flat that morning.

The night air was thick as the oncoming storm slowly built. Danny was sitting on the sand in the darkness. He could just make out the shoreline as the heavy swell relentlessly lifted and turned against the shingle.

Fergus was in the shed, checking the kit and the route for the morning trek to Meacher's house.

From further along the beach the sound of voices and laughter drifted up from the hippy encampment. Four figures sat hunched around the bonfire. The kids had obviously been packed off to their beds. The firelight was inviting and Danny watched for a moment and then stood up.

At first he thought all four people huddled around the fire were women, but as they heard his approaching footsteps and turned towards him, he saw that two of the fire-gazers had beards as well as long hair.

'Hey, man, welcome,' said the closest hippy. 'Come and join us.'

Danny mumbled a 'thanks' and sank down on the sand, close by the fire.

'We saw you arrive earlier,' said the one of the woman. 'I'm Columbine and that's Rosemary. And those two layabouts are Rupert and Clive.'

They were all smiling, waiting for him to reveal his own name. 'Oh, oh yeah. I'm Da— I'm Dean.'

'Nice to meet you, Dean.' They all said it together, and it sounded like they all meant it sincerely.

'Is your dad not coming over?' asked Rosemary.

'He's not my dad,' said Danny, 'he's my uncle Frankie. He's a bit tired – probably turned in by now.'

'We're making a stew,' said the smiling Rosemary. A huge pot was suspended on four metal rods over the open fire. 'Will you join us?'

'Yeah, thanks,' answered Danny. 'It smells good.'

'It's vegetarian,' said Columbine.

'Great. I love vegetarian.'

Danny had never eaten a vegetarian meal in his life, but he was hungry and the stew did smell good. A few minutes later he was tucking in as heartily as the others.

He told them he and his uncle were taking a walking trip along the coast and then listened as the hippies explained how they worked during the winter so that they could spend their summers travelling and 'chilling'.

'None of us particularly like working,' said Rupert as he replenished Danny's bowl from the steaming pot. 'We see it as a necessary evil.'

'An evil that earned us enough to go all the way to northern Spain last year, but only as far as East Anglia this summer,' added Clive. He smiled. 'We didn't work so hard.'

They were friendly, gentle people. 'How long have you been camping here?' asked Danny.

'Four days,' replied Columbine. Danny didn't notice the slight change in her voice as she glanced at the others before continuing. 'It's probably time to move on tomorrow though. The summer's almost over.'

They ate in silence for a few moments. Perhaps it was the sound of the waves against the shore, or perhaps it was the way he moved, but they didn't hear Fergus as he approached. But suddenly he was there, on the edge of the light from the fire, his eyes firmly fixed on Danny. No words were necessary. Danny knew exactly what his grandfather was thinking.

'You must be Frankie,' said Columbine. 'Come and have some stew.'

'No, no, you're all right,' replied Fergus quietly. 'I just came to get Dean.'

'Oh, please stay for a while,' urged Rosemary. 'There's plenty left in the pot. Dean's been telling us about your walking trip.'

Fergus appeared to relax a little, sensing that Danny hadn't given away any secrets.

'Well, all right. It's kind of you.' He sat by the fire and took the bowl of stew that Columbine offered him and smiled as Rosemary made the introductions for a second time.

'On holiday from work, are you?' asked Rupert.

Fergus didn't hesitate. 'No, I don't work. Used to be a mechanic but I took early retirement when I got the chance.'

When they'd finished eating, Rupert and Columbine

stood and went to the Transit van. They were back a couple of minutes later. Rupert was carrying an acoustic guitar covered in Greenpeace and Save the Whale stickers and Columbine held a cardboard box. 'We usually have a bit of a sing-song after dinner,' she said as she took a tambourine from the box and gave it to Rosemary.

She delved into the box again, took out what looked like a little tortoise with holes in its shell and offered it to Danny. 'Do you play the ocarina?'

Danny shook his head, relieved to see that the tiny instrument she was holding was actually made of clay. Columbine smiled. 'You just put your fingers over the holes and blow.'

Fergus stood up. 'We ought to be getting back. We're making an early start in the morning.'

The hippies tried to change his mind, but this time Fergus insisted they leave. Back in the gloom of the shed Danny took the bollocking he was expecting. 'What the hell were you playing at? How many times do I have to tell you, we never, ever go off SOPs!'

'I know! I just wanted to be with some normal people for a while.'

'Normal? You think Parsley, Sage, Rosemary and Thyme back there are normal?'

'They're a lot more normal than you.'

'Look, Danny,' said Fergus angrily. 'You talked me into this, and I'm glad, because I can't run away for the rest of my life. But we have to do things my way, and that means sticking to SOPs.' He picked up

Danny's sleeping bag and unravelled it. 'Now get some sleep. I'll take first shift on stag.'

Danny crawled into his sleeping bag and lay in the darkness. The sounds of the sea mingled with the music of the hippies. One of the men was singing a song that droned on and on, and every so often the others joined in loudly, singing something about the times changing.

They're wrong, thought Danny. The times already have changed.

Getting into Eddie Moyes's room took Mick no more than a few seconds. His MOE wallet was about the size of a Filofax. Inside were basic master keys. The old-fashioned two-lever didn't even resist Mick's first selection as he turned the lock.

Inside the room he used his mini Maglite and found what he was looking for in less than a minute. The notebook was inside Eddie's overnight bag.

Mick put the notebook on the bed. He had plenty of time to work. Downstairs, Brian and Jimmy were keeping an eye on Moyes as he worked his way through his steak. Fran was outside in one of the vehicles.

Hidden beneath the sweatshirt tucked into Mick's jeans was a hand-held digital scanner. It was about half the length of a sheet of A4 paper and a little wider. He pulled out the machine, switched on the power and pressed the scan button. A blue light shone through a semicircle of glass at the bottom of the scanner.

Mick picked up the notebook with his free hand and began the quick and simple operation. He placed the scanner at the top of each page and ran it evenly down

191

the paper. Every word on every page was captured and retained. As he worked, Mick felt twinges of pain from his back and his broken teeth. He managed a smile as he thought of the revenge he planned to take on Fergus Watts when he caught up with him.

He scanned the final page and then carefully replaced the notebook exactly where he'd found it. Then he went on the net.

'That's Mick finished. I'm coming out.'

Eddie had finished his steak. He sat back in his chair, licked his lips and then drained the last of his pint. He was too content for the moment to go to the bar for another.

The bar was getting rowdy. A group of leather-jacketed bikers had turned up earlier and had gradually got louder and more boisterous, especially the big one with the beer-soaked ginger beard. Drops of beer were dripping down onto his grubby Hell's Angels T-shirt.

Eddie heard the sound of a glass breaking as the waitress arrived to take his dessert order. He frowned. 'Not the sort you'd expect in a nice place like this.'

'Bunch of yobs,' replied the waitress. 'They act like they own this village. We've barred them once before and I can see it happening again before the night's out.'

'You get them everywhere,' said Eddie with a sigh. 'I'll have the Death by Chocolate.'

27

George Fincham and Marcie Deveraux were waiting in London when the scanned pages of Eddie's notebook came through. Mick had gone back to the car, plugged the scanner into the lead from his Blackberry and sent it by e-mail.

Fincham read the pages quickly, looking for a sign, a clue, anything that would help unravel the mystery of what Eddie Moyes was up to and why he was in Norfolk. And then he saw the name. 'Meacher. Of course, Meacher.'

'Meacher, sir?' asked Deveraux.

'Watts's CO when he was in the Regiment. He would have known that Watts had been recruited as a K.'

'It must have been a kick in the teeth to him and the Regiment when Watts turned traitor.'

Fincham didn't reply immediately and Deveraux watched her boss intently. His face remained impassive when he eventually spoke. 'There are security issues here, Marcie, and I don't want Moyes stirring up things with Meacher. These Regiment men stick together. Who knows what he might say?'

'What could he say, sir?'

The question was straight and direct but Deveraux didn't get a straight and direct answer.

Fincham was looking through the scanned pages of the notebook, reading Eddie's notes of his conversation with Mrs Meacher. 'We'll go up to Norfolk in the morning and speak to Meacher. Remind him of his loyalties. Official Secrets Act, that sort of thing.'

'If you think it necessary, sir.'

'I do.'

'Then shouldn't we go now?'

Fincham was still looking at the notes. 'Meacher is away sailing. Coming in to Blakeney on the morning tide.'

He went to the window and looked out into the darkness and the slow-moving river Thames. 'I've sailed there myself. It's a difficult entry at the best of times, but highly dangerous in the darkness at low water. He won't risk it tonight; he'll be anchored on the bar just off Blakeney Point now.'

'And this is significant, sir? Only I'm not much of a sailor myself.'

Fincham turned from the window and smiled. 'Highly significant, Marcie. It means that we can both go home and get a few hours' sleep. Be ready to leave first thing.'

Deveraux got up from her chair. 'Very well, sir. I'll see you in the morning then.'

Fincham nodded a goodnight and Deveraux left the room. Fincham waited in the silence for a few moments and then picked up his mobile phone and punched in a number. The call was answered after two rings.

'Yes, sir?'

'Fran, good work tonight, well done.'

'Thank you, sir.'

'But it's brought to my attention a serious security risk. There's more for you to do.'

The last diners had left the hotel restaurant overlooking Blakeney Quay. The last drinkers had made their way from the pub. The last lights in the waterfront cottages had been extinguished.

The team was ready, about to 'borrow' one of the RIBs moored to the quayside. It would have been easy just to steal the boat, power up the engine and hurtle off down the creek towards the sea. But the job Fincham wanted carried out had to look like an accident, so taking the boat had to be done covertly.

The plan was simple. The RIB had been identified and selected an hour earlier, when there was still movement on the quayside. Now it was deserted.

Jimmy had done a walk-by to check that nothing had changed since the boat was chosen. Now he was standing in the shadow of a building on one side of the quay. Mick was out of sight on the opposite side. They had the whole area covered. Fran and Brian were sitting in their vehicle waiting for the go-ahead.

Jimmy got on the net.

'Jimmy's static. All clear.'

'Mick's static. All clear.'

It was time for Fran and Brian to move. Fran went on the net.

'Fran and Brian foxtrot.'

They got out of the vehicle. No interior light came on to attract inquisitive eyes. On the back seat of the car were two red plastic fuel cans. There was an outboard on the RIB but no owner in his right mind would have left fuel in it.

Fran locked the car and they walked towards the RIB. There was no need to talk or look around: Jimmy and Mick were covering them.

Brian climbed down into the boat and then turned and took the fuel containers from Fran, who followed Brian into the RIB. He was already sitting on the boat's rubber side, starting to connect the fuel line that led from the massive Yamaha 75 engine to the first fuel container.

The RIB was tied up to the quay in the conventional way with a knotted bowline, but then doubly secured with a motorbike lock and chain. Fran got busy with her MOE wallet. She put her Maglite in her mouth so she could use both hands and quickly found a key that worked.

The RIB was almost ready to go. All Fran needed to do was study and remember the bowline knot. It had to be retied in exactly the same way when the boat was returned.

Brian slowly removed the two paddles that were latched down on each side of the boat as Fran untied the knot. Then she went on the net.

'That's Fran ready to go.'

'Jimmy's foxtrot.'

He picked up the sports bag at his feet and headed towards the RIB.

Mick was also carrying a bag.

'Mick's foxtrot.'

They reached the quayside together and slowly got down into the boat before opening the bags. Inside were four sets of Gore-Tex jackets and trousers taken from their ready bags.

Fran and Brian pushed the boat away from the quayside and began to paddle gently towards the sea while Mick and Jimmy started to get changed.

28

For a few seconds Fergus thought he heard the deep rumbling of distant thunder out at sea. But only for a few seconds. Then he realized what was actually happening. The throaty roar of the leading motorbike, instantly followed by the sounds of other engines, told him it was an early morning attack.

Instinctively he dived for his day sack and the pistol he had kept hidden from Danny since the fight outside Foxcroft.

Danny watched, speechless, as his grandfather pulled back the top slide all the way and then let it go, to crash forward back into position. He pulled back the top slide again, but this time just a few millimetres to 'check chamber'. He needed to see that the shining brass case of a round had been picked up when the top slide sprang back into position and was now pushed into the chamber of the barrel, ready to fire. If he had to pull the trigger the last thing he wanted was to hear the 'dead man's click' as the firing pin went forward but had no round to fire.

He let the slide push back into position and, with his right thumb, pushed the safety catch up to safe. He checked the magazine was firmly in place before crouching at a gap in the wooden planking wall to peer outside, trying to get some idea of the number of attackers they were facing.

Danny said nothing, unable to take his eyes off the black pistol nestling comfortably in his grandfather's right hand.

Outside the shed, the roar of the engines got louder and merged with the sounds of shouting voices.

But then Fergus stood up and turned back to his grandson. He saw Danny staring at the pistol but offered no words of explanation about where it had come from. He simply removed the magazine and pulled back on the top slide. The round from the chamber was ejected and went spinning in the air. Fergus caught it in mid air and placed it back in the magazine. The weapon was now made safe and Fergus put both pistol and magazine back in his day sack. 'Come on, we're leaving.'

'But what is it? What's happening?'

Fergus was rolling up his sleeping bag. 'Local dispute. Gang of bikers don't seem to like the Peace and Love brigade as much as you do. Nothing to do with us.'

Danny crouched at the gap in the wall. Across the beach he could see five motorbikes circling the two vans on the beach, their riders shouting and jeering.

It looked like a scene from an old Western movie where the Indians circle the wagon train.

As Danny watched, one of the hippies – he thought it was Rupert – emerged from the Transit van and tried to talk over the noise of the roaring engines and jeers. It was useless. A biker rode closer and, without stopping, lashed out with a boot and kicked Rupert in the thigh. The peace-loving hippy crumpled onto the sand.

Danny turned back to Fergus. 'They're hurting them. We've got to help.'

Fergus finished packing his day sack and stood up. 'None of our business and we can't get involved. We'll go the other way up the beach.'

Danny stared in disbelief. 'But we can't just leave them.'

'We can and we are! Now, get your gear and let's go. I told you last night, stick to SOPs.'

'You can shove your SOPs,' snarled Danny, and before Fergus could stop him, he opened the shed door and went running across the sand.

The bikes had come to a standstill and their swaggering riders had switched off the engines and dismounted. Their ginger-bearded leader still reeked of last night's beer. 'We told you to clear out, we warned you, but you didn't listen. Now we're gonna have to show you we won't stand for weirdo scum messing up our beaches.'

Clive was standing over the fallen Rupert and the two women were by the VW van, trying to keep the children inside. 'Please let us go,' shouted Columbine. 'You're frightening the children.'

'Better keep them in the van then, darling. And stay in there yourself – this won't be for the squeamish.'

One of Ginger's mates saw Danny hurtling across the sand towards them and shouted a warning. 'Look out, Ginge, reinforcements.'

When Ginger turned, Danny was almost on top of him with no idea of what he was going to do. He just kept running and thudded into the biker's gut, bounced off and ended up on his arse.

Ginger glared down at him with a look that said he was about to be ground into the sand. Then he saw Fergus limping towards them. Ginger laughed. 'Hello,' he shouted. 'It's Dad's Army. Don't panic! Don't panic!'

The rest of the gang thought it was hilarious, but Fergus wasn't smiling. 'Leave them alone, eh, lads? They're not hurting anyone.'

'Piss off, Granddad,' said Ginger menacingly. 'While you've still got one good leg to stand on.'

Fergus sighed and spoke quietly to Danny. 'Don't do or say anything. You've got us into enough trouble.' He walked towards Clive and Rupert, still hoping he could calm down Ginger and his gang. 'Come on, lads, you've had your fun. Just let them go, eh?'

'I told you to piss off, old man,' said Ginger. 'Or do you want some as well?'

Fergus ignored the threat and just kept walking towards Clive and Rupert. 'It's all right, Clive, get him into the van. I'll give you a hand.' The two hippies looked petrified, their eyes going back and forth between Fergus and Ginger.

The gang leader was used to his word being law. He moved towards Fergus. 'Right, that's it. I warned you. Who the fuck do you think you are? Batman?'

They were just five paces from each other. Fergus kept his head down, jaw clenched and body tensed to take any hit. He couldn't count on his injured leg holding up in a fight, and this time there was no element of surprise to help. He had to depend on speed and experience.

He kept walking, staying just to the left of Ginger, and as they met, he quickly grabbed him behind the neck with his left hand and at the same time rammed his right palm under the big man's chin. Ginger's head cracked back as Fergus held onto him and kept walking. When he let go, Ginger couldn't stop himself from toppling back onto the sand.

There was a stunned silence as the other bikers stared in surprise. Then they started to jeer and laugh.

The big biker stood up and shook the sand from his hair and beard. Eyes blazing, he ran at Fergus, who waited, legs bent and spread and feet firmly planted in the sand, ready to take the impact of the giant lumbering towards him.

Ginger lashed out with a kick as he approached, but Fergus just stepped aside, grabbed the leg with both hands and twisted it, sending the big man sprawling for a second time. He tried to kick out at Fergus as he fell but missed and ended up looking like a crab flailing around on its back.

The rest of the gang sat back on their bikes, enjoying the spectacle. 'You're the one wanted to come and sort out the weirdos, Ginger. You can't even sort out an old dosser!'

Ginger picked himself up again, realizing that his status as gang leader was declining fast. 'You're dead, old man! Dead!'

Fergus was bored with the unequal contest now. He smiled at his lumbering opponent. 'Come on then, son, give it your best shot.'

Even Danny smiled at that. Ginger lunged towards Fergus, throwing a wild punch at his face. It was a sloppy attempt, Fergus didn't even have to move to avoid it. He brought his left forearm across his body to deflect the blow and the biker toppled forward under his own steam. He was halted mid fall as a hand gripped his throat like a vice. He crumpled to his knees, struggling and choking and clawing helplessly at the hand clamped around his neck.

Fergus looked towards the rest of the gang to make sure they were still laughing and not coming to join in as he bent down and whispered into Ginger's ear, 'Give it up, son. I don't want to hurt you. What's that going to prove, eh?'

The bikers were getting restless. Their leader had been humiliated and all the motivation for the attack on the hippies had gone. One by one they got onto their machines and rode away. As the bikes disappeared through the gap in the sand bank, Fergus released his grip on Ginger's neck and let him fall to the ground.

He walked back to Danny. 'Did as you were told, for once. Come on, let's get out of here, before we're thanked with rosehip tea and carrot cake.'

Danny looked over at the hippies. They were gathering their things together and quickly packing them into the vans. Ginger was still sprawled on the sand, gasping and gulping in oxygen.

'But why didn't you stop him straight away? Why let him keep attacking you?'

'Sometimes it's better not to meet force with force,' said Fergus as they walked back to the shed. 'The rest of the gang saw old Ginger being made to look stupid so they laughed. That's what I wanted. If I'd hurt the lad they might have joined in, and I couldn't have handled that.'

They went into the shed and began to pack their day sacks. Danny stared at his grandfather. 'Have you ever really been scared?'

Fergus went to the doorway and looked out. Ginger had stumbled back to his motorbike and was riding away, a lot slower than when he had arrived. 'There's nothing wrong with being scared. It's natural and I've always owned up to it. Apart from once.'

'When was that?'

'Later, Danny. We need to get moving.'

They stepped out onto the sand and Fergus replaced the combination lock on the door. As they walked along the sand, the storm that had been threatening for the past couple of days suddenly broke. Thunder rumbled overhead, and out at sea a jagged flash of lightning arced down to the water. Danny felt the first heavy drops of rain on his face.

29

Elena slept before making her second attempt at cracking the Firm's Intranet. She was desperately tired and knew she had to be wide awake and alert when trying again. She used the excuse of a raging headache to escape from her dad and went for an early night.

The headache wasn't invented. Joey had been driving her insane since they left Sonny's, droning on and on about how they needed to get in quickly on the wonderful investment opportunity.

The alarm was set for three thirty in the morning: Elena wanted to allow herself at least four hours online before the rest of Foxcroft started to stir. She put the clock under her pillow so that the girls in the adjoining rooms wouldn't be disturbed when it rang. But Elena was awake even before the alarm sounded.

Back online, she spoofed her IP address again, but

this time she gave herself the screen name of Gola. She just liked the sound of it.

She went quickly to attrition.org, started to hit links and was bounced around for nearly an hour as she searched for someone who had made the Firm their exploit.

A hacker by the name of Red Dawn had posted some information about his exploit into the Firm's internal system at Vauxhall Cross but there was no script to show Elena a way in.

Elena read the information that was posted and was about to go elsewhere when a pop-up window came up on her screen:

YOU REALLY WANNA GO FOR IT? IT'S PRETTY COOL IN THERE. READ WHAT BLACK STAR HAS FOR YOU!

Elena stared. Someone was there. Someone was watching her, tracking her attempts to get to the Firm.

She pressed the link that took her to Black Star's page. There was a list of exploits, ranging from British Nuclear Fuel to Ticket Master – Black Star never paid to see a band!

Elena went to the link giving details of his exploit into the Firm.

He said he had found root access to the internal system by tunnelling over the firewalls. Firewalls were almost like fire doors in the real world, and sometimes they were not securely closed but propped open, leaving them vulnerable to tunnelling.

Another pop-up came onto the screen:

YOU WANNA TRY IT GOLA? I KNOW YOU WANT TO. I GOT THE SCRIPT. Y OR N?

Elena sat back on her chair. Black Star was offering her a way in. She knew there was no way she could talk back to this genuine hacker somewhere out there in the Deep Web; she just had to make a choice. She hit Y.

A download progress bar popped up and the files began to download.

Black Star sent another pop-up page:

TRY THIS COOL SCRIPT. IT'LL FIND THAT OPEN FIRE DOOR FOR YOU AND GET YOU IN WHERE YOU WANNA BE. HAVE FUN IN THERE!

When the script was downloaded, Elena opened up pages of numbers and coding.

YOU WANNA SEND IT? Y OR N?

This time Elena didn't stop to think. She hit Y again.

There was a delay of a few seconds and then the progress bar came up on the screen and the download started.

REMEMBER GOLA, YOU GET CAUGHT IT'S REAL JAIL TIME.

The pop-up disappeared as the bar slowly filled. About halfway it stopped; nothing was happening.

Elena kept her hands off the keyboard, fearing she might mess up if she tried to intervene. She was nervous and the thought struck her that perhaps she'd been discovered and the police were on their way.

But Black Star came back:

GOLA, YOU'RE IN! YOU WANNA EXECUTE THE SOFTWARE?

She knew what that meant. A firewall had been tunnelled and the script was about to be placed into the Firm's system. She hit Y, the pop-up disappeared and the bar began to move again.

Elena glanced at the time bar at the top of her computer. It was already seven fifteen. There were sounds of footsteps from the floor above. Another day was beginning at Foxcroft.

The bar filled and then disappeared.

Black Star came back for the last time:

YOUR PRIVILEGES HAVE BEEN ELEVATED SCRIPT KIDDIE AND YOU HAVE ROOT ACCESS! I LOVE MY JOB, HAVE FUN IN THERE. THAT'S ME OUTTA HERE.

The pop-up disappeared as pages of index bounced onto the screen. Elena was in, free to roam what was supposedly one of the world's most secure sites. The temptation to explore was almost irresistible but Elena did resist and concentrated on the task she'd been given by Danny.

Fincham's e-mail was easy to locate and access, but

at first it looked as though the whole exhausting process would lead to nothing.

Fincham wasn't a big e-mail user. Elena checked his sent mail. There was nothing much of interest – internal memos and replies to invitations to various functions, including an acceptance for a reception at the House of Commons for that very evening. But there was nothing at all about Fergus Watts.

She moved on to his inbox, and again quickly discounted most of the mail. Then she opened an e-mail received the previous night. It was blank, but there was an attachment.

She downloaded the file and the first thing she read, in bold handwriting was, *July '97 – SAS Traitor Watts*. At the bottom of the first page was another name, written in the same hand: *Eddie Moyes*.

Elena scrolled to the next page, quickly realizing that these were the scanned pages of a notebook belonging to the reporter. His handwritten notes of the original Fergus Watts stories. There were pages and pages: details, different events, government statements, highlighted quotes from various sources. And each separate note had an identifying dateline. It was like seeing a notated version of the stories Danny and Elena had read online. She scanned through as quickly as she could, trying not to miss anything that might be important.

The notes jumped from the battle in the jungle to the escape from the Colombian prison, and then, in the turn of the page, came into the present time. The final note, on the last page, bore the previous day's date.

Elena's eyes widened as she saw the name Meacher, his address, phone number – all the details she had given Fergus and Danny. She read of his sailing trip and of his scheduled arrival at home that morning. Moyes had underlined it three times and then written, *'Must be there!!!'*

Moyes was planning to see Meacher. But worse, much worse than that, Fincham had read the notes; he was probably on his way there too. To the very place that Fergus and Danny were heading.

Elena exited the Firm carefully, hoping desperately she hadn't left any telltale signs of her exploit. Then she shut down her computer and hurried from the room.

Joey was sitting in the garden, drinking an early morning cup of tea and smoking one of the disgusting black cheroots he'd brought with him from Nigeria.

'Morning, darling,' he beamed as Elena approached. 'Sleep good?'

'Can you drive, Dad?' asked Elena urgently.

'Drive? Sure I can drive, honey.'

'Have you got a licence?'

Joey gave his daughter a reproachful look. 'Elena, you should know by now, I don't do nothing illegal.'

'I need you to drive me to Norfolk.'

'What!' Joey almost choked on his cheroot.

'It's in East Anglia.'

'I know where it is, darling, I lived here, remember? But why—?'

'My best friend is in trouble and I have to help. The

house is in the middle of nowhere so I can't get there quickly by train. We'll hire a car – I'll pay, but we must—'

'Slow down, slow down,' said Joey, getting up from the bench. 'We have things to do, Elena. Sonny's waiting for a decision and we can't just leave—'

'You can have the money!'

Joey stared. 'What?'

'You can have the money,' said Elena again. 'Some of it. And you can do what you want with it. Spend it, invest it, give it to Sonny, I don't care. But first you've got to take me to Norfolk.'

Joey took a last drag of his cheroot and threw the butt onto the ground. 'I'll go get my driving licence.'

Thunder rolled around the sky as Eddie Moyes sat in the hotel overlooking Blakeney Quay and watched the rain beat against the windows.

Eddie was in a foul mood. He'd woken up with indigestion and a well bad hangover, but had forced himself out of bed and driven to Blakeney to meet the incoming tide, and Colonel Meacher.

But although the tide arrived, Meacher didn't. Eddie waited and watched on the quayside, and when the storm broke he retreated to the hotel and a much needed black coffee. But still not a single boat came up the creek.

Eddie sat and nursed his coffee as another clap of thunder boomed out overhead. He knew what had gone wrong. Meacher must have had a mobile phone on the boat and his wife had called to warn him that a reporter would be waiting when he returned. So he'd gone into one of the other little harbours along the coast. And no doubt Mrs Meacher would have been waiting in the car to drive the colonel home.

So Eddie sipped his coffee and worked out Plan B. He was going to drive over to the colonel's house and doorstep him if necessary. And he wouldn't leave until he had the information he wanted. But not just yet. He needed at least two more black coffees. And maybe a couple of biscuits.

The windscreen wipers on George Fincham's Mercedes were going at double speed. They were already in Norfolk, having made good time along the M11 and then the A11 trunk road through Cambridgeshire and into Norfolk. They reached a place called Brandon, where they were held up for the first time as a train passed over a level crossing.

They had spoken very little since leaving London, Fincham preferring to listen to the rolling news on Radio Five Live. That suited Marcie Deveraux. This was a difficult and delicate job, and the more time she had to think and prepare herself for all possibilities the better.

The car phone rang as they cleared Brandon and the last stretches of Thetford Forest. It was already switched to hands-free and Fran responded instantly to Fincham's curt 'Yes?'

'Last night's job completed with no problems, sir. The body was discovered early this morning and the police are treating it as an accident.'

Deveraux turned to Fincham. 'Body? What body?'

Fincham took his left hand from the steering wheel and gestured for Deveraux to wait. 'And Moyes?'

'Still in Blakeney, sir.'

'Well done, Fran. Wait out, I'll call you back.'

The rain was beginning to ease. Fincham ended the call and switched the windscreen wipers back to normal speed. He kept his eyes firmly fixed on the road as he spoke to Deveraux. 'Meacher was a serious security risk, an old man who knew too much. Had Moyes talked him into revealing details of the deniable operators policy it could have led to severe embarrassment. Questions in the House, newspaper scandal. Best avoided.'

'So we killed him?' Deveraux was struggling to keep her temper in check. 'Just in case he said the wrong thing?'

Fincham still didn't look towards her as he replied. 'Meacher died in a tragic boating accident, Marcie.'

'But you could have consulted me on this, sir. Asked my opinion.'

This time Fincham did turn to Deveraux when he spoke. His eyes were cold and hard. 'I have high hopes for you, Marcie, very high. But I run the section *my* way and *I* make the decisions. Remember that.'

Deveraux didn't respond. There were many things she could have said, and wanted to say, but her on-going mission was more important. So she held her tongue and regained her usual composure before speaking again. 'Sir, as you knew what was happening last night, why are we going through with this trip?'

'We're going to offer Mrs Meacher our condolences and at the same time we can establish exactly what she does or doesn't know.'

He saw Deveraux glance quickly towards him and smiled at her. 'No, Marcie, I'm not anticipating any sort of unfortunate accident as far as Mrs Meacher is concerned. Get back to Fran, will you? Tell her to lift off Moyes for now. I want the team to get a trigger on Meacher's house so that it's secure for our arrival. I don't want any interruptions.'

Deveraux reached for the car phone. 'And what about Moyes, sir?'

'We'll pick him up later. Once he learns of Meacher's demise, he'll concentrate on finding Watts, which is exactly what we want him to do.'

The rain had stopped and the windscreen wipers squeaked over dry glass. Fincham switched them off. 'And then we can bring this operation to a satisfactory conclusion.'

'Yes, sir,' said Deveraux softly. 'Exactly.'

30

According to the map Elena had provided, the derelict brick and flint barn was less than a mile from Meacher's house. Fergus decided it was the perfect place to carry out the final preparations for the OP on the house.

The storm had rolled on inland but water was still tipping through the holes in the remaining roof tiles as Fergus and Danny started to unzip their day sacks.

'We'll make this place the ERV,' said Fergus. 'If we get split up make your way back here and wait for six hours. If I don't show up you get out and go to the press. Remember that – and *don't* go back to Foxcroft.'

'There was a reporter at the Victory Club when I was there,' said Danny. 'Bloke called Eddie Moyes. He wrote stories about you when you were in Colombia.'

'Then find him. But you make sure you get the story to one of the nationals.'

Danny nodded and took the food they'd bought on

their last shopping trip from his bag. 'So what do you want me to do with this stuff?'

'Take the Mars bars from their wrappers and open the cans of luncheon meat and wrap everything in cling film.' He saw Danny's puzzled look. 'We can't just walk up to Meacher's and knock on the door, we need to know exactly who's there. We might be waiting a long time, and I get hungry, even if you don't.'

'Yeah, but why the cling film?'

'Noise. The OP could be close enough to the house to spit at. And that's why we're taking still water in plastic bottles – no cans of fizz to give us away. Until this morning we've been staying away from danger areas; now we're going into one. We've been *re*acting; it's time to act.'

Danny felt a surge of fear as the reality of what his grandfather had said hit home. But Fergus seemed unconcerned; he was checking the items he'd bought from the garden centre and a hardware store. He looked up and saw that Danny was staring at him. 'Something wrong?'

Danny hesitated before he replied. 'You said you'd tell me about the time you didn't own up to being scared.'

Fergus's clipped reply was tinged with irritation. 'Why d'you want to know all this? We need to get on.'

'Because . . . because *I'm* scared.'

Fergus dropped the hammer and bag of nails he was holding into his day sack. He nodded. 'Yeah. Yeah, course you are,' he said a lot more gently. 'Look, leave that stuff for a minute. Come and sit down.'

The steady flow of rainwater streaming down the

ancient walls was beginning to slow, and they sat side by side on a pile of fallen brick and flint. 'I was nineteen, a lance corporal in South Armagh leading a foot patrol. Reckoned I was dead hard with my bayonet and my tin hat. Suddenly I turned a corner and there's a group of guys wearing masks, getting ready to ambush another patrol.'

He shook his head as he remembered the chaos of what had followed. 'All the training, slick weapons drills, everything just went out of the window because I was shitting myself. The terrorists were too. One guy – I saw his eyes go wide under his mask, we were that close – I was firing at him; he was firing at me. Firing and firing, until he went down. I killed him, but it could just as easily have been me dead in the road.'

Danny was staring down at his trainers, unable to look at his grandfather as he finished the grisly story. 'After the contact, none of my mates wanted to talk about fear. That's what young infantry battalions are like, all bravado. They just wanted the war story, maybe because they were frightened of their own fear. I wasn't man enough to say I'd been scared, terrified, I just told them what they wanted to hear.'

Fergus got up and gathered together his sleeping bag and spare clothes. 'What I learned later, as I got older, is that everyone is scared in a contact. It's fear that makes you react when you're being fired at, it's fear that makes you move towards the enemy, and it's fear that makes you do what you do to survive.' He looked at Danny. 'Being scared is good. Anyone who tells you they're never scared is a liar.'

Danny went back to his bag and continued wrapping the food in cling film. But there was something more he needed to ask. 'How many people have you killed?'

'Blimey, you don't want much, do you?' said Fergus. 'Look, that's . . . it's private . . . personal. Something I have to live with, and something I don't talk about, not even to you.'

'But how do you cope with seeing someone killed?' said Danny. 'I'm trying to understand.'

'You just deal with it,' answered Fergus as he gathered together the spare kit and clothes. 'You don't have a choice. You just deal with it.'

He hid the kit and clothes behind the pile of brick and rubble. 'We'll take only what we need, in the day sacks. We can pick up this stuff later, but I'll take the rest of the cash, just in case someone finds what we leave here. Now, let's go.'

They were still both soaked to the skin as they neared the driveway leading to Meacher's house. Danny's jeans were heavy and clung to his legs; his skin felt cold and clammy. Back at the barn he had been about to ask why they hadn't changed into dry kit, but had decided to keep his mouth shut. He knew he would find out soon enough.

The house wasn't visible from the road. The narrow, tree-lined drive bent away from the road, and thick hedgerows protected the property from prying eyes. Fergus and Danny avoided the drive and walked on further down the road.

There were no immediate neighbouring properties,

and after about a hundred metres Fergus said they should push their way through the bushes and make their approach from one side of the house. They stepped over a grass verge and a small ditch and began to ease their way through brambles and thorns. Every step brought a fresh soaking as the foliage showered them with rainwater. Danny smiled to himself. Now he knew why they hadn't changed into dry kit.

Fergus wanted to carry out a three-hundred-and-sixty-degree recce of the target and find the best position for watching the front of the house. But once they broke through the scrubby stand of wild bushes and caught their first glimpse of the house and part of the gardens he realized there was a problem.

The large, double-fronted, red-brick house and its manicured gardens were entirely surrounded by a combination of tall brick wall and metre-and-a-half-high chain-link fence where the wall had crumbled away. The fence had obviously been standing there for years as thick ivy and climbing roses scrambled their way up to the top. There was no way they could get a full view of the front of the house without going into the garden itself.

Fergus whispered to Danny, 'When we approach a target we don't want any confusion over where we are, so we use colours for the different sides of the building. No matter which direction you see a building from, the colour system stays the same. The front is always white and the back is black. The right side, as you look at the front, is red and the left side is green. Understand?'

Danny nodded.

They moved along the fence, approaching the red side of the house. They reached a section where a row of evergreen shrubs on the other side screened the fence from the house.

'We'll go through here,' whispered Fergus, taking a pair of secateurs from his bag. 'Those bushes give us good cover. It's not perfect – the cut in the fence could be discovered while we're in the OP – but we'll have to chance it.'

'Can't we just climb the fence?'

'You could, but with this leg of mine I might never get over. And anyway, we'd make too much noise.'

Fergus pulled out some green fibre material, the sort normally used for putting under gravel paths to keep weeds down. He got Danny to wrap it around the bottom link, so that as he cut through the mild steel with the secateurs, the pinging sound of the steel snapping was hardly audible. When he'd finished cutting he stood up and pulled the fence apart to reveal an upside-down V shape. Rainwater from the storm-soaked plants came cascading down as the chain links gave, and they both got another drenching.

Fergus held up the cut section of fencing and told Danny to crawl through the gap with his kit. Then Danny pulled the cut fencing to his side so that Fergus could follow him through.

They pushed the cut section back into position and left it unsecured for a quick escape if necessary. They were ready to move towards the house but Fergus had one last instruction: 'We do this in bounds.'

'In what?'

'Stages. And we crawl – I can still do that. Stick to my route like glue. OK?'

They crawled on their stomachs back along the line of shrubs, with Danny following exactly as instructed. Fergus stopped behind the cover of a bush every few metres, and then looked and listened for two or three minutes before deciding on where to move to next.

After several bounds they got their first full look at the roof and brickwork of the red elevation of the house. To the right of the building itself was a moss-covered, high wall that looked even older than the one on the perimeter. Built into it was a wooden door that appeared to lead to a rear garden.

Fergus told Danny to stay with the kit and crawled further to his left. Soon he could see the gravel drive and a small Nissan that was parked in front of the house. He guessed he was looking at Mrs Meacher's run-around. Maybe the colonel wasn't at home.

Then Fergus spotted what he needed: a huge, thick bush sprawled over an area of lawn about thirty metres from the front of the house. He crawled over to the back of the bush and tuned in to the area. The field of view was perfect – he could easily see all of white, including the large front door, and there was also a good field of vision on red until the rear garden wall got in the way.

It was the perfect OP point, but before Fergus could beckon Danny over he heard a noise to his right. He froze, unable to see what was happening as the bushes were in the way.

But Danny could see. The door in the wall had creaked open and, as he watched, an old man in a flat cap and wellies walked through. He was pushing a wooden wheelbarrow that looked even older than he did. The wheelbarrow was loaded with plant cuttings, probably destined for a flowerbed somewhere at the front of the house. But not right at that moment. The effort of pushing the barrow through the gate seemed to be as much as the old boy could take. He parked the barrow close to the wall, slowly and carefully straightened up, and with a rub of his aching back, retreated through the gap in the wall and closed the door behind him.

Danny signalled to Fergus that the coast was clear and his grandfather beckoned him over.

'You never go in front of your OP because that's the area the enemy can see,' said Fergus when Danny reached him behind the bush. He motioned for Danny to look at the route they had taken. 'And on a day like this, they'd see all that.'

The marks in the wet grass were clearly visible. 'That's why you always have to think about the route you're taking and keep behind the OP.'

'So how do we see through the bush if we have to stay behind it?'

'We don't need to see through it, we'll be in it.'

Twenty minutes later they were inside the bush with a clear view of the house. Using the secateurs, Fergus cut a small hole about half a metre in diameter at the bottom of the leafy shrub. He placed the small cut branches behind him and then told Danny how to make a bung from the offcuts.

While Danny worked, Fergus tunnelled his way into the centre, carefully cutting away inside the huge, old plant, and pushing the cut branches further into the bush, making the interior denser and gradually forming a cave.

When he'd finished they moved into the bush, taking their kit with them. The bung was ready to be pulled into position. Danny had tied the branches together with the garden string. It looked like a pagan bunch of flowers with a metre-long length of string dangling from the tie. Fergus pulled the bung by the string and it neatly plugged the gap in the bush. Then he took the remaining fibre material and snagged it on the branches so that it lined the inside of the OP.

'Without the material, if the sun hit the bush, anyone outside would be able to see through to us,' he said. 'Our biggest weapon isn't the 9mm pistol, it's concealment.'

'What about the nails? You didn't use them.'

'As a last resort, for climbing, we could have made dumars. But like I said, I'm not up to climbing any more.'

He explained how to make dumars while continually looking through the bush towards the front of the house.

After a while the wooden door in the wall opened again and the old man reappeared, pushing an ancient black bicycle. The flowers were going to have to wait. He carefully mounted the bike and pedalled slowly down the drive.

'One less person for us to worry about,' whispered

Fergus as the old boy passed within a few metres of them. The crunch of the bicycle on the gravel faded but was replaced almost immediately by the sound of an approaching vehicle.

'Maybe it's Meacher,' said Danny.

But he was wrong. A police car passed them and came to a standstill outside the house.

Two uniformed officers got out, a man and a woman. They went to the front door and rang the bell. In less than a minute the door opened and a tall, upright, grey-haired woman appeared.

'Colonel's wife,' whispered Fergus. 'I remember her.'

Mrs Meacher spoke briefly to the officers and then led them into the house. They went into a room on red and were clearly visible to Fergus and Danny through a tall window. After a couple of minutes Mrs Meacher sat down on a high-backed chair. The female officer pulled up another chair and sat next to her. It didn't look like a routine visit.

31

The team were on their way to Meacher's. Fran checked her map and gave her orders over the net as she drove.

'Mick, it looks like a long driveway. I want you to get a trigger on where it meets the road. I want to know who drives in and out.'

'Mick, roger.'

'Roger that. Jimmy and Brian, I want you to get a trigger on the house itself. I want to know who's in there before the boss arrives. Roger so far?'

'Jimmy, roger.'

'Brian, roger.'

All four members of the team were taking different routes towards Meacher's house. Fran was in the area first. She pulled her VW Polo into a lay-by next to a small river and parked near where a couple of families were feeding the ducks.

'That's Fran static about seven hundred metres south of the target. At the bridge over the river. I'll stay complete.'

Fran knew that Jimmy and Brian would have to go foxtrot to do their job. Mick might need to do the same, so someone had to be with their vehicle, ready to react if there was a drama. She opened the glove compartment and took out a sweaty cheese and onion sandwich bought from a garage the previous day for the journey to Norfolk. There had to be an innocent reason for stopping in the lay-by, so she walked towards the ducks, breaking off bits of the sandwich and throwing them onto the riverbank.

Some of the ducks came waddling towards her, squawking and flapping, but after a few half-hearted pecks at the bits of sandwich they turned away and went back to the other food on offer. Maybe they just didn't like onion.

Jimmy parked up about a hundred metres from the driveway, down a muddy track that led into a wooded area. The track was just wide enough for a vehicle and was deeply rutted with tyre marks. Where it petered out, flies buzzed around an overflowing bin surrounded by tied-up plastic bags. This was dog-walking territory.

Jimmy got on the net to organize an RV with Brian, who was parking up nearby.

'Jimmy's foxtrot.'

Fran went back to her car as the families drove away. She sat in the driver's seat with the door open. A few of the ducks waddled around nearby in the hope of picking up something more appetizing than cheese and onion. Fran got on the net.

'Mick, you there yet?'

He was working his way through the undergrowth

opposite the entrance to the driveway. It wasn't ideal – Fran would have preferred two cars ready to react to any situation – but it was the only way he could get a trigger. His Gore-Tex gave him some protection from the wet foliage and leaf litter but it was hard going. Finally he could see the driveway.

'Mick has the trigger on the driveway. I can't see all the way up to the house but I can see in both directions along the road.'

Jimmy and Brian settled on a place to climb over the garden wall on the green side of the house. The wall was over three metres high at that point, but there were trees still in full leaf on the far side that broke the line of the top. They would give them cover as they crossed.

Jimmy got his back against the wall, bent his legs and cupped his hands between his thighs. Brian stepped back a little, jammed his right foot into Jimmy's hands and, using his partner's hands as a stepping stone, launched up at the wall. He grabbed the top and hooked his arms over to anchor himself. As Jimmy pushed Brian's foot upwards, he turned to face the wall.

It took a few seconds before Brian was bent over the wall. He stayed low, using the tree foliage for cover and turned round so that his legs were dangling down on the garden side and his top half was bent down towards Jimmy. Then he held his arms out. Jimmy jumped up and, like acrobats, they grabbed each other's wrists. Jimmy walked up the wall, almost turning upside down before he got one leg over the top so that Brian could let go of his wrists and grab his body to pull him up.

They dropped gently into the garden and then stopped, and listened, and tuned in to their new environment.

'That's Jimmy and Brian garden side. On green side of house.'

'Roger that.'

The two men began crawling forward, staying behind a row of shrubs that mirrored those on the opposite side of the garden. They decided on an OP at the end of the shrubs. It gave them an adequate view of the front of the house, the garden on the opposite side of the drive and the two parked vehicles.

'Jimmy and Brian have the trigger on the house. No sign of life. Two vehicles. Silver Nissan Micra, November Papa Charlie six-four-zero November. The other's a police patrol car.'

Jimmy could clearly see the wet gravel beneath the police car.

'It arrived after the rain; the Nissan hasn't moved all night.'

In Fincham's car Marcie Deveraux was also listening in on the net through her earpiece. She relayed the information to her boss.

Fincham shrugged. 'The local plod giving Mrs Meacher the news of her husband's unfortunate accident. I do hope she's not the hysterical type, I want to get this over quickly.'

Jimmy came on the net.

'Stand by. Stand by. That's the front door opening . . . two police, towards their car. A possible Mrs Meacher at the door. She's gone inside, door closed. That's the police complete . . . engine on . . . wait, now mobile towards the main. Now unsighted.'

Deveraux listened intently while checking the map on her lap. They were just a few miles away. 'The police have just left Meacher's house.'

Fincham nodded. 'Tell Fran that if the team give the all clear we'll go straight there.'

Deveraux had to wait while the police were taken out of the area by the team. Mick picked up the patrol car as it reached the end of the drive.

'That's the police at the main. Wait. Wait. That's gone right towards you, Fran.'

He continued watching until the vehicle disappeared along the road.

'That's now unsighted.'

In their OP, Fergus and Danny watched as Mrs Meacher went back to the side room, picked up the telephone and dialled a number.

'What's going on?' whispered Danny.

'Dunno. But I'd like to know what that call's about.'

Mrs Meacher spoke for about five minutes. Soon after she had put down the receiver, the Mercedes swept up the drive and came to a halt where the police car had been a little earlier. Fincham and Deveraux stepped out of the car and went to the front door.

'Him,' breathed Danny. 'How could he know we're here?'

'He doesn't. Maybe they've come to warn the colonel about us.'

Mrs Meacher came to the door. Fincham, looking solemn and concerned, shook hands and then introduced Deveraux. Mrs Meacher led them into the house and they entered the side room.

On the other side of the garden, Jimmy and Brian kept the rest of the team informed of everything they were seeing.

'That's all three complete the house. Now unsighted.'

Caroline Meacher was old school, army officer's wife, born and bred to accept even the worst of news with the stiff upper lip of the ruling classes. If she was surprised at the swift and sudden arrival of Fincham and Deveraux, she didn't mention it. Her years of close contact with the Regiment had taught her to expect the unexpected.

She offered them tea, which they politely refused, and Fincham spent the next couple of minutes telling her what a great man and servant to his country her husband had been and how he would be missed by everyone who knew him.

Fincham oozed charm and concern but Mrs Meacher didn't appear to be impressed. 'Did you actually know my husband, Mr Fincham?'

Fincham smiled his most sympathetic smile. 'Sadly, only by reputation, Mrs Meacher, and I consider that to be my own personal loss.'

Deveraux cringed inwardly. 'Is there anything we can do for you, Mrs Meacher?'

'Thank you, but no. I've telephoned my son; he and his family live nearby. They were the reason we retired to Norfolk. We wanted to see more of our grandchildren.' She was silent for a moment and her eyes grew moist. 'My son and his wife will be here within the hour.'

Fincham glanced at Deveraux. He wanted the questioning over before the other mourners joined the party.

Fergus had to know what was going on inside the house. He started to push himself backwards towards the rear of the bush. 'I need to find out what they're talking about. Pull the bung back into position when I'm outside.'

'Wait,' said Danny. 'Let me do it. I can get there quicker than you.'

Fergus hesitated, reluctant to let his grandson move into more danger. But he knew what Danny said was true. 'Be quick, but don't rush.'

Danny pushed himself back, carefully kicked out the bung, and crawled out. As he moved away, Fergus pulled the bung back into position and watched as Danny used the tracks already made in the grass to go behind the line of shrubs and get closer to the window.

The damp from the cold, wet grass seeped through to Danny's skin but he ignored it and focused on his route to the window. He reached the end of the row of shrubs and moved into open ground to cross to the window.

Jimmy and Brian spotted him instantly.

'Stand by. Stand by. That's Danny in the garden. Danny in the garden.'

Deveraux's eyes widened as she heard the words in her earpiece. Fincham was cautiously questioning Mrs Meacher, totally unaware of what was happening outside.

By the bridge, Fran had slammed the car door shut and started the engine on the first 'Stand by'. Ducks squawked and scattered and flew into the air as the Polo hurtled away towards the house. Fran pressed her gearstick pressel.

'Roger that. Marcie, what we doing? Leaving, lifting or killing?'

There was no immediate answer. Fran knew that Deveraux couldn't speak on the net with Mrs Meacher in the room.

'Use click system, Marcie. Repeat, leaving, lifting or killing?'

32

Norfolk was losing its appeal for Eddie Moyes, even though he was feeling a little better. He'd enjoyed a couple of coffees and had even managed a prawn sandwich, just to settle the stomach. But he'd had more than enough of Blakeney, of boats and of sea air. Personally, he'd never seen the attraction of a life on the ocean wave; he liked the feel of solid earth beneath his feet.

It was time to get on with the job. Meacher would be at home with his wife by now. Eddie had given him plenty of time to settle in.

He strolled over to his blue and rust Sierra; the old girl had done wonders getting him all the way up to Norfolk. Eddie was looking forward to returning to London. He'd write his story tonight and then tomorrow he would open negotiations with the tabloids.

The door creaked open and Eddie lowered his bulky

body into the driver's seat. Realizing he was puffing and blowing a bit, he decided that he really should start that diet. The Atkins Diet – the one where you eat as much fried food as you like – sounded just the business. Tomorrow would be soon enough, after he'd sold his story.

The car coughed into life at the third attempt and Eddie took his last look at the coast and drove away.

A huge lorry went steaming past the hire car. Elena sighed in frustration; her dad was driving at Sunday afternoon speed. At this rate it would take hours and hours to get to Norfolk.

'Can't we go a bit faster, Dad?'

'Faster? Why, sure, darling,' smiled Joey. 'I was just enjoying the view, and these wonderful British roads. Drivers here are so much more courteous. Back home it's every man for himself.'

Joey put his foot down. A bit. He was having a good time. A nice little trip into the countryside was fine by him. He had his daughter's promise of some of her cash, and although they hadn't yet settled on the amount, Joey was confident he could talk her into being generous. After all, he was helping her out in a big way.

'So this friend – Danny? – boyfriend, is he?'

'He's my friend, Dad, my best friend.'

'Mmm,' said Joey as he nodded his head. 'Must be in big trouble if we're going all this way to help him out.'

'He is, Dad,' said Elena softly. 'Big trouble.'

33

Deveraux had given two clicks for 'lift'. It was her only option. The order was clear: *lift* Danny.

Jimmy and Brian broke cover, ran across a stretch of grass and crunched onto the gravel of the drive-way. Danny had slipped from their view as he reached the red side of the house but they knew exactly where he was.

Fergus turned and saw them the moment he heard the noise. His decision was instant. He had to save Danny.

He kicked back at the bung, grabbed the kit and forced his way out of the bush, making as much noise as he could. Leaping to his feet, he made sure that Jimmy and Brian spotted him. Then he ran, as best he could, down the drive.

The two operators instantly changed direction, chasing full speed after Fergus.

'We got Watts on the drive! Watts on the drive! Towards you, Mick.'

Mick had already moved across the road and got into the bushes just off the track. He held his pistol in both hands as he waited to hear the runner on the gravel. He was looking forward to meeting Watts again.

Danny was just to the side of the window when he heard the shouts and then saw Fergus hobbling down the drive as the two men chased after him. He saw the pistols in their hands. Instinctively Danny stood up and started to run to help his grandfather. But he could almost hear Fergus shouting at him: 'Stick to SOPs! Get to the ERV!'

He looked towards the window. A woman was standing there staring at him, the woman who had gone into the house with Fincham. 'Go,' she mouthed at him silently. 'Run.'

She held his gaze for a few seconds more before turning her back on him. But she didn't move away from the window. It was as though she was deliberately hiding what was going on outside to the others in the room. Danny turned and ran. Hard.

They were gaining on Fergus quickly. He strained every muscle and pain jarred through his leg with each stride. But every extra metre meant a few more seconds for Danny.

And then Mick stepped out of the bushes, pistol aimed at Fergus's head. 'Stand still! Drop the kit, hands up!'

Fran's car screeched to a halt at the end of the drive at the same time as Jimmy and Brian pushed Fergus to the ground. She left the engine running and the door open as she sprinted over to the group. 'Leave him!' she shouted to Jimmy and Brian. 'Find the boy. Go, go!'

They went. Without a word. Tearing back towards the house as Mick started kicking Fergus in his stomach. There was nothing Fergus could do but grit his teeth, tighten his body and take the pain. But it didn't last long.

Fran pulled Mick away. 'There'll be time for that.'

Mick covered with his pistol as Fran dragged Fergus towards the Polo. 'Get in the back and cover him,' she shouted to Mick. 'We'll pick your car up later.'

She banged Fergus's face a couple of times against the roof before shoving him into the back of the car. 'Fucking arsehole!'

Danny reached the fence, dived at the cut and pushed himself through, ripping his jacket free as it snagged.

At the same time Jimmy and Brian got to the OP, checked inside and then started following the tracks in the grass that led away behind the bush.

Danny was running towards the road, pushing through brambles and thorns. His jacket snagged again and he tore it free and then he could see the narrow road just ahead. He burst through the final bush and almost fell as he reached the tarmac.

There was a screech of brakes. Danny glimpsed a flash of blue to his left before the car hit him and he was sent flying back into the bushes. He lay there on his back, his head spinning, flashes bursting in his eyes. He wanted to get up but his legs wouldn't function.

Eddie Moyes flung open the door and pulled himself from the driver's seat. 'Oh, shit, shit, shit! I didn't see you, you just ran out and—' He reached the body sprawled on ground. 'Danny! Oh, my . . .'

Danny's head was beginning to clear. He opened his eyes and saw the panic-stricken face staring down at him. 'Get me in the car. We've got to go, fast – they'll get us.'

Jimmy and Brian were at the fence, having heard the squealing brakes and the shouting. They pushed their way through the gap and started to run.

Danny was on his feet. He shrugged off Eddie's helping hands and dragged open the passenger door. 'Come on! We're dead if they get us!'

Eddie didn't argue. He ran to the driver's side and jumped into the car. His trembling right hand reached for the ignition key: the car had stalled at the moment of impact. He turned the key. The engine didn't start.

'Come on!' yelled Danny.

Jimmy was ahead of Brian. They were both gasping for breath as they heard the vehicle start at the second attempt. But they were close now.

Eddie revved the engine and shoved the car into first.

'The other way,' yelled Danny. 'The way you came.'

Eddie puffed and panted and started a three-point turn. The car stalled again on the third turn and Danny thumped down on the dashboard. 'Stop flapping! Come on!'

As Jimmy and Brian pushed through to the road the car skidded off the way it had come, with dark smoke pouring from the exhaust. Jimmy could see Danny looking back as the car made distance.

'That's Danny in Moyes's car! They're heading away from the river!'

There wasn't a flicker of emotion on Fran's face as she hit the gearstick pressel.

'Fran's checking.'

She was approaching the bridge. She stood on the brake and clutch at the same time and the car skidded to a halt in a cloud of burning rubber. The ducks scattered in terror as Fran put the car into reverse, left hand across the passenger seat as she craned round. Right hand on the wheel, she released the clutch, and the tyres smoked again as the Polo screamed backwards. She slammed both feet on the brake and clutch again, this time yanking the wheel all the way to the right. The front of the car span round to the left as the rear wheels stayed where they were. As the car turned completely she jammed the gearstick into first and hit the accelerator.

A couple of minutes later she was racing past the driveway to Meacher's house, passing Jimmy and Brian as they ran back for their vehicles. In the back of the Polo, Mick was controlling Fergus with his 9mm stuck into his mouth. Blood from Fergus's nose was dripping onto the top slide. Mick smiled at his prisoner. 'Looks like we'll have the boy soon as well, eh?'

Fincham and Deveraux had said their farewells to Mrs Meacher and were getting into the Mercedes. Fincham started the engine and heard its gentle and reassuring purr. 'You dragged it out somewhat, Marcie. It was obvious early on that she knew nothing.'

'I did realize that, sir,' replied Deveraux. 'But there was a spot of excitement out here in the garden. I thought it best that Mrs Meacher remained unaware.'

Fincham was about to slip the car into gear but he turned and looked at Deveraux. 'Excitement?'

'We have Watts, sir,' said Deveraux calmly. 'Shall I tell Fran to take him to the nearest safe house?'

Fincham stared. And then he smiled.

34

The sweeping, tree-lined driveway, the elegant lawns and garden, the brand-new Range Rover parked close to the beautiful double-fronted red-brick house were all very impressive. Joey sat back in the driver's seat of the hire car and nodded. If this was the sort of place where Elena's friends were to be found then his daughter had obviously inherited many of his own ambitious characteristics.

It was a perfect picture of peaceful English country life. Joey guessed that probably the most exciting thing that ever happened in this garden was a gentle game of croquet followed by high tea in the shade of one of those huge shrubs that sprawled across the lawn.

Elena was standing at the front door, having told her dad to wait in the car. Joey didn't mind; he reckoned that once the house owners learned they had driven all the way from London to find his daughter's friend, they'd be invited in for 'refreshments'. And then maybe asked to stay the night. The English were famous for their manners and hospitality.

The front door opened and a youngish man appeared and began talking to Elena. Joey saw him look over in his direction so he smiled broadly, raised his right hand and gave a friendly wave. The man ignored him and went back to talking to Elena. Joey wasn't disappointed. He knew the man was just following the rules of proper, polite etiquette and was waiting until they were formally introduced.

Joey was partly right. The man was being polite but there was no chance of an introduction. 'I'm afraid I have no idea what you're talking about,' he said to Elena. 'The only visitors here today have been . . . have been official visitors. And the police.'

Elena felt her heart thud in her chest. 'The . . . the police?'

The man took a deep breath and Elena could see that he was struggling to hold back tears. 'My father died last night, a boating accident. So if you'll excuse me, I must get back to my mother. I hope you find your friend, but I'm afraid we can't help you.'

'I . . . I'm sorry.' It was all Elena could say.

The man nodded and closed the door. Elena turned away and walked slowly back to the car. Meacher was dead. A boating accident. It had to be too much of a coincidence. They'd killed him. They must have. Before Fergus and Danny could get to him. But what had happened to Danny and Fergus? Where were they? Elena could only hope they had seen the police at the house and got away quickly.

'What's going on, darling?' asked her dad as she fastened her seat belt. 'We not staying for tea?'

'No, Dad,' said Elena softly. 'Danny's not here, and he won't be coming now.'

'Not even a cup of tea? What happened to English hospitality?'

Joey started the car. 'So what now?'

'We find somewhere to stay for the night. I might be able to contact him online in the morning.'

Joey sighed. At the end of the driveway he turned right onto the narrow road. The car crossed a small bridge across the river and a few minutes later they passed a derelict brick and flint barn set well back from the road.

'Where are you, Danny?' whispered Elena.

Danny was in the barn, his back pressed against the wall as he glanced out through a broken window and watched the car as it passed. That was all that mattered to Danny. The vehicle kept going. It didn't stop. No one jumped out to check the barn.

They'd been at the ERV for over three hours and Danny was determined to stay there, as instructed, for three more. He knew there was little chance of his grandfather having escaped, but he was going to stick to SOPs. His body was battered and bruised; he hurt everywhere, but he ignored the pain. He knew it would go.

Somehow, and it was purely down to luck and had nothing to do with Eddie's driving skills, they had shaken off their pursuers. At the first T junction Danny had shouted, 'Left!' Minutes later, Fran skidded to a halt at the junction, instantly weighed up the fifty-fifty choice and chose to turn right. It was a crucial error and gave Eddie and Danny the time they needed to twist and turn their way through the countryside and eventually reach the ERV.

They hid the car out of sight of the road and then staggered, exhausted, into the barn.

Eddie was a total wreck. Shaking and sweating and pacing around and blurting out that they had to go to the police for protection.

Danny told him that if he wanted to stay alive he'd better sit down and shut up.

'Don't tell me what to do!' yelled Eddie. 'You nearly got me killed back there! I'm just a reporter, this is nothing to do with me.'

'That's what I said at first,' said Danny calmly. 'But you're in it now, Eddie, and believe me, there's no way we can go to the police. My granddad made a plan, we have to stick to it. We wait for him here for six hours. If he doesn't turn up, then I tell you everything.'

'Six hours,' groaned Eddie, glancing around the derelict building, 'but—'

'You don't have a choice,' said Danny. 'I promise you, if you leave here now, you're dead.'

The safe-house compound was like a concrete island, enclosed on all sides by a tight-mesh steel fence, seven metres high. It was surrounded by an open area of ferns and drainage ditches; about eight hundred metres further out in every direction, the dark mass of Thetford Forest blotted out the skyline.

The compound was in the MoD training area, but no squaddies ever went inside and it wasn't marked on any map. It was reached via a mud track leading from the main road into the training area. The track forked to the left and then went through the forest before breaking out into the open area, where the first of many signs gave the stark warning: DANGER KEEP OUT. MOD PROPERTY. DANGEROUS BUILDING.

Eight hundred metres away, along a cracked concrete roadway, were the imposing double gates to the compound. They were as tall as the fence itself. More signs, on the gates and on every side of the towering fence, warned off unwelcome visitors. These ones read: DANGER. UNSTABLE BUILDING − KEEP OUT.

The compound was entirely surfaced with concrete. Straggling weeds grew from the cracks. A drainage ditch ran along the right-hand side of the compound, outside the fence. It cut across the open ground and went back towards the forest.

The safe house sat at the centre of the concrete island. Every window of the two-storey building was covered by the same tight-mesh steel. There was only one door into the building, in the centre, at the front. Behind the main building, and to the right, was a large Nissen hut where the vehicles were hidden.

The steel door opened and Marcie Deveraux emerged, just as a pair of American fighter jets passed overhead as they made their landing approach to the base at Lakenheath.

Deveraux pulled the door shut and stood for a moment breathing deeply. Then she walked behind the Nissen hut and made sure she was out of sight of any of the windows. She took out her mobile phone, checked again that she wasn't being watched, and then punched in a number. It was answered almost instantly.

Deveraux spoke softly. 'Fincham doesn't like the sight of blood so Fran and Mick have had the first crack at Watts. He's not talking yet, sir. It's a pity he was taken this early on in the operation.'

Another pair of jets passed overhead and Deveraux waited until the noise of their engines had died away. 'No, I haven't seen him myself, but Fincham's going to speak to him before he goes back to London for the MPs' reception at the House. He's as determined as we are to find out who else outside the Firm knows that Watts was operating as a K. But if Watts doesn't talk I'm not sure how long I'll be able to keep him alive, sir, not without compromising my own situation.'

She checked out the windows and door as she listened to the voice at the other end of the line. Then she nodded. 'Yes, sir, that was my thought too. At this stage it's worth trying.'

Deveraux ended the call and then took a piece of paper from her jacket pocket. A mobile phone number was written on it.

The six hours were almost up. Danny was outside the barn and Eddie was reading through his notebook when his mobile rang. There was no number displayed on the screen, and without thinking he answered the call.

'Mr Moyes, don't speak, just listen and write this down. Do you have a pen?'

'What? Who is this?'

'I said don't speak. Are you ready?'

Eddie fumbled for the pencil in his coat pocket. 'Yeah, I'm ready, but—'

'Fergus Watts is being held near Thetford. Landranger Map, sheet one-four-four. Grid reference eight-two-five-eight-two-five. I'll repeat that once more, Mr Moyes, write it down.'

Eddie scribbled down the map reference as the words and numbers were repeated.

'Read that back to me, Mr Moyes.'

'Landranger Map, sheet one-four-four. Grid reference eight-two-five-eight-two-five.'

'That's correct. It's unlikely that Watts will be alive tomorrow morning, Mr Moyes. You do understand that this isn't a police matter, don't you?'

'Yes, I understand,' said Eddie as Danny walked into the barn.

'Eddie, no. Hang up! Hang up!'

But the caller had hung up even before Eddie moved the phone from his ear.

'It was a woman. She told me where they're holding your granddad. She said he'd probably be dead by the morning. Now, I want some answers, Danny. Why do they want to kill him, and what the hell is going on?'

Danny looked at his watch. The six hours were up. 'Sit down, Eddie. I'll tell you why.'

He told him everything, exactly as Fergus had ordered. About his grandfather's true role in Colombia and Fincham's treachery, and all that had happened since his first meeting with Fincham at the army RCB board. Eddie listened, incredulously at first, but slowly realizing that it all made too much sense to be a lie. All the missing pieces fell into place.

'It's got it all,' he murmured, already seeing the headlines and world exclusive by-line blazed across the *Sun*. Or the *Mirror* – it didn't matter. 'Drugs, death, cover-ups, corruption in high places. I won't just get a job with this, I'll win awards.'

'Yeah, but not yet, Eddie. First, we're gonna get my granddad out.'

'What? Are you mad? That call was a set-up. They can't find us and they're using your granddad as bait. If we go there, they'll kill the lot of us.'

'No,' said Danny urgently. 'The call must have been from the woman who saw me at Meacher's. She told me to get away. She helped me then, and I think she's trying to help us now.'

'You think! You *think*! You're asking me to risk my life again because you *think* someone is trying to help us? I may look stupid, Danny, but I'm not fucking crazy. Let's get in the car and go back to London before they pick us up.'

'If they'd wanted to pick us up they could have done it hours ago.'

'Yeah, how?'

Danny pointed at the mobile that was still in Eddie's hand. 'I should have thought of that before. They can be located to within a few metres – I did it myself to trace my granddad. Look, Eddie, you'll have a much better story if you help me rescue Fergus.'

'You're a brave kid, Danny,' said Eddie, shaking his head. 'But I'm no hero. I'm a coward, son, always have been.'

Danny sighed. 'Will you at least drive me to Thetford, so I can get close?'

Eddie delved into his coat pocket for his car keys. 'Yeah, I'll drive you to Thetford. It's on my way.'

'And can I use your mobile? I need to phone a friend.'

35

From the outside the safe house looked derelict, but inside, the building was clean but basic. The concrete floors, walls and ceilings were all painted white. Stairs leading from the entrance door led up to two interrogation rooms situated behind closed steel doors on either side of the stairwell.

The interrogation rooms were bare, apart from a couple of chairs, a desk and a wooden pallet. In one corner was an exposed toilet.

The building was not designated purely as a safe house for interrogation; it could also double up as an FOB. The hard-standing outside, with sufficient space to land a helicopter, meant it could be used to house Special Forces in the event of a terrorist incident in the area.

The entire compound was protected by a sophisticated security system. Along the mud access track, UGSs were buried at hundred-metre intervals. Their warning sensors could be set for vehicles or for people. Those in the track were set for vehicles; the lighter setting could easily lead to them being tripped by forest wildlife.

More UGSs were buried at fifty-metre intervals in the ditch running alongside the compound. These were set for humans: no deer would walk the length of the ditch, only someone using it as cover to get close to the house.

The UGS wiring was also buried and ran back to a monitoring system in the ground-floor, left-hand room of the house. The room was equipped with little else – just a sink, a kettle, portable electric heaters, an electric student hob and camp beds. The room opposite had further camp beds, rolled up, and a shower and toilet.

Fran's team were in this room. Jimmy was preparing an instant meal of Pot Noodles, sliced bread and cheap, thin ham, to be followed by muesli bars.

Fincham and Deveraux were in the room opposite.

Jimmy poured boiling water onto the Pot Noodles just as the door opened and Fincham and Deveraux appeared.

'Grub's up, sir,' said Jimmy to Fincham. 'Sure we can't tempt you to one of these? We usually throw in a dollop of brown sauce and some Branston pickle to spice them up a bit.'

Fincham made little attempt to disguise his look of distaste. 'Thank you, but no. I'll eat later in London.'

'Won't be anything like this though, sir.'

Fran and Mick were sitting on camp beds. They

shared a smile. Everyone knew exactly how uncomfortable their boss was in these surroundings and Fran
couldn't resist joining in the wind-up. 'There's extra
camp beds in the other room, sir. You could always
doss down with us if you'd rather stay.'

The suggestion was ignored. 'I'll see Watts now.
Brian, bring some of that . . . food. We won't starve
our guest to death.'

Brian grabbed one of the Pot Noodles and followed
Fincham up the stairs, winking at Deveraux as he
passed.

Fergus was in the room to the left of the stairs. Mick
and Fran had enjoyed themselves interrogating him
and he wasn't a pretty sight. His face was a swollen,
bloodied mess. Blood that hadn't dried into his stub-
ble had dripped over his shirt and onto the floor. His
lips were split and fresh blood ran from his nose into
his mouth. He was blindfolded with photographic
blackout material and he wore no shoes. Both wrists
were plasticuffed to the pallet and his hands were
swollen where the cuffs had cut into the skin.

Fergus heard footsteps on the stairs and the key
turning in the lock before the door opened. He felt his
legs being dragged sideways and back towards his body
and his feet were plasticuffed to the pallet. Only then
did Brian free his hands and rip the blackout material
away from his eyes. Fergus flinched and then squeezed
his eyes tightly together; the glare of the fluorescent
light was dazzling.

The door closed and Fergus heard footsteps going
back down the stairs. Slowly he opened his eyes. As

they gradually adjusted to the light, a figure sitting on a chair a metre away came into focus.

Fergus and Fincham were face to face for the first time in years.

'It's been a long time,' said Fincham quietly.

Speech came painfully for Fergus. 'Not long enough.'

Fincham indicated the steaming Pot Noodle on the floor next to Fergus. 'My colleagues assure me that it is edible.'

Fergus knew the tactics. Fincham in control, relaxed, sitting back in the chair, watching silently while he dug pathetically at the food with his fingers. All meant to increase his sense of despair and humiliation. But he didn't care. He was hungry, despite the beating he'd taken, and he knew he had to eat and keep his strength up to have any chance of survival.

Fighting back the pain as the hot spices burned into the cuts on his lips, Fergus swallowed the food as quickly as he could, just in case Fincham chose to kick it away and get on with the interrogation. Fincham watched in silence as Fergus tipped the container up to his mouth to make sure every last scrap went down his neck.

At last Fincham leaned forward in his chair. 'I'm going to ask you this just once. Who else knew you were operating as a K?'

'Even if I knew I wouldn't tell you,' said Fergus through a mouthful of noodles. He forced a smile. 'Maybe there *are* others. You'll have to sweat it out, Fincham, like I have for all these years.'

The room smelled stale and fetid. Fincham got up and walked to the window. The metal frame would open only a few centimetres before hitting the steel mesh fitted on the outside. But Fincham needed what fresh air he could get. The smell of blood offended him just as much as the sight of it. He stared through the mesh towards the forest. 'You're going to die, Watts, you realize that, don't you?'

When Fergus didn't reply Fincham continued without looking back. 'Of course I should have had you killed in Colombia, but after you'd ruined my little operation I quite enjoyed the thought of you rotting away in squalor. And I didn't anticipate the jailbreak. That was remiss of me.'

'You won't have the balls to kill me yourself, Fincham,' said Fergus, spitting blood and noodles from his mouth. 'But before your trained monkeys do it, I'll make sure they know what you really did in Colombia.'

Fincham took a deep breath of fresh air, turned away from the window and went back to the chair. 'The last desperate ramblings of a man who knows he's about die and will say anything to save his life. You'll be wasting your final breaths, Watts. But I am going to give you a chance.'

He saw Fergus squint at him through bruised and half-closed eyes. 'Oh no, Watts, not to live, your death is inevitable now. No, I'm going to give you the chance to *not* have to watch your grandson die.'

Fergus felt the hairs on the back of his neck stand on end. 'You really are an evil, sadistic bastard, Fincham. But you won't find Danny, he's long gone.'

'Oh yes, I'll find him,' said Fincham calmly. 'Tomorrow, or the next day. And he will have to be eliminated. But you won't have to watch, Watts, not if you tell me what I need to know.'

He stood up. 'Think about it. There was Meacher, and he's no longer a problem. Who else was there?'

When there was no response, Fincham glanced at his watch. 'I'm expected at the House for a reception. Goodnight, Watts. I'm sure my friends will look after you.'

He left without looking back. A few minutes later the Mercedes purred into life and Fincham drove away from the compound.

Fergus heard the clang of the gates as they were closed. He glanced towards the window, desperately hoping his grandson had followed his orders.

36

'So where exactly are you?'

'Place called Sheringham; it's not far from where you are.'

Elena and Joey had booked into a B&B and were walking around the seaside town when Danny called Elena's mobile.

When she answered and heard Danny's, 'It's me,' Elena couldn't stop herself from screaming, '*Danny!*'

Half of Sheringham turned to stare and Elena realized she needed to be just a bit more discreet.

Before making the call, Danny told Eddie he wanted to find out if his friend had managed to hack into Fincham's e-mail. He figured any information at all might be helpful as he prepared for the rescue attempt. What he didn't tell Eddie was that, despite his brave words, he was totally petrified at the thought of what lay ahead and he desperately needed to hear Elena's voice before he set out.

Elena listened as patiently as she could while Danny told her what had happened at Meacher's house and in the hours since.

'You know Meacher's dead, don't you?' said Elena, unable to stop herself from interrupting. 'They killed him before Eddie Moyes or your granddad could speak to him.'

Danny turned to Eddie to relay the news. 'Meacher's dead. That must be why the police were at the house.'

He went back to the phone and Elena explained what she'd discovered online and how she'd made her dad drive to Norfolk in the hope of warning Fergus and Danny off.

'But I was too late. I stayed here because I hoped I'd get you online in the morning.'

'Elena, I'm gonna try and get my granddad out.'

'I knew you'd say that. I'm coming with you.'

'No, you can't.'

'Don't argue with me, Danny. You can't do it alone, and if that reporter bloke won't help, you'll need someone.'

Danny glanced towards Eddie, who tapped his watch, indicating that he was anxious to get on the road.

'But . . . but what about your dad?'

Joey was sitting on a bench, looking perfectly content as he sat in the late afternoon sunshine and smoked one of his cheroots. Elena moved a little further away and spoke quietly into the phone. 'I've been to the building society and got him five hundred quid. That's just for a start – I had to order the rest to collect tomorrow. I'll tell him I'm staying the night with you and . . . and your dad. He won't care; it'll give him a chance to start spending his money.'

Danny hesitated. 'Are . . . are you sure. It'll be—'

'Dangerous. Yeah, I guessed that. Where do we meet?'

'I'll ask Eddie. But can you go to the shops for me first?'

'Shops?'

'There are a few things we might need.'

They rendezvoused just outside Sheringham. Joey was happy enough to let his daughter go off for the night, especially after listening to Elena's elaborate lie about how Danny and his 'dad' had got back together after a long separation – 'just like we have'.

'You see, that's what I was worried about. Danny had come all this way to Norfolk and there was a message at Foxcroft saying his dad couldn't see him. But everything's fine, now they've met up.'

'Mmm, I understand, darling,' said Joey, lighting another cheroot. 'But that other place we visited, what was that all about?'

Elena thought quickly. 'That was . . . that was where I thought Danny's dad was living. He's a . . . he's a vicar, just started at a new parish. But I got the wrong village.'

'A man of the cloth, eh? Well, that's fine then, darling. I couldn't leave you in safer hands. So, we meet back in London tomorrow and—'

'And go to the building society, yes, Dad. I'll be there.'

While Elena bought the things Danny had ordered,

Joey sat in the car and thought about the different ways he could enjoy making inroads into the five hundred pounds burning a hole in his pocket.

They met Danny and Eddie in a lay-by soon after. Joey pulled the hire car to a standstill and walked back with Elena to where the old Sierra was parked.

'Evening, reverend,' said Joey, extending a hand to Eddie as he got out of the car.

'This is my dad, Joey,' said Elena, spotting Eddie's bemused look. 'I told him all about your new parish, Reverend Watts.'

'My new—?'

'Travelling incognito, are you, vicar?' smiled Joey.

'Incog—?'

'No dog-collar,' said Joey. 'Well, I'm all in favour of the modern ways.' He glanced over at Danny, who was looking equally confused, and then turned back to Eddie. 'Glad to see you and the boy have made things right, reverend, just like me and my darling Elena. And I can see the family resemblance. He's the image of you.'

'Well, we'd better get off, then,' said Elena hurriedly. She went to Joey and kissed him and then nodded to Danny to get into the car.

'Right, bye then,' said Eddie, as he climbed back into the driver's seat. 'And, er . . . God bless you.'

'Praise the Lord,' called Joey as the Sierra stuttered into life.

Elena waved through the back window as the car pulled away from the lay-by and then turned and smiled at Danny.

'Don't ask,' she said.

37

They were on their way. At last. Eddie counted the miles taking them closer to the target and worried about the suicidal rescue attempt, while Danny and Elena sat in the back, packing Elena's purchases into a day sack.

They were animated, excited. Elena's arrival seemed to have given Danny fresh confidence and assurance. Eddie drove in silence, partly cursing himself for his own cowardice and partly thinking that he should just head straight for London without stopping. But he knew it would be pointless. Danny was so set on trying to rescue his grandfather, he would probably fling open the door and leap from the car.

Danny had given Elena a long shopping list which included two hand-sized blocks of wood, a hammer and some five-inch nails.

He took one of the blocks and started hammering a nail into it as Elena watched, and Eddie looked in his rear-view mirror to see what was going on.

'I didn't ask why when you said you wanted this stuff,' said Elena over the sound of hammering, 'but, er . . . why?'

'Shit!' said Danny, as he missed the nail and hit his thumb with the hammer. 'I'm making climbing dumars. My granddad told me how to do it.'

'Climbing? Danny, you may not have noticed, but this is Norfolk. There's no mountains.'

Danny ignored her and hammered a nail into the second block of wood. When both nails were all the way into the blocks, with their heads flat against one side, he took out his Leatherman knife and pulled out the pliers attachment. He bent over the ends of the two nails to form hooks, leaving a straight section of nail between hook and wood block.

Next he took two orange nylon straps, the sort normally used for securing things to roof racks, from his day sack. He wrapped one end of each strap around the straight part of each nail. Then he formed one-metre loops and wound the other end of the straps around the nails and secured them with the buckles. The dumars were finished.

'I think that's right,' said Danny, as he packed them carefully into the day sack.

'If they don't work you could always hit someone with them,' said Elena. 'They look lethal.'

Just outside Thetford they pulled into a filling station. Danny told Eddie to park off the forecourt because of the security cameras and then went into the garage shop in search of Landranger Map 144.

'Can't you get him to give up on this stupid idea?' said Eddie to Elena as they waited in the car.

Elena laughed. 'When Danny wants to do something, he does it. Doesn't matter what anyone else says. Don't worry about us, vicar, we'll be all right.'

The reporter turned in his seat, glaring angrily at Elena. 'You think this is all a laugh, don't you, like a game! It's not. You could get killed! Killed! Can't you get that into your head!'

Elena looked away and stared out through a side window. 'I know it's no game,' she said quietly.

They sat in silence until Danny returned to the car. 'Last one they had,' he said as he opened up the map and found the six-figure reference Eddie had written in his notebook.

'There's nothing there,' said Elena, looking up from the map. 'It's just forest.' She pointed at two words printed in the target area. 'See that?'

The two words read: DANGER AREA.

'It's an army training area,' said Danny. 'They put that to warn the public off.'

Eddie started up the car. 'Yeah? Well, it's working on me.'

'You're sure you wrote down exactly what the woman said?'

'I'm a reporter, that's what I do.' Eddie made one last attempt at warning them off the rescue attempt. 'Look, it's dark, it's late, and you've got no idea what you're up against. Come back to London with me. I can probably get this on the television news tonight and in the papers tomorrow. They won't do anything to Fergus then.'

'We're wasting time, Eddie,' said Danny, refolding the map. 'Just get us as close as you can to the map reference.'

Eddie crunched the gears as he shoved the Sierra into first gear and pulled away.

They parked in a firebreak in the forest, just past the track leading into the army training area. Danny used his Maglite to read the map. 'This is it; we walk from here.' He grabbed the day sack and reached for the door handle. 'Thanks, Eddie. Write the whole story, and get the facts right.'

'Wait,' said Eddie. He hadn't spoken since they'd driven away from the filling station, but he had been thinking. 'Look, I'll come with you, just to see what's there. Then if you still want to go through with this crazy plan, you're on your own. OK?'

Danny simply nodded. They got out of the car, crossed the road and walked back to the MoD track. It was the closest manmade feature to the map reference so it made sense to think it might lead towards wherever Fergus was being held.

'We'll make the ERV five metres into the forest and twenty metres up the road from here,' said Danny, pointing in the direction he meant.

'The what?' asked Elena.

'Emergency rendezvous. If anything goes wrong, go to the—'

'Danny, I've told you,' said Eddie interrupting. 'I'm coming to find out what's there, that's all. If it all goes wrong you won't see my arse for dust, so there's no point in telling me about ERVs or ETAs or even ETs. I'm a coward, remember?'

There were fresh tyre marks in the mud where the track met the road. But as they moved into the darkness along the left-hand side of the track, the ground got harder and they lost sight of the tyre marks and almost everything else.

The black night engulfed them. Danny and Elena walked on either side of Eddie, clutching at the reporter as he stumbled with almost every step. 'Use your torch, Danny, I can't see a thing.'

'Stand still for a while and wait for your night vision to kick in. You stay with him, Elena.'

Before Eddie or Elena had the chance to stop him, Danny moved on. He stopped after twenty metres, then crouched down and listened. His own night vision was working now; he could make out individual trees on the other side of the track. As he tuned in to the area and heard the light breeze shifting the treetops, Eddie and Elena came hurrying up.

'I'm not here just to look after him,' complained Elena without looking at Eddie. 'Don't go wandering off like that.'

Beads of sweat were standing out on Eddie's forehead. He already looked ready to give up and turn back. But Danny wanted to hang onto the reporter now, realizing that if they did manage to rescue Fergus, Eddie was the one with a vehicle.

'I need your help, Eddie,' he said. 'Count your paces and tell me when you reach twelve hundred.'

'Twelve hundred? That'll take—'

'You too, Elena,' said Danny. 'So we're certain it's right.'

'But why?'

'We need to know how far we're travelling. One hundred and twenty paces is about a hundred metres, so twelve hundred is around a kilometre.'

'How do you know that?'

'Army RCB,' said Danny as he moved on. 'At least I got something useful from it.'

Eddie followed. 'One, two, three . . .'

The first twelve hundred paces took an hour. They moved in bounds, just as Fergus had taught Danny. The second kilometre took even longer. When Eddie breathlessly blurted out, 'Twelve hundred,' Danny saw that he looked totally exhausted.

'You're doing great, Eddie, we're nearly—'

He stopped mid sentence as he spotted vehicle lights on the track behind them. They were closing. Quickly. 'Vehicle. Off the track, quick!'

He pushed them both into the forest. Branches scratched at their faces and snagged on their clothes as the vehicle's headlights bounced off the trees and came closer. Danny fell into the leaf litter, pulling Eddie and Elena down with him.

The vehicle passed their hiding place and the trees around them turned an eerie red as the driver hit the brakes and turned left onto a smaller track. Danny lifted his head and watched the small car bounce away and then disappear.

'He's showing us the way. Must be going somewhere, Eddie. Less than a kilometre, I reckon.'

'A kilometre!'

'Oh, stop moaning!' said Elena as she stood up and brushed the leaf litter from her clothes. 'Just walk!'

38

Jimmy was at the wheel of the car. He'd been to an all-night Tesco to get more supplies. He hit the gear-stick pressel.

'That's Jimmy approaching the house.'

Brian was on stag, monitoring the surveillance devices protecting the compound.

'Roger that, Jimmy, I have you now.'

One of the screens in front of him showed a line drawing of the mud track leading to the house. Jimmy had driven over the first set of UGSs and set off the alarm. A second white light blinked on and off, followed by the third, as Jimmy got closer to the compound.

He stopped the car just after the third set of UGSs and switched off his lights. Then he drove slowly into the clear area and along the concrete track. He took his time, waiting for Brian to come out and unlock the gates.

Fran and Mick were also in the surveillance room.

They'd moved on to sandwiches now that the supply of Pot Noodles was exhausted. They weren't particularly hungry, just bored. Eating helped pass the time on a long, routine job like this.

Marcie Deveraux was alone in the room opposite. She knew she had to stay awake, but rest was important. She turned off the light, lay down on the camp bed and clasped her hands together behind her head. As she stared up into the darkness, Deveraux heard the door to the surveillance room open and then footsteps going up the stairs.

Fran had taken over on stag. Her first job was to check on Fergus. At the top of the stairs she unlocked the door, pushed it open and then smiled mockingly at the prisoner sprawled on the floor with his feet plasticuffed to the wooden pallet. 'Comfy?'

Fergus stared back defiantly as Fran walked into the room, casually removed her Glock 9mm from its holster and pointed it at the spot directly between his eyes. 'I'm looking forward to finishing you. It's always a pleasure to get rid of another drug trafficker.'

She touched her still bruised nose with the Glock's barrel and then checked that Fergus was securely cuffed to the pallet before going back to the door. 'We'll pick up the boy soon enough. Shame about him, but he'd probably turn out like you, anyway. It's in the blood, I reckon.' She grinned. 'You sure you've got nothing you want to tell the governor?'

Fergus made eye contact with her. 'Fincham set me up. He's the one who should be sitting here. He's the real—'

'Yeah, I was waiting for that one,' interrupted Fran. 'Now, you got anything sensible you want to say, or what?'

Fergus knew he was wasting his time. He looked away.

'Suit yourself, it's your funeral, although you won't exactly get a funeral.' She stepped out of the room, closed the door and re-locked it, leaving the key in the lock so that there was no chance of it getting lost.

Downstairs, Fran went outside and checked the padlock on the gate before walking a circuit of the fence line, looking for cuts. It was routine SOP at the start of a two-hour stag and she was soon back in the surveillance room, staring at the UGSs on the monitors.

The kettle was coming to the boil and Mick was spooning instant coffee into mugs lined up on the worktop. 'You want one, Fran?'

'Yeah,' she answered, turning away from the monitors. 'Oh, by the way, our friend upstairs reckons he's an innocent man and the governor's the one who should be in the frame.'

'Yeah, course he should,' said Mick as he poured the steaming water into the mugs. 'And you're the Queen of Hearts.'

Danny heard noises in the bushes ahead just as they completed another bound. He stopped, his eyes narrowing, trying to penetrate the darkness. Eddie was breathing too hard to hear a thing. He blundered into Danny. 'Sorry,' he said, far too loudly.

The noise from the bushes increased, as if someone

was running away, and this time Eddie heard. 'What's that?'

'Ssshh,' breathed Elena, grabbing Eddie's arm.

'Just a deer,' said Danny. 'We scared it.'

Eddie wiped a hand across his sweating brow. 'Not half as much as it scared me.'

Danny knelt down on the track, tuning in again to the area, and his knee rested directly on top of a circular UGS buried just a few centimetres under the mud and leaf litter. Fortunately for Danny, it was calibrated to take the weight of a vehicle, and inside the house Fran took a sip of her brew and stared at the blank monitor.

Danny stood up and led the others on until they reached the edge of the open, treeless area. And then, through the tall ferns, they saw the start of the concrete road.

Elena whispered to Danny, 'You were right.'

'But there's not meant to be anything here but forest,' breathed Eddie, peering into the gloom.

Danny turned to him. 'You staying or going?'

'Staying. Just for a bit longer.'

They crept onto the concrete road, keeping to the left-hand edge. Soon they could see the dark shape of the building ahead and the tall fence and gates. 'There,' whispered Danny. 'That's where they've got Fergus. We need to do a CTR.'

'Baffling me with letters again,' moaned Eddie.

They took a clockwise route around the fence line, approaching the white side of the building first. The solid steel fence was made up of rectangles, too small even for a foot or handhold.

269

A dull light shone from the left-hand bottom window of the building and more light leaked from the window directly above. They moved on to green: there were no windows here. On black they saw light from the right-hand-side bottom window, and again, light from the room above. Passing the Nissen hut, they moved on to red and spotted the drainage ditch on their side of the fence.

'Now what?' asked Eddie, sitting down on the mud. 'I can't see how you'll get in there.'

Danny checked his watch. Finding the compound and doing the careful CTR had taken hours.

Elena knew exactly what he was thinking. 'Probably only four hours or so till it gets light. We can't afford to be stuck out here then.'

'Better get on with it,' said Danny as he started off towards black. Elena followed and Eddie dragged himself to his feet and trailed after them.

Behind the shelter of the Nissen hut, Danny took the climbing dumars from his day sack and glanced at the fence. 'Not a mountain, but high enough.'

Eddie looked up at the towering steel barrier. 'You'll never make it.'

'I'll make it.'

'We'll both make it,' said Elena firmly.

'Oh, no,' said Danny, untangling the nylon straps. 'You haven't used these before.'

'Oh, and you have, have you?'

It was getting a bit too loud and heated. 'Sssshhh,' hissed Eddie. 'Will one of you just get over the bloody fence!'

'I thought you weren't staying,' snapped Elena.

'I'm not. I'll see you into the compound, that's all.'

'Look, I'm no use to you out here,' said Elena to Danny. 'Get over and throw the straps back. If you can do it, I can.'

There was no point in Danny arguing, and anyway, he knew Elena was right. There was little point in her staying outside the compound like a spectator. She'd come to help, not to watch.

He made sure his day sack was tight against his back, went to the fence and hooked one of the blocks into the steel at about shoulder height. The nylon loop hung down from the block. Danny placed the second block a little higher on the fence, keeping the blocks about shoulder-width apart.

Gripping the blocks with his hands, he placed his right foot in the lowest loop and, using both arm and leg muscles, pulled himself upwards, letting the loop take all his weight. He felt it creak and stretch and the sturdy fence buckled slightly and made a rattling sound. It wasn't loud, but in the still, quiet night, it sounded as though Danny was hitting a cymbal.

But the loop held. Danny put his left foot into the other loop, transferred his weight to the left side and pulled himself up. He was moving upwards, but now came the difficult part. He had to take the right block out of the fence and move it higher so that he could continue climbing. His first attempt was hopeless. As the nail came free, Danny swung to the left and ended up suspended in mid air with his back to the fence.

Elena rushed over, grabbed Danny's legs and turned him so that he was facing the fence again. He pushed the hooked nail in higher up the fence, transferred his weight, and took another upwards step.

'Get it right, will you?' breathed Elena.

She watched in silence as Danny climbed steadily and carefully up the fence. But the minutes were passing swiftly and each move was difficult. As he neared the top, his leg and arm muscles were yelling in protest as they worked overtime to get him to the other side. His clothes caught on the sharp steel stretched along the top of the fence. Carefully, he freed the material, and swung himself over. The descent of the fence was almost as hard as the upward climb but eventually Danny made it to the ground and freed the nails from the fence.

He stepped backwards and threw the two dumars over, one after the other. Within seconds Elena had hooked them onto the fence and was starting to climb. She looked through the fencing towards Danny. 'Easy,' she whispered.

It was almost time for Mick to take over on stag. He was dozing on his camp bed when Fran gently shook him by the shoulder. He opened his eyes.

'Stag in five,' said Fran quietly. 'Kettle's on.'

Mick nodded and yawned. 'I'll check on Watts while I'm waiting.' He stood up, stretched and headed for the stairs. When he returned, Fran had made the brew. Mick pulled on his jacket for the routine check outside. 'I'll be back for that in a minute,' he said, going towards the door.

Danny and Eddie saw the light spill from the exterior door as it opened, and then watched a dark figure walk across the compound towards the main gate. Elena was inside the compound, about halfway down the fence. She couldn't see the gate but knew she was in trouble when she heard the rattling noise as Mick checked the padlock.

Elena had no choice. She shook her feet free of the loops and let go of the blocks, there was no time to worry about leaving the dumars on the fence. She hit the concrete hard but didn't feel a thing; fear was pumping adrenaline around her body. Danny pulled her up and they ran into the Nissen hut as Eddie disappeared into the ferns.

Mick started his circuit, checking the bottom of the fence by torchlight. Danny and Elena were huddled close together behind one of the cars. They couldn't see Mick approach the point in the fence where the loops dangled down against the steel. But Mick was looking forward to his coffee; he didn't look up at the top of the fence. He passed the dumars and continued on towards the Nissen hut.

The footsteps came closer. Danny and Elena kept perfectly still, both unconsciously holding their breath. Mick stopped. He was no more than three metres away from them. The torchlight flicked over the corrugated iron of the hut and then bounced from one car to another, settling momentarily and then flicking on.

The footsteps started again and the torchlight moved along the base of the fence and eventually faded. Danny and Elena heard the door to the house open and close and the compound was silent again.

'Check the car doors,' whispered Danny as he stood up. 'We might need one of them.' Elena moved swiftly from one car to another. They were all locked.

'Let's move,' said Danny.

Keeping low, they crossed the back of the compound and crouched under the right-hand ground-floor window. Danny slowly lifted his head and through the mesh, saw a man with his back to him at the far end of the room.

Two more men were asleep on camp beds and a woman was getting into a sleeping bag on another bed. It made sense. Four cars, four people.

But the woman crawling into the sleeping bag was white; the woman Danny had seen at Meacher's was black. He'd been hoping to find an ally in the enemy camp but it looked as though Eddie was right: they were on their own.

Danny looked up at the light coming from the window above him. 'He's got to be up there,' he whispered to Elena. 'And there's only one way up.'

The exterior drainage pipe from the toilet in the room looked secure. Danny pulled on it to check, wiped his hands on the wall to dry them, and began to climb. After the dumars it was easy. Within seconds he was at the window. He gripped the metal sill sticking out from the steel mesh and jammed his feet between the pipe and the wall. Slowly raising his head above the sill, he peered into the room.

Fergus heard the movement at the window. He sat up, thinking for a moment that it must be a bird. But the soft tapping against the mesh was slow and constant. It was no bird. He looked, and then he stared as he made out the flat of a hand gently banging against the steel.

Danny watched as his grandfather carefully dragged the pallet across the floor, making as little noise as possible. Fergus reached the window and got to his knees. He pulled at the metal frame and it opened a few centimetres before being halted by the mesh. But it was enough for him to see Danny smiling in at him.

Fergus looked stunned, and then furious. 'You . . . you bloody fool!' he hissed. 'Get out! Go. Now. Go!'

39

Danny was going nowhere – at least not as long as he could hang onto the drainage pipe. He reached down, pulled out his Leatherman and carefully slid it between one of the rectangles in the mesh. 'You're only as sharp as your knife,' he breathed.

Despite his fury, Fergus grabbed at the knife and pulled it through.

'Four guards,' whispered Danny. 'All in the room under this one. And four cars. Can you hot-wire?'

Fergus nodded.

'Elena and Eddie are with me.'

'Elena and . . . ? Danny, what the hell do you think—?'

'I couldn't do it on my own,' hissed Danny. 'I'm not perfect like you.' He was finding it hard to hold onto the pipe; his legs were shaking under the strain. 'Wait out until I give the signal, then try to get out of there and down to the cars.'

'What's the signal?'

'I don't know yet, and it may be quite a while. But you'll know when you hear it.'

He couldn't hold on any longer and began slithering down the pipe.

'Danny, just get away and—'

But he was gone. Fergus closed the window and carefully moved the pallet back to its original position. He hid the knife in his jeans and fixed his eyes on the door and the lock. He could see the tip of the key, held in the key well.

Five minutes earlier he'd been thinking about dying, preparing himself as well as he could. He'd been in many near-death situations. This time there had seemed no hope and too much time to think about it. Now there was hope. Faint, slight hope. But there were no experienced, highly trained SAS veterans out there fighting for him. Fergus's life was in the hands of his seventeen-year-old grandson.

Danny waited until his legs stopped trembling and then moved with Elena back to the fence, where the dumars were hanging. Eddie came bustling through the ferns towards them. 'What did you see? Is he there?'

'Upstairs,' nodded Danny. 'And four guards downstairs. But no sign of Fincham or the woman who was at Meacher's.'

'Four?' breathed Eddie. 'Look, get out now while you still can. At least you know your granddad's alive. We'll get back to London and—'

'I'm not going anywhere without Fergus,' hissed Danny. 'We have to create a diversion to give him the chance to get out.'

'We?'

'Oh, don't worry, Eddie, we'll do it,' snarled Elena. 'You clear off back to London and don't give us a thought. You just think about yourself. We'll probably get killed, like you say, but you'll be all right. You and your precious story. And that's all that matters, isn't it, not someone's life?'

The words came flooding out but eventually Elena fell silent.

Eddie stared at her. 'You finished?'

She nodded.

'Look,' said Eddie, 'it's no good you appealing to my better nature because I haven't got one.'

'Yeah, I'd noticed.'

'And anyway what could *I* do?'

'You could use your car.'

'To do *what*?'

Eddie and Danny were both staring at Elena now.

'Drive it down the track towards the compound. Sound the horn, flash the lights, play the radio, do anything to get the four of them out of the house. Once the gates are open, you turn the car round and get away as quick as you can. We'll do the rest.'

Eddie turned to Danny. 'Was this your idea?'

'No, it was not, it was mine,' snapped Elena. 'He's not the only one with a brain.'

'Will you do it?' said Danny. 'It's probably our only chance.'

'But it'll take hours for me to get back to the car.'

'We've got at least two hours till daylight, three maybe.'

'But . . . What if . . . ? But . . .' He was weakening.

'Do it, Eddie,' said Elena softly. 'Please?'

The big reporter shook his head and sighed. 'The minute I see them get to those gates, I'm off. Away. Out of it. Michael Schumacher won't have nothing on me.'

He pulled up the collar on his coat, turned away and began walking. After a few steps he stopped and looked back. 'Crazy,' he murmured. 'Crazy.' And he pulled his coat tightly around his bulky body and hurried off into the night.

There was nothing more Danny and Elena could do but wait. And hope. They crept over to the shelter of the Nissen hut and sat down on the concrete. The night was at its coldest and they huddled closely together.

'Bit hard on him, wasn't I?' said Elena.

'Yep.'

'D'you think he'll come back?'

'Dunno.'

'But what if he doesn't? What do we—?'

'I don't know, Elena. Let's wait and see.'

They were silent for a few moments. The cold was beginning to bite.

'You tired?'

'Knackered.'

'Yeah.'

They lapsed into total silence, both of them thinking of Eddie blundering his way through the forest, both of them hoping he wouldn't give up. They battled the cold and tiredness, speaking only occasionally, sometimes dozing lightly and then suddenly waking with a start.

After two hours the door to the house opened and another of the men came out. They were both instantly wide awake, listening to every footstep as he checked the gates and made his inspection of the fence. He walked straight past the dumars without looking up, quickly completed his circuit and went back into the house.

Danny looked at his watch and then up at the sky. The first slight hint of daylight was beginning to crease the darkness above the treetops.

'He's not coming back, is he?' said Elena.

Danny shook his head. 'Looks like it's down to us.'

They stood up and moved cautiously over to the back of the house.

40

Eddie was on the way, gunning his car through the forest as quickly as the rusty chassis would take. He was scared, terrified, but he was on his way. And he was eating, chewing on the last of the emergency Mars bars he kept in the glove compartment.

The trek back through the forest had been a nightmare, but he'd kept going, knowing he only had to follow the track to be sure of the direction. He'd stumbled, tripped, fallen, cursed, snagged his clothes on branches and been petrified by the hooting of an owl. But he hadn't rested. Not once.

The car bounced and clattered on the mud track and Eddie switched the headlights onto full beam. He wanted everyone in the house to see the car when he arrived. If they didn't, he'd sound the horn, and as soon as they came running from the building, he'd turn the Sierra round and clear out. With any luck, and Eddie reckoned he was due some luck, he'd be back on the main road and away before they got near him.

Brian was on stag. He switched on the kettle for a brew. The rest of the team were asleep and the monitors were blank. Nothing was moving outside. The kettle came to the boil at the same time as the first set of UGSs started to blink on the screen. Brian did nothing but watch and wait. It could have been a malfunction. Then the second set of UGSs further along the track started to blink.

'Stand to! Stand to! We got a vehicle!'

The team jumped from their maggots and grabbed their weapons. Fran was first out of the main door as they bomb burst from the building.

Danny and Elena heard the shouts and then footsteps coming their way. Danny grabbed Elena's hand and dragged her along the back of the building and they turned into the dead ground of green. It wasn't meant to happen like this. They should have heard Eddie's car approaching.

Vehicles started up in the Nissen hut and the gates rattled as they were pulled open.

Fergus also heard the 'stand to', and the engines starting. It had to be the signal. He cut the plasticuffs and crawled to the door, his legs stinging with pins and needles as blood began to circulate freely. He pulled the nail-file from the Leatherman, knowing that if a key is in a lock it can be turned from either side.

Marcie Deveraux sat on her camp bed. And waited.

Safe house SOPs had kicked in. Fran and Mick were already in their vehicles, speeding out of the compound,

MP5s on their laps and pistols on their belts. Jimmy had his MP5 and was running out of the gate and heading towards the ditch to check if anyone was hiding there, and Brian was at the gate, his eyes scanning the open ground around the compound.

As Eddie drove out of the forest and onto the concrete track, he saw two cars heading straight for him. His eyes widened in horror. 'Oh, shit!'

There was no chance of turning the car. He stood on the brakes and clutch and the Sierra screeched and skidded to a standstill. Eddie jumped from the car and dived into the ferns.

Danny peered round the corner of the building and saw that all four of the team were outside. 'We're going in,' he said to Elena.

Elena nodded and they ran along white and into the house. They went straight into the room where Danny had seen the team. 'Look for keys!' yelled Danny. 'We need a car.'

They heard footsteps coming down the stairs and Fergus came into the room. He saw them frantically rifling through bags and jacket pockets.

'Keys!' yelled Danny. 'We're looking for car keys.'

'No time!' shouted Fergus. 'Go! Go!'

As they started to turn, they glimpsed the movement in the doorway. 'Hands up! Get 'em up! Now!'

Brian had his pistol aimed at Danny's head. 'Do as I say, Watts, or I'll kill him first and then—'

'All right!' shouted Fergus, beginning to raise his hands.

'Nice and slow,' said Brian. 'Don't move or do—'

He got no further. There was a double tap from the hallway. Brian lurched forward as though he had been punched in the back of the head, and then dropped like liquid.

Danny and Elena had no chance to take in the horror of what had happened as Marcie Deveraux moved into the doorway, her Glock pointing at Fergus. 'Me! Look at me!' she screamed at them, knowing that if they looked down at Brian's body and saw the blood pumping from the shattered skull they were likely to panic and run.

They stared at Deveraux, eyes bulging. Deveraux fixed her eyes on Fergus. 'It isn't time for you to die yet, Watts. Go. While there's a chance.'

Her eyes flicked down to Brian. 'He drove the Toyota. Keys must be on him. Take them.'

Fergus reached down, grabbed the keys from Brian's jeans and bundled Danny and Elena towards the door.

'Wait!' said Deveraux, dropping her pistol and turning to Fergus. 'You know what you have to do,' she said. 'Make it look good.'

She closed her eyes and Fergus pulled back his arm and punched her hard on the side of the chin. Deveraux went down, spitting out blood.

Fergus grabbed the weapon from the floor. 'Move,' he yelled to Danny and Elena.

Outside, in the ferns on the other side of the ditch, Jimmy had heard the double tap from the building. He was sprinting back towards the compound when he saw three figures in the gloom of the Nissen hut.

Fergus pressed the fob and the lights on the blue Toyota began to flash. They jumped into the car, Danny and Elena in the back seat, and the engine roared. 'Down! Keep down!' shouted Fergus. He put his foot down and as the vehicle leaped from the hut it took out the wing mirror of the green Renault parked alongside.

Jimmy was nearly at the gates as the Toyota thundered out of the compound. He brought his MP5 up into the aim and got his sights just ahead of Fergus's head, hoping that the moving vehicle would bring him into the line of fire.

They heard the dull *ping, ping, ping* as the rounds hit the vehicle. Fergus stayed as low as he could, and kept driving. A side window shattered and glass sprayed over Danny and Elena.

Up ahead, the track was blocked by three cars, doors open.

'Hold on,' shouted Fergus. He steered the car onto the mud at the right of the track. The Toyota bounced about, flattening the ferns as Fergus fought with the wheel to bring it back onto the track.

They were almost into the forest when Danny lifted his head and looked back through the rear window. Fran and Mick had found Eddie; they were dragging him through the ferns towards the cars. 'Stop! Stop!' yelled Danny.

Fergus instinctively stood on the brakes, but before he too had time to look back, Danny had grabbed the pistol, leaped from the car and was running towards the three vehicles.

'No, Danny! No!' screamed Elena while Fergus slammed the car into reverse and sent it hurtling backwards.

Fran spotted Danny as he ran past the Sierra. She instantly released her grip on the terrified reporter and sprinted for Danny as the Toyota skidded to a standstill by the three vehicles and Fergus leaped out. 'Stay there and stay down!' he yelled at Elena.

Eddie saw his chance. He kicked and punched himself away from Mick and started to run. He got no more than three steps. Mick clinically raised his pistol and double tapped the reporter in the head.

Eddie was dead before he hit the concrete.

Danny stopped running. Shock and horror, numbing and overwhelming, swept through his entire body. He couldn't move; everything became unreal and distant. His ears buzzed – he didn't hear the shouts or the noise as his brain struggled to make sense of what was happening. The pistol hung limply from his right hand as he stared at the lifeless body sprawled on the ground.

Fran was less than twenty metres away. As she raised her own pistol there was a burst of automatic fire from behind Danny. The thunderous noise exploded in his brain, dragging him back to reality. He glimpsed Fran diving into the ferns for cover and turned to see Fergus firing a second short burst from behind the Sierra. In his hands was the MP5 he had grabbed from the passenger seat of Fran's car.

The thump of the automatic fire echoed away through the trees and Danny heard a more urgent, screaming noise. He looked back along the track towards the compound. The green Renault was coming straight at him.

Fear, absolute terror, made Danny turn and run, harder than he had ever run before.

Fergus fired short, three-round bursts into the car's windscreen. The brakes screeched and smoke burned from the tyres. Jimmy was at the wheel. He took a round as Fergus fired again. The car lurched and swerved and ploughed into the back of another of the vehicles. But it was moving too fast to be stopped. The front end lifted and the car bucked and span and flipped over onto its roof. Fuel spewed from the ruptured fuel tank.

As the car burst into flames, Danny tore past his grandfather and flung himself into the back of the Toyota. Fergus fired into the tyres of the other cars and then, as he stood to follow Danny back to the Toyota, sent a final burst into the ferns to keep Fran and Mick's heads down.

He reached the car and jumped into the driver's seat. The tyres smoked as he put his foot down and they tore into the forest. 'Never go off SOPs!' he yelled furiously, as he battled to keep the speeding vehicle on the mud track. 'How many times have I told you! How many times!'

Danny still had the pistol gripped in his right hand, although he hardly knew it was there.

'Put it down!' shouted Fergus. 'Put the weapon down!'

Without speaking, without even acknowledging that

he'd heard his grandfather's order, Danny slowly released his hold on the pistol and let it drop to the floor.

The car reached the end of the mud track and they emerged from the dark and gloom of the forest into early sunlight. It was morning.

Fergus turned the vehicle onto the main road, heading south, and then looked into the rear-view mirror at Danny. 'The man down,' he said. 'He was the reporter, right?'

Danny hadn't uttered a single word since flinging himself into the car. He looked at the mirror and saw his grandfather's eyes boring into him. 'Eddie,' he whispered eventually. 'Eddie Moyes.'

Fergus nodded. 'You deal with it, Danny. Like I told you. Remember? You deal with it.'

Danny didn't reply, but gazed out through the shattered side window and fought back the tears that were beginning to sting his eyes.

They drove on in silence; Fergus planning, Danny and Elena desperately tired but unable to force from their minds the nightmarish visions of the forest.

Fergus skirted around the town of Thetford and crossed from Norfolk into Suffolk. 'Anyone else know you were in Norfolk, Elena?' he said at last.

'Just my dad,' she answered. 'I'm meant to be meeting him back in London today.'

'You will. Go back as if nothing happened. Fincham doesn't know about you, the survivors back in the forest didn't see you, and as for the other woman . . .' His voice trailed off.

'What about her? Why did she let us go?'

'I don't know. But it means she won't be talking to Fincham about you. Danny and me have to go away – we might need your help again.'

Traffic was beginning to build, most of it travelling in the opposite direction – trucks, cars, some of them towing caravans. The normal, everyday world was closing around them.

Elena looked at Danny, and reached out and took one of his hands in hers. 'Of course,' she said. 'Anything.'

EPILOGUE

Six months later

The spring morning was not just warm, it was hot. Shirtsleeves weather.

The flags hung limply over the burger bar in the still, humid air. Business was brisk, with regulars as well as early season holidaymakers on their way to the south coast.

Burgers and bacon sizzled on the hotplate. Dean was cooking and Frankie was pouring tea.

Two of their regulars, young Londoners called Paul and Benny, were tucking into bacon sandwiches. They were builders, recently arrived in the area with a get-rich-quick plan to buy derelict houses, do them up and sell them on for a big profit. But so far they seemed to be spending most of their time at Frankie's.

'I'm glad we found you, Frankie,' said Paul, stirring sugar into a steaming mug of tea. 'This is the only place round here where you can get a decent cuppa.'

Benny nodded. 'Yeah, and Dean's cooking is almost as good as my mum's.'

Frankie smiled. '*No hay ningún lugar como el hogar.*'

Benny swallowed a mouthful of tea. 'What's that mean, then?'

'There's no place like home,' said Dean, turning over a burger on the griddle.

'True. Very true,' said Benny. His friend nodded and they bit into their sandwiches and turned to watch the traffic go by.

Elena had been true to her word. She'd helped, mainly with cash. After Joey had taken his share, much of her remaining money went into funding the escape and the setting up of the new business.

And business was booming. Elena was already getting her cash back, paid through various banks directly into her building society account.

Frankie glanced over at Dean as he refilled the brown sauce bottle on the countertop. He'd seen that distant look many times over the past six months. 'You'll see her again one day,' he said.

'So you keep telling me,' answered Dean. 'But when?'

Frankie turned away; they'd had this discussion before. 'When it's safe.'

The two builders came back to the counter as they finished their sandwiches. 'Two more of these, Dean. You are one great cook.'

Dean smiled and tossed more bacon onto the griddle. As it sizzled and spat he whispered to himself, '*No hay ningún lugar como el hogar.*'

*

It was a warm day in London. George Fincham was, as always, in his office early, drinking coffee from his favourite bone-china cup and gazing out of the window, downriver.

There was a knock on the door. 'Come.'

Marcie Deveraux entered, looking as elegant as ever, her face showing no sign of the extensive dental work she'd had since her encounter with Fergus Watts.

She was holding a single sheet of paper. 'Watts and the boy, sir, there's been a possible sighting.'

Fincham remained calm, but he felt his heart quicken. The coffee cup trembled slightly in his hand. 'Where?'

Deveraux slid the sheet of paper across the desk. 'Spain.'

THE END

Some time later . . .

Danny stared at the printed sheet and sighed with irritation. 'Look, what's the point in learning this stuff?'

'Because some day we might depend on it. If we can't communicate, we can't operate efficiently. So you need to learn to tap out at least five words a minute.'

Danny laughed. 'Five words! There's mobiles, and e-mails, and MSN, and satellite phones – we can talk for hours. But you've got me learning dots and stupid dashes just so I can send five words in a minute in Morse code. Big deal!'

Fergus wasn't smiling. 'If you spent a bit less time taking the piss and a bit more doing as you're told, you'd make things a lot easier for both of us,' he snarled. 'Those five words could mean the difference between life and death. It works, Danny, always has and always will. Modern technology can let you down, even if you're lucky enough to have it, which we're not.'

'Yeah, but—'

'Just shut up and listen. I was on a job in the Middle East when the sat phone I was using got soaked in a flash flood. That was it, end of sat phone, almost end of me. It was Morse code that got me out in one piece.'

He picked up a pencil and pulled a sheet of paper from Danny's notepad. 'We'll need a couple of code words.'

'Code words? Why?'

'Questions,' sighed Fergus, 'always questions. If ever we do make contact using Morse I'll start with my code word, and that's all I'll give you until you come back with your word. That way we'll be certain we're talking to each other, and no one else.'

'So what are they then, these code words?'

Fergus began writing down the Morse code, groups of dots and dashes, each short series representing a single letter.

−... ..− .−. −−. . .−.

'That's my word,' he said. 'Now yours, and I'll keep it short.'

−... .− .−.

'So what's it mean?' asked Danny as his grandfather passed the paper to him.

Fergus put down the pencil and sat back. 'Work it out,' he said. 'And then remember it.'

GIVE
YOUR DAD
A McNAB

Perfect for birthdays, Christmas and Father's Day

Available wherever books are sold

ABOUT THE AUTHORS

Andy McNab joined the infantry as a boy soldier. In 1984 he was 'badged' as a member of 22 SAS Regiment and was involved in both covert and overt special operations world-wide. During the Gulf War he commanded Bravo Two Zero, a patrol that, in the words of his commanding officer, 'will remain in regimental history for ever'. Awarded both the Distinguished Conduct Medal (DCM) and Military Medal (MM) during his military career, McNab was the British Army's most highly decorated serving soldier when he finally left the SAS in February 1993. He wrote about his experiences in two phenomenal bestsellers, *Bravo Two Zero*, which was filmed in 1998 starring Sean Bean, and *Immediate Action*. He is the author of the bestselling novels, *Remote Control*, *Crisis Four*, *Firewall*, *Last Light*, *Liberation Day* and *Dark Winter*. Besides his writing work, he lectures to security and intelligence agencies in both the USA and UK.

Robert Rigby began his career as a journalist, then spent several years in the music business as a songwriter and session musician. He turned to writing for radio, television and the theatre and has also directed and performed in children's theatre throughout the country. He has become an established young people's playwright and his award-winning work with youth theatre companies has been seen in Britain, Europe, the USA and Africa. He now works mainly in television and his scripts include the long-running BBC children's drama series *Byker Grove*.